HELLVERSE

SHADOWS OF THE ABYSS

SEAN WALUSKO

The following is a work of fiction. All characters and events

portrayed in this story are a product of the author's imagination.

Table of Contents

This tale has been translated to a native tongue of mortal men so that we too may know the cruelty of the gods.

I. The Price Of A Soul

The Abyss; An endless void of blackened silence engulfed in the essence of living shadow. A dimension ruled by creatures born of bloodless pain, and the name by which these countless terrors were whispered. With skin laced in the blackest suffering, upon sullen and hollow eyes, shrieked voices layered over countless ages of torment. They swam in a sea of darkness, breathing pain and exhaling hatred, for their instinct fueled a need to consume and hunt.

Throughout the infinite of this celestial chasm, they swam. Across shadowed malevolence, trapped in a place of unknown origin, they followed the scent of blood and further aroma of confusion. Their home, the muddled space between life and death.

From out of the darkness, they pulled and scratched. Charred hands tipped with crimson talons dug into newly formed flesh. Once living, now dead, fresh arrivals fell deeper into the nothingness of eternity. Souls were lost in this endless void as they lay torn limb from precious limb. Screams made haste as the creatures silenced their calls. The echoes rang about the nightmare dreamscape, only to be accompanied by more futile efforts of survival.

The beasts fed and gorged themselves on whatever came through. Man, woman, child, and other beasts were shown no mercy nor held any sacred sway to nurse the hunger. All were equal in the consumption of flesh. With their eyes focused on incoming prey, they flew across time and space as if they were a single being. Wings spread wide and tails moved like barbed whips as they engaged in their hunt. Hundreds of them overtook the poor souls, leaving no more than a faded memory behind in their wake. They did this at constant, without end, because they too are cursed. Cursed to feed and thrive on the life of others. Cursed to seek refuge in those dark corners of the infinite. Their rhythm came in pulses set to the beating screams of protest. Their cycles played out like a predestined harmony that followed the simplest of nature's rules.

As more new arrivals made their entrance, the beasts struggled to keep up with their routine. From outside the dark walls of this dimension, blood shot into bellows while sharpened steel followed. Around each geyser of crimson expulsion, a new body formed. The blood gave way to bones, organs, meat, and skin until the soul was complete. Some were more tattered than others, but in the fresh grasp of death nonetheless. The tearing of dimensions was commonplace in the void. It was a place where the newly dead awoke after their last breath was left behind, only to find their next one on the backs of creatures that hungered for punishment. These poor beings knew not of their crossing. Some struggled to keep a fastened gaze, at times disappearing from the creature's grasp. Others failed or simply gave in to their final moments and accepted consumption by the Abyss.

Deeper they flew into the void, falling in every direction as bearings had little meaning in this place. Only a heightened sense of fear is what newly entered lost souls relied on to navigate through the madness. And even deeper still, some ventured. Past the nightmare creatures, past the tombs of flesh, past the rape of all things natural, leaving the waking world behind. Death here was not the end, but the beginning. So must the cycle continue to bear the fruits of these harbingers. Death feeds off life. And where there is death, new life will soon follow.

Behind the veil of darkness, in a time before the last creation, a single world showed its red crescent sliver of light. War had overtaken the now lost world, for it had come upon the eve of its final days. Between gaping valleys and beneath mountainous peaks, men spilled blood for reasons long forgotten. The sun had been blotted from the sky with black clouds that spread sparse pockets of red light from the shadowed sun. Caught in a permanent eclipse, the red world was on the brink of death, and in death, so must it fall into the Abyss.

A torrent of nightmares swirled about like a plague, spilling from the prisons that kept them trapped. From out the mind of a single assassin, the nightmares reflected back and into the eyes of another, fallen to his feet. The fallen warrior looked up at his reaper, eyes set ablaze by victory. He gripped the intruding blade and tried to release it from his chest while the assassin tightened and dug deeper. The fallen one released his last breath as his hands went cold. Above him, the assassin's eyes grew tired and fell deep as he loosened the grip his hands had on his spear. Through his own heaved breaths, the assassin listened to the roaring thunder of steel and flesh entwined in battle. He ground his teeth and jerked his spear from the corpse at his feet. The four-foot-long blade shined with the entrails of his victim as the blackened sky provided the perfect veil for his murderous glory. With his head raised, he looked out from behind his blood-caked hair and scanned the horizon. The battle was magnificent. Bodies were torn and mutilated as swords released their tangled flesh and spears rose them to the heavens.

Men from both sides raised their arms and gave out war cries. Earth split as quakes were released through the pounding of war hammers in the forms of shields, spears, swords, and axes, all painted with their previous victim's blood-drenched escapades.

The assassin wasted no time and made haste to the next closest opponent. He raised his spear behind his back and charged forth to ready himself for the next kill. Behind him, another opponent made his charge. He turned his body and swung his spear around, introducing the blade to his opponent's throat. A velvet geyser of hot blood shot across the assassin as it followed the movement of his blade before crashing on the rocks beneath his feet. Before the decapitated head could reach the ground, he made a swift turn, sending his red-stained spear through the gut of his previous target. When the head did reach the cold stone surface below, he vacated his blade, intestines pulled out while still attached to the spearhead, and sent off for another kill.

Like a man possessed by war itself, the assassin twisted and turned his way through the battlefront, mutilating all that stood in his path. He roared and yelled, sending a chill up the spines of all those around him. His blade pierced the armor of his enemies, sending their crimson life force in every direction. Amongst him, other warriors of modern death followed. The sky soon unveiled its black cloud portrait with blood falling back down like a rainstorm. The assassin lifted his head high and basked in the scent of iron and methane released from the freshly made corpses fallen at his feet. Before long, there was nothing left to quench his blood thirst.

He stood tall, his chest burning from rage amidst the ruins of a once great city. The assassin looked on past the carnage, past the suffering, and into a red sun rising from the unwavering sacrifice of his enemies. It was raised high above the horizon as it set the sky on fire. He looked on as the flames came closer to purge the battlefield of its impurities. As the flames whipped against his flesh, he closed his eyes and took in the pain. As one battle ended, another began.

* * *

The tides of fate twisted and turned their every movement around a soft pearl shell of nude milk-white flesh. The water was a magnificent clear blue-green set below an open dome roof from which rays of hot white sunlight penetrated through. Waves rippled and turned as a body of near perfection exposed itself to the surface. Midnight black hair became a series of living tendrils, while ruby lips and ample breasts rose above the surface. The surrounding statues and adoring young subjects that accompanied them magnified her attention.

With her body fully exposed for all to see, Sophia emerged from the pool and looked around at her adoring pets. Two of them came over to dry the water beading from her neck down to between her thighs. Another gifted her with a transparent black robe to cover her precious form.

Sophia made her way towards the large double doors that housed the only way in, or out, of this grotto. She was summoned not by force, but by fate. A fate that clenched its cracked and clammy fist and called itself 'savior.' And so she marched on past the halls of men and up the rising path to salvation. Up an endless flight of stairs she walked, a journey all too familiar to her. Ignoring the empty hollows of this great cavern, all she could do was stare upwards, away from the silken red carpet, which her feet tainted on the way to her lord.

With a feverish patience, Sophia waited, staring at the terrifying statues adorning the gates to the throne room. Its onyx doors opened and slowly creaked while hands plated in golden-showered armor pulled them apart. She lifted her head high as she made her way past the entrance guards and through the gates. Surrounded by no more than a few dozen men dressed in black and gold royal fatigues, her master sat and watched her every sultry movement. His eyes were as black as the midnight oil that fueled the flames of his machines of war. Cracked and coarse was his skin, mostly seen by the sneer plastered across his pale face. In contrast was the shimmering golden crown laid upon his head, tainted from its nobility by the triad of horned bones protruding from its circumference. Bones taken from the bodies of rulers he had conquered ages ago. His royal cloth, a black and red robe stretching from his neck down to his gold-booted feet, hid the grizzly exterior of a man cursed by time and madness. And so he sat atop a blackened throne, sculpted to resemble the skulls and flesh of his enemies. Sophia stopped at the foot of the crescent-shaped staircase that led up to his throne and looked up at her lord. With his eyes closed, he slowly rose, giving off a low-toned hiss few wished ever to hear. Still, she continued to look up, undaunted by his demeanor. With great audacity, she decided to speak before him.

"My Lord Daemos, you have summoned me. To what purpose may I ask?" Sophia asked with cocky assurance as she stared into the blackened soul of her master.

Daemos opened his eyes and stared down at his pet. It was not her decision to speak before him that raised his temper, but her tone. It was swift and to the point, almost spiteful of the fact that she was called away from her lustful engagement.

As Daemos raised his arms towards the white dome above, the lights in the throne room dimmed. With this setting more to his liking, he spoke, "Your arrogance is almost flattering. I thought you to be more mindful of the escapades you indulged in," Daemos said.

Sophia, now under the veil of her own impotence, lowered her head and gave her lord the floor to speak. Daemos, now in full thrall of his sanguine doll, lowered his arms and raised his head to the heavens.

"You take too easily from the hand that feeds you. Those that you call pet, I call vermin. They are to serve a single purpose and that purpose is not yours," Daemos said, as he turned his back to Sophia. "You would do well to remember that."

Sophia clenched her teeth and sliced deep into her palms with fingernails pointed to a razor's touch. Her complacency was already broken the moment she entered the ornate throne room, but now it was decimated. She rolled her eyes up and defied the very fabric of her existence. "I will not be ordered around like some rabid lapdog held in your thrall. I know what fate awaits those women. They are not pets." Sophia stopped and waited for a response. None was given, though. "If they were, I would see them set free."

Sophia turned around and stormed out of the throne room and into the halls of obscurity. Past the pain and promises of creating a renewed sense of hope for her people and into the endless nightmare that she had no warning was to come.

Cold and uneasily quiet, the throne room became. Not a shattered echo ruined by the hiss of a dying whisper stirred in the stale air. The clatter of feet striding away died off as she marched toward the shadows. Solitude reclaimed its place as the rightful owner of the room's atmosphere. Daemos stood alone by his blackened prodigy, marked with etchings of malice and tyranny. As he stroked the ebony skulls lining its outer rim, he closed his eyes and shot deep past the shattered mask of his memories. Creatures with flesh charred and cracked to demonic perfection wielding the power of eternal grandeur invaded his mind. They twisted and turned about his every thought. Screaming and bellowing out a thousand crazed voices at once with each movement, they swam in a sea of blood and fire. It was beauty defined.

* * *

The assassin's body was wrought with hunger and fatigue. The taste of charred black flesh still sat upon his tongue as he breathed in the now cold tarnished winds of war. Step after step, he caught his balance on the well-cooked trees that surrounded him. As he got deeper into the rotting corpse of a forest, he began to feel the weight of his armor take its toll. For hours he walked, slowly dropping each piece of ruined steel from his weary body. His lungs filled with ash as he looked up at the bleak red sky above. As he moved his long tar black hair from out of his face, he looked at his blood-soaked hands. The blood dripped down from his palms and onto the scorched earth below. He could not tell his own blood from that of his victims, considering some of it was, in fact, his own. Looking back at the battlefield, he saw the results of his ravenous outburst. Without a wound to call his own, he attributed his survival to more than just mere luck. He knew the true nature of the beast inside and clenched his calloused fingers against the rigid armor shielding his flesh. His will grew weaker with each passing moment and soon his eyes gave in to their own accord. As they closed shut, he saw the same nightmares that always appear when darkness is induced by his mind. Creatures winged and soulless sprinted across his vision. They clawed and hissed at his reality, threatening to break through if not properly fed. Nothing, it seemed to him, was enough to keep them at bay. He continued on, though, past the thick of burnt foliage and over the blood-tarnished rivers and swamps of nature's cauldron. Everywhere he set foot seemed to house traces of some sort of battle. A landscape cursed and shattered by war. Soon he would leave this world. He would find a new place to call home and take with him only memories of pain and retribution left behind in his wake.

His flesh grew weary and cold. The ground beneath his feet seemingly gave way with each step he took. He continued, carrying upon him the burden of remorse, not for those he had killed, but for those he had yet to slaughter. Eventually, his body faltered. His eyes sank deep into his skull just moments before he fell to the dirt below. Darkness came over him. It swirled around and comforted him as a mother would her dying child. Time at this point had no meaning. Neither did the laws of reality. Whether it had been mere seconds or endless days when he finally awoke was irrelevant. The heat from the growing flames that had overtaken this world now tore away at his flesh. Piece by piece, he felt himself get ripped apart. The breath in his lungs had been replaced with a cleansing fire. No longer was he able to see the charred remains of this world as his vision turned black.

His next waking moment was one of bondage. A swirling torrent of liquid shadow held his arms and legs in place. His bonds twisted and danced with themselves as they held down their victim. Eventually, his entire body was covered with blackened liquid smoke. Soon everything was engulfed in this living darkness. The shadows themselves came to life and teased each other with quick jabs and snapping jaws. Wings, claws, and tentacles danced around him as they came and went from the shadows. Before long, they completely encased him in the blackened stench of the shadow world. All around him was a dimension made of madness. There was nothing left for him to focus on as the creatures examined their new friend. Beyond the madness and blackened void, he felt something familiar. It was a voice. A voice with ancient blood tethered to its raspy tongue. It rang out towards him and said in a deep otherworldly tone, "Do not forget who you are."

In that instance, the very fabric of reality that the assassin knew existed shattered as his mind separated from his body. Once again, his skin felt as if it was on fire and his insides twisted and collapsed in on themselves. His very essence was torn apart while the laws of creation were broken one bone at a time. From being witness to the inner workings of the universe to crashing back into reality, he gave in and accepted his fate. Then the voices came. Faint at first, then more noticeable.

"Hold her down," said a voice echoing in the dark.

The warrior assassin was confused. He felt alive once more, but not as himself, as someone else. He knew something was wrong. Very wrong. Yet his transcendence held a note of familiarity.

* * *

Sophia looked on in horror as one of her pets struggled. The girl was no more than fifteen years of age. She was kept chained to a stone altar in the middle of a star-shaped symbol painted in blood on the floor below. Five clerics in black robes stood at each point as they chanted in an ancient tongue. The girl panicked and convulsed while they kept their empty gaze to the heavens above. She tore away at her flesh and tried to break free of the chains that held her hands and feet. Sophia turned away and wept as the girl begged for mercy. Daemos watched from the shadows as Sophia stared back at her master in disgust.

Soon the girl's screams changed from that of fear to anger. Her body began to tear itself apart from the inside out. Her muscles tightened and her newfound strength allowed her to break free of one of the chains. A guard in the room gave his concern. "My Lord..." the guard said.

Daemos answered, "Keep your patience."

The chanting hum grew louder as the clerics concentrated their energies onto the girl. With her free hand, she tore away at her clothes. A split second later, she ripped the flesh off her cheeks and neck. Her hands were soon torn apart from the inside out as a new set of hands emerged. With a new set of claws, their wet red muscle exposed, she continued to tear away, revealing her nude chest and stomach. As each piece of flesh was thrown from her body, a new surface began to show itself. Sophia looked on as the girl ripped away her old body in replace of a new one. Within mere moments, the girl was reduced to no more than a pile of ripped flesh and pulverized bone. In her place lay a man. A warrior assassin who only moments ago was held captive by the darkness of an ancient battleground. The warrior looked at his body and saw the remains of the girl still sitting upon his skin and on the floor beneath him. His breathing got heavier as he broke free from the other chains. He grabbed one of the clerics and threw him across the room. Before he had the chance to grab another, he felt the sharpened edge of a crescent blade break through his rib cage and drag him to the floor. Another hit him in the leg and another again in his ribs. With all of his strength gone, he fell face-first onto what used to be the girl's skull. Collapsing in on her thoughts, Sophia ran over to the warrior and whispered into his ear. "I am sorry it has to be like this," she said.

Daemos took in the scent of fresh blood and the stench of exposed entrails as he walked toward the man born from the flesh of sacrifice. Sophia collected herself and left the warrior's side. She gave one final look of disgust at Daemos before taking her leave. The warrior, held in place by rusted chains and hooks, looked up at the king. Daemos stared back into the warrior's eyes and spoke, "Welcome home, Azrael."

II. A Dire Meeting

Like an endless torrent spilling forth into a lake of madness, did the nightmares invade. Over fields of ash-covered mountains, the blackened clouds shot down their discord. The crimson luminescence aborted itself from the mist and rang down to the scorched earth. And with a roar of newfound life, the creatures of the Abyss defied their gods. One over another, they crawled and slithered their way around. Masses of bodies clutched by the throes of snapping jaws and leathery tails intertwined. Again, the lightning crushed its way down toward the earth it so seemingly wished to scar. Only in those slight flashes of bright red did the Abyss show its face. An eyeless race of serpentine beauty, hungry to feed their ripened muscles and venomous fangs. Razor-sharp claws dug into the edge of a mountain on the brink of falling in on itself. And with the next strike of thunder and lightning, its wings spread and mouth dilated, exposing its twin sets of flesh-defying teeth.

As the screaming call of an ancient race tethered its way around his mind, Azrael shot forth his weary eyes and stared back into reality. Nary a sound did he make as he sat, quaint and silent. He stared ahead towards a weathered and rusted wall. In its center sat a large tank of crystal blue liquid. Surrounding him were eight walls total, every other one holding a large rectangular tank at its core. Aside from the pristine sight of the living water, the other three held combinations of living fire, acid, or smoke. Each danced in mostly unnatural ways. Rippling and falling in on themselves as they sprawled in directions that seemed to be motivated by fear rather than nature. It was the clarity of the blue and the combative nature of the liquid itself that kept his gaze. Although confined to a sizable tank in the middle of a cold and callous surface, it moved freely as it pleased, and for that, he was jealous.

Neither a free man nor a prisoner, Azrael was merely a tool, a weapon forged in the depths of the unknown by his Lord Daemos. At least, that was what he believed. With the outside world waiting for his entrance, Azrael decided to stay within the comfort of the octagonal room. It was what he was accustomed to and what he felt was appropriate for someone with the social bearings of a rabid dog. He sat, unmoved by any celestial decisions, in his torrid state of meditation. He would be given the luxury of food and a bath and would leave it at that, for he knew it would be a wasted effort to avoid being sent to yet another world to cleanse it of its sins. Deep in thought, he was when the door behind him creaked. The sound of chains pulling against giant gears shifted his focus. He stood up and turned to the rising door, and awaited his visitor.

Sophia entered, strutting her angelic body across Azrael's vision. Her footsteps sent shrill echoes across the catacombs. With her gaze fixed on Azrael, she circled him and addressed her attention to break his solitude.

"Why are you here?" Azrael asked Sophia, as she stopped to adorn the same liquid flowing across his eyes.

With her body perched against the wall, she turned and addressed him, "Do you never tire of this?"

Azrael moved his attention away from Sophia. His eyes fell to the floor and thoughts of war masked in routine played out in his mind. "I have no respite for the gestures of mortal fears," Azrael said, moving his gaze back up to Sophia. "My reasons are mine alone."

"And what would those reasons be?" Sophia asked with a slight smirk.

"I am looking for something. For someone." Azrael held back at his tethering unhinged outburst.

"And you think that by going to distant stars and killing all in your path that you will find what you are looking for?" Sophia asked.

Azrael stood up and walked over to Sophia, confining her within his outreached arms. He looked into her dark red eyes and saw a hint of empathy hiding behind the bloodlust. "You act as if I have a choice in the matter. Why ask me this now? Not once in the time since our beginnings have you ever held concern for my actions. So I ask of you again, why are you here?"

Sophia slid Azrael's arms off hers and stepped away from the wall. She held out her hands and gripped deep her fingernails into her palms. As the blood left her body, the tanks of gas, smoke, fire, and water rustled about in the dark and muggy room. Azrael felt her heart surge with a potency he had only felt in battle. "I thought I could satiate my connection to the living. Seeing my surrogate daughters ripped apart each time you come back hurts worse than the last."

"Why do you tell me this now?" Azrael asked.

"Your future intertwines its fate with my own and the threads of fate weave their markings upon your favor," Sophia exclaimed.

"My question still stands," Azrael demanded.

Azrael studied Sophia's posture and felt her blood run with a nervous twitch. The anticipation of what she was about to say was not well hidden. "The Seraphim consort will arrive in seven days' time to give Lord Daemos their blessings. With their blessings, they will tell him stories of heresy and blasphemy. You, of course, will be sent to purify the blasphemers. A harbinger of death sent by the Lord himself," Sophia said.

Sophia looked down at the drops of blood let loose from her palms to the steel grate below. The dark red pool of crimson expulsion reflected to her an uncertain future. A future held in sway by the actions of a single thought. She kept her mind aloft and stared up at Azrael. Being her elder by a full century kept Sophia's tongue silent out of intimidation. All she has known of Azrael are centuries filled with murder and bloodlust led. Sophia let loose her tongue and spoke her own blasphemies. "In all this time, I have never actually met a Seraphim in person. I am accustomed only to the stories you and Lord Daemos have told me over the years," Sophia said.

"This will be the seventh time they have visited Abaddon," Azrael said.

"And it will be the first time I will have the honor to grace their presence," Sophia said sarcastically.

"And I take it you wish me to use this, your first meeting with them, to impress upon them a gesture of goodwill. To what purpose?" Azrael asked.

Sophia paced behind Azrael and thought out loud to sedate his curiosity. "I may not have the same influence as you on the Seraphim. I wish you to speak to them, as I am sure you have before. Ask them why they wage this war. Why my daughters must be ripped to shreds so that you may cleanse a world that might or might not be committing atrocities benign to us?"

"You wish me to tell them to end their crusade?" Azrael almost could not believe what he was hearing. "The Seraphim are able to conduct their war because they have the will to do so. They visit our world on the rarest of occasions to be sure that we are still on the righteous path. Even if I could convince them, they will just find someone else. I have no choice."

Expecting such an answer, Sophia turned back to Azrael with a rebuttal of her own. "We always have a choice," she said.

With her leaving, the room once again sat still and cold. Azrael pondered upon her words as they stung like the sharpened claws of a rabid beast. The lights dimmed, and so too did his allegiance to Daemos. For too long, he thought, did their alliance seem to benefit from a corrupted architecture based on lies and manipulation.

* * *

As the days passed, the cities of Abaddon slept silently. Their rustling engines sedated out of the sheer anticipation of a once-in-a-lifetime experience. And so the people waited. Promises given by the gods of peace and severance were what the people expected, but at what price is where their ignorance lay? Only a few held within the closest respite of the gods knew the sacrifices made to ensure an entire civilization's survival. The gods gave to the people their prayers in tandem, in turn reminding the sinners how justice is handed from above.

And from the heavens above they came, riding on the blistering light of a distant star. They swam in the dark reaches of space, gliding and flowing over each other while the stars and gas giants acted as their backdrop. However, they had become bored and hollow. By pitting worlds against each other, they found respite. Physical life had little meaning to them. The planet Abaddon was but a tiny sparkle in the eyes of the Seraphim. A world of no more use to them than a playground stage made to bully other worlds. With their glowing tendrils spread, they set their empty, soulless eyes upon Abaddon and rode to it on the winds of creation.

* * *

Night fell as the seventh day approached. The altars of obscurity in which the people held their faith would be washed clean with the coming of the bringers of the light.

Daemos washed his flesh clean of any imperfections to welcome his guests. He lay in his steel coffin and charred his skin with the white flames of purity. His eyes opened anew to a younger, fresher body. His mind was still his and his flesh intact, but the time elapsed from his age had gone. Pale and lifeless was his skin. Light blue veins leading to dead white eyes reached out and touched those around him. His servants covered his searing molten body with the white robes of ceremony. His very touch sizzled and cooked the robes as they were laid upon him. He left down the path out of his bathing room and, with each step, smoke rose and trailed behind. Short bursts of malevolence clenched about his aura with invisible tendrils lightly wiping their stain upon his guests.

Daemos left the baptismal waters behind and marched on. He headed for a large cathedral fueled by lost souls and wanton criminals, making his way down a suspension bridge that connected his fortress to the gateway. He was alone. Neither guards nor any other accompaniment halted his stride. He was bare and without any sign of royalty. Simply covered by no more than a white silken robe, golden armored greaves, and boots to match.

The holy tower was held in place at the castle's center. From out of the red stained glass windows, one could see beyond the landscape for miles. A land covered by black brick and towering superstition.

Azrael and Sophia looked on from behind a crimson portrait as they watched their lord approach. They stood at the head of an altar lit by hundreds of candles that were littered throughout the antechamber.

The roaring of a boundless thunder echoed throughout. Catching deep the hollows of the horned god's halls while whispering their faint machinations to the fates. Daemos, now joined by Azrael and Sophia, marched forth with his sights set on destiny. Destiny being an age-old creature of timeless beauty and unadulterated malevolence. Their metaphysical bodies existed as no more than a source of pure white-hot light radiating with raw energy. The Seraphim were, as it seemed, perfect.

Large double doors gave their invitation to Daemos as he made his entrance to the black-spire church. Sophia, wearing an open-cut ceremonial black dress, looked on with complete apathy. Azrael kept his composure hidden beneath the royal red cloth he wore around his waist that fell down to his knees. He wore the same steel-plated royal armored boots as the soldiers of Abaddon to match his chest guard.

As Daemos approached, both Azrael and Sophia stepped aside and allowed their lord to take seizure of the altar. In the center of the altar lay a bowl, accompanied by a short blade. Daemos grasped the blade and sunk it deep into his wrist. Blood flowed out from his veins and flooded the large metal bowl. With a single touch, he dipped his forefinger into the fresh pool of nectar. The blood began to boil, and the room echoed a stark delivery. Statues that lined the walls of the room began to move and pulsate. They twitched and screamed as stone twisted and broke to reveal mortal flesh beneath. Held in thrall by chains, wire, and bandage, they struggled for release. Above them, the skies opened up as the stars lay stillborn. The winds of plague reared their menace and presented an immense source of light. The gateway had been opened. Glass shattered and an ocean of liquid smoke overtook the room. The bodies continued to twist and contort, their features unrecognizable. Sophia trembled, but kept her composure. Azrael tensed his muscles and reared his teeth. Daemos stood, bored and anxious, waiting for this circus to come to an end. Trapped within a swirling torrent, the three of them caught glimpses of lightning and living flame. It whipped and beat their skin. It was merciless and painful. A fitting

introduction for beings bent on following prophecy and fanaticism.

The Seraphim had arrived.

The room, now calmed and vacant of any deistic typhoon,

showed a clear view of the night sky from beyond a series of

shattered windows. Of the six now living statues, three of them

began to spew up their own innards. Their eyes burned hot and their

skin cracked and peeled. With immense strength, they broke free of

their bonds. The other three began to revert back into oblivion; their

flesh hardened and their bodies were stone once more. Covered in

blood, chains, and torn cloth, the three men approached Daemos.

One of them looked over at Sophia and slanted his head at her

disgusted visage. She sighed in deep as she witnessed a new unholy

act of possession. Daemos took notice and addressed her, "Pity you

feel for these lowly creatures. Mortals, they are no more than vessels

and food for us. Embrace it, for you have no choice." He stepped

forward and examined the three men, now possessed by the pure

light of a truly worthy creature. "My brothers. I hope you accept my

gifts with an unwavering reprieve, for we are at your mercy."

The three men looked at each other. Their eyes burned white, and their cracked skin blistered cold as a winter chill. "We accept," one of them spoke.

Sophia whispered into Azrael's ear, "Why must they revert to a barbaric act such as possession?"

"They are not wholly physical beings. Once they join with a host, only then must they succumb to the rules of the mortal world as well," Azrael answered.

Sophia stared at the newly possessed corpses and saw how their muscles fought against the tyranny of possession. The Seraphim were in full control though, as each movement they made was both graceful and littered with mortal pain. "What are they?" Sophia asked with a concerned look on her face.

"The Seraphim are creatures of habit bent on instinct and survival. It is what drives them to choose what lives and what dies. It is and has always been like this. Once they leave here, they will shed their skin and once more become the physical embodiment of light that they truly are. Only memories and base instinct from their time as a mortal will remain."

"They are soulless," Sophia said.

"No. They are nothing more than a soul," Azrael answered.

Daemos reared his attention back to the three men. "What is the purpose of your visit on this our greatest eve?"

"We have seen the undoing and rebirth of existence. No more than a trite musing of pointlessness are these creatures that serve you. They have followed willingly. All of them. There is, however, little incentive for them to continue their civilization." Once he finished speaking, another continued.

"We have come to tell you that the crusade is over. We see no reason to continue other than to divulge in some war-mongering pleasure." The three men stepped up to Daemos and awaited their answer.

Azrael leaned into Sophia and whispered into her ear, "I guess this negates the need for persuasion." As quickly as any hint of relief swept Sophia's body, so too did it leave. She felt a cold chill across her bones as the three men gave off their apathetic prose.

"Why this decision?" Daemos asked.

"You of all know there need not be a reason," another one of them said.

"Then what of Abaddon? What of all that we have accomplished to drive the Abyss back into obscurity? Am I to believe that because we are no longer needed, we are to be destroyed?" Daemos continued.

"No. Not you..." The man then turned his attention to Azrael and Sophia. "Them."

Azrael spoke out against his lord's wishes and broke his vow of silence. "I am tired of these games. I have cleansed countless worlds only to have these puppets undermine my actions. I am sick of this. Two thousand lifetimes. For two thousand beats of a mortal life, have I embarked on your pointless crusade. Never once did I question you, and now this world is to be destroyed simply because you have no use for it?"

"What heresy is this?" one of the possessed men shouted.

"Daemos, we had a deal. Remember your promise," Azrael said.

Daemos turned to Azrael, with his eyes pierced and searing. "Keep your tongue, Azrael," he said.

Sophia slowly began to back away from the ensuing confrontation. She hid behind a pew no more than a few feet away. Although immortal, she still feared for her existence.

"You allow this? For a flesh and blood creature to address us in this way?" asked the man. He stepped closer toward Azrael, who was already gripping tightly the hilt of his sword.

Daemos replied, "No. He is an insolent child that speaks out of turn. He will be punished for his actions. Why your decision, though? What more is there than terrorizing an entire planet with no more than a simple story passed down through generations?"

"You mock us?"

"What am I to do? Hand over what I have slaved to build for the past millennia?" Daemos asked in defiance.

"No. You are to return to us."

Azrael looked at Daemos with a stark line of confusion. "What is he talking about?"

"Nothing, Azrael. He knows not of what he speaks," Daemos said.

The three men reared their posture and gripped tight their weapons. Sophia closed her eyes and called out to the ancient gods of prophecy in the hopes that they would hear her prayers. The Seraphim were a lie. They were not the beings of light she had heard of in the tales of old. They were monsters disguised as men. Their white auras and majestic halos only hid the horrors of their true nature. A nature bent on the destruction of others to ensure their own survival. As she opened her eyes, the cold grip of a dead man's hand held her throat. She was lifted up above his head and held in place by his unnatural strength. Azrael growled at the man holding Sophia and pulled his sword from its sheath.

"Put her down or I shall have your head," Azrael remarked.

"A threat? From a creature such as you?"

Daemos intervened and tried to make sense of the situation. "Put your weapons at bay. Now."

"Your use has run its course," said the man holding Sophia. Within an instant, he released his grip and threw her to the ground. A sickening twist of her spine sent her body into a series of painful convulsions. By the time she gathered her strength and was able to turn and face her attacker, she felt the shrill cry of the afterlife call out to her. Azrael watched in shock as the Seraphim beast ran his sword through Sophia's gut, spilling her precious lifeblood to the floor. Upon seeing this, Azrael sent his sword through the killer's chest, puncturing his heart. It took a mere second for Azrael to remove his blade, slicked in dead blood, and lift it high above his head. As he brought it back around, he released the Seraph's head from his body.

"Uriel," One of the men said as he looked down at the decapitated blood-spilled corpse of his brother. As torrents of thick, viscous plasma poured out from the gaping wound, mortal flesh burned away, revealing the creature's true nature. Its head glowed with white-hot light and held two large, black, sharpened eyes. Its body glowed with the same luminescence while tendrils whipped and twitched sans a head to guide them. Soon after, all movement stopped and the Seraph's body became a husk of gray flesh.

"There are still two of you and I still hunger," Azrael said with a snarling growl.

Daemos knew that the future he had planned would come to fruition sooner than later. With the threat of inevitability, he grabbed Azrael's throat from behind and ran his fingernails deep into his neck. "I am sorry it had to be this way," Daemos whispered into Azrael's ear. Azrael fell to the ground and held onto the gaping hole that had been ripped into his throat. Knowing that this was his end, he crawled his way to Sophia.

Her words were faint and her motion was all but gone. "We are the same Azrael. The gods have answered my prayers. I am free now. You are free as well. Learn of the truth, for all of us." With her last breath, she pulled him close and set her lips upon his. She let forth a trail of blood seep out from between her lips and onto his tongue. It burned and tasted of a darkness he was all too familiar with. As the light faded from his vision, he watched as Daemos and the remaining Seraphim gathered around their fading corpses. He was no longer able to see or hear them, only feel their presence. He held on for as long as he could, hoping beyond hope to make sense of this madness.

"It is time you came back with us," one of the possessed men said to Daemos.

"No. This world is mine," Daemos said.

"This world was never yours to begin with. You have been in that shell for so long that you have forgotten your true face," another one said.

"Come, let us show him who he really is." The two men walked up to Daemos as he stumbled back against the altar. With each step, their skin began to harden, chunks of corroded flesh falling to the ground, exposing cracks and rivers of light. Tendrils escaped from their backs and appendages. Where they used to have legs, instead, grew a pair of serpentine tails emitting a bright glow of pure energy. They floated seamlessly toward the frightened Daemos. In a flash of blinding light, he and the other two beings were gone, stripping with them any evidence of their existence.

The church was no more than an empty shell. The statues had been placed back in their native arrangement while the bodies of Azrael and Sophia lie cold and still. With one last breath, Azrael closed his eyes and felt his heart stop. Its final beat tore a rift through time and space. The very foundation of the cathedral itself came crashing down into a void of nothingness. Windows shattered and its pieces flung into a vortex of nonexistence. The surrounding walls were erased from all forms of reality. Azrael fell for what seemed to be an eternity. All around him was the darkness that had haunted his mind as he was finally its slave.

III. Leviathan

Chaos. The Abyss. Words for this place were meaningless. There was no direction, no sense of any difference between reality and hallucination. All around was a never-ending blackness. Echoes of mercy and pleading voices rang throughout, yet fell farther and farther into oblivion. The hissing of smoke and scent of iron passed across like a buffet of flayed flesh. There was nothing to call a foundation to stand upon, only the floating mass of terror that awaited and hungered. It was the very definition of a realm of lost souls. It was home to the Abyss.

He felt them as they pulled at his flesh. They scratched at his wounds, yet they did no harm. He felt their hunger, and it was the same as his. Azrael opened his eyes and shook awake his senses. He was still falling, but at the same pace as the sky around him and the souls beneath. Their tails and claws avoided him. He reached out in the hopes to be punished, to be erased, but none would answer. He watched as they fed upon the freshly dead that entered this realm. They tore and chewed at their meat and sucked dry the marrow from their bones. Like a strike of lightning, he felt a hit from behind. He turned and saw a man with a gaping hole in his chest. The man screamed at Azrael and pleaded for mercy. Inadvertently knowing what to do, Azrael let his true nature take over. He grabbed the man and pulled him close. Azrael opened his mouth and sunk deep his teeth into the man's throat, tearing and vacating his flesh. The hunger was gone. Fear, however, had taken its place.

Azrael swam across the void and witnessed more acts of this feeding frenzy. The newly departed were no more than a meal to the creatures of the Abyss. He tried to pretend to wonder why he was spared being fed upon, but he already knew the answer.

Below, in the deepest recesses of damnation, prying eyes watched the evisceration play out. A mass of flesh and bone held together by ancient blood called this place home. Its very breath sent quakes of rumbling echo throughout the liquid darkness. Like a snake slithering in the dirt, it moved and swayed its massive form with otherworldly grace. It came up from below the pits of damnation and up towards the surface where new life had arrived. The god beast reared its vague monstrosity into Azrael's vision. From out of the blinding shadows, it came up. Tentacles jettisoned out forth and pierced through Azrael's hands and feet. Another came up and burrowed its way through his chest. Azrael was now held in thrall by a creature that ruled the darkness from beyond a tattered veil. Like the prelude to a ground-shattering earthquake, he heard its body rumble beneath his feet. The tentacles swayed back and forth as the creature rose up from the bowels of this nightmare. Towers of flesh-melded corpses shot up in front of him. He gazed up as he watched people caught in a mass pillar of blood, skin, and bone scream out to him for mercy. When he brought his attention back down, the towering creature had stopped its ascension. Azrael looked straight ahead and realized that he was staring into the hollowed,

blackened eyes of a god. Eyes that screamed a furious terror in their

callous malfeasance streamed into a cosmic breath of creation. Not

for one to stare into the face of reason did this god of un-creation

look into the very soul of his warrior in thrall.

"What light blinds this creature behind his halo shroud?" the

self-proclaimed god spoke. Its mouth; a random mass of charred

flesh made bone and synapse, slid and crumbled apart while words

were expelled.

"I answer to no one," Azrael exclaimed.

Orbs of eternal damnation made their presence ever-known

as they wandered across Azrael's tattered body. He was examined

and inspected. Tendrils of rock-hard flesh dug deep into Azrael's

skin, yet he never bothered to fight them away.

"I am a god. But I am not your god. You are no creature of my design. Your soul is null and void. You have been sent here on incident, a traverse duality. But by whom?" the towering god of the Abyss asked, reeling Azrael closer to his senses. "Abyss. Yes, you are a child of creation. An oddity born even prerequisite to my arrival. These are your brothers and sisters, the creatures that gnaw and pull at you. It is affection through bloodletting." The god pulled Azrael closer. "I see now, poor oddity. An Abyss child born into a man's tethered flesh. Thus stands the question of why. Why do you exist? Why are you not a charred flesh beast of shadow like your siblings? Your existence alone begs to question the fabric of life and its pretenses. I see all. I see that you have no place in this sanctum of death and feasts."

"You see nothing," Azrael shouted out to the towering god as the bondage made tentacles squeezed him tighter.

"I see the living. You are in a place of death. Now is not your time young death dealer yet you have no destination. Your line has been severed."

Azrael immediately thought of the poor souls that were used time and time again to pull him back into reality. This time he had been killed and left for dead with no blood scripture to guide him. The Seraphim had trapped him, so it seemed.

"What is this?" the towering god asked, as he leaned his planet-sized eye up to Azrael's face. With another tentacle, the god sniffed around Azrael's mouth. "Blood? So a destination was set."

The kiss. Azrael remembered Sophia's soft sticky lips press against his as their blood crossed between one another.

"She gave you a map. Her blood will guide you. She was special, I take it. Yes. You will like this place, young warrior. She is sending you across the void of time and space to the birthplace of your ascension. There, your fate lies in waiting. Do not disappoint us. The Abyss must thrive on fresh life and you must provide."

Azrael's body reveled in the burning ache of a kiss left behind on his callous lip. The blood spilled out and forth in bellows, expelling all thoughts of pain, fear, and the exquisite release of death. He had lost what he held onto for so long. Only the blood was left behind. Only blood would be his saving grace. His hunger for it would defy them. He peered deep into the non-existence of this self-proclaimed god and aided it to his whim. He had no more need for the blood, as it would be his final echo.

The towering god slid away his leathery grasp and loosed his grip on Azrael. "Go then, my immortal pain seeker. Feed the Abyss," the god spoke.

As his release came, Azrael felt the sharpened sting of his sibling's claws race across his flesh. Piece by piece, his skin was torn to shreds. He held back the need for a vocal expulsion and instead bit into his tongue. His hands found their way to his eye sockets and dug deep his fingers into those soft white jellied orbs. Within seconds, they burst. Soon all of his skin would be no more than a shroud for the darkness to play with. He was set adrift, floating throughout the black smoke of his own tortured soul asylum, a skinned and eyeless living corpse.

* * *

The daylight suffering of Abaddon swept across its surface. Daemos watched as his Seraphim brothers lay waste to the cities of man. A true force of divine intervention sent bodies rippling through to their demise. The young, the old, the innocent, the guilty, none of them held sway in the decision to cease destruction by their guardian angels. It mattered not if the people prayed to or cursed them, as there was only one outcome; death.

"You are still upset about Uriel's death at the hands of my assassin, are you not, Moloch?" Daemos asked as he lorded over the slaughter of his people. His once great palace was now nothing more than a burning pile of rubble in the distance behind him. To his side stood the self-appointed general of the Seraphim armies, Moloch. His form was that of a middle-aged mortal man sculpted to muscular perfection.

Moloch adorned his physical body and the armor that lay upon it with ethereal royalty. His skin glowed pale as snow and his sword raged with the flames of a tepid inferno. Around his waist was a dirty, blood-stained sash that had once shared the same pearlesque purity as a set of overcast clouds. The white cloth had been subject to fire and execution and was now the tainted color of rotting flesh. Still clean, though, were his golden and silver boots, tempered in the flames of his forefathers. They held a delicate design resembling that of mortal royalty, but their function was much more rigid and could withstand the strongest of attacks. He kept his stride as he watched the world around him burn in a glorious inferno.

"Uriel was careless," said Moloch.

Daemos stayed by the general's side as he moved with the same pretentious grace and determination. "Was Sophia's death entirely necessary, though? Was any of this necessary?" Daemos asked.

Moloch took in the ashes of his onslaught and kept his thoughts clean and pure. He knew that what he was doing, on this world, was for the greater good of all of creation. "Nothing is necessary. Once we are done here, we will move on to the next world and so forth. Physical life is a disease. It is a curse. You of all should know that. Just look at yourself, brother. Your body is broken. It crumbles as you walk. Each day, you must shed your flesh and cover your true form with a new rack of meat. It truly is disgusting," Moloch answered.

"Disgusting? Much in the same way that you mercilessly slain my greatest weapon and his guardian?" Daemos asked with a tone of contempt.

"What weapon? Azrael? You were the one that took his life. Either way, that fool was no weapon. He was a tool used out of your own cowardice. It was your job to cleanse those worlds. Why you sent a mere man to do it is beyond even my understanding. And how he survived for so long is a question all on its own." Moloch looked over Daemos with conspiracy. Trust was not something the Seraphim were known to abide by.

The two of them continued to walk down the stone pathway. All around them, blood was shed and bodies fell. The murder and wanton violence had little effect on their composure. Men, women, and children ran up to their king and his angelic companion. Daemos shoved them aside as Moloch brought down his fiery blade of rapture through their unsuspecting skulls.

"Our brothers are preparing a meeting to determine the fate of this world. Gabriel and I will attend as your consort. This world is finished," Moloch said.

"You are wrong about one thing, Moloch," Daemos interjected.

"And what is that?"

"Azrael was no mere man."

* * *

Emptiness filled the air as Azrael floated amongst the
shadows. His skin had grown back and his eyes opened anew. The
hair on his head had returned to its full length and swirled about as if
caught under a tidal wave. Slowly, his lungs began to feel the
pressure of the void. The Abyss had almost seemingly disappeared
and left him to wander the black depths of this inner space all on his
own. Where was he to end up he wondered? He thought of the Abyss
god and the sweet taste of Sophia's blood trail. With that thought,
Azrael laid himself open to the void and closed his eyes. His body
began to tingle as the slow rising of liquid touched his skin. Soon it
covered his whole body. As he re-opened his eyes, all he saw was
red. Thick boiling blisters of coagulated blood floated amongst the
newly formed sea of plasma that he was caught under. He had left
the land of the dead and entered the world of the living. One hundred
feet above, he could see the surface. He swam his way up through
the molten sea of blood and headed for air.

He shot his way above the sticky surface and threw forth an explosion of crimson nectar as he gasped for his first breath in this new world. With his body aching and his mind broken, he swam for hours in the red sea. Not once did he look to the skies, nor did he ever scan the horizon for a sign of land. He just swam and pushed away the blood and bone that made up the whole of this ocean. He ignored the crashing of thunder and jettison bolts of black lightning. It merely fueled his determination to escape another doomed life. With one last stroke through, the liquefied remains of his arrival shoved its way aside as his hand hit something solid. His feet caught the warm grain of sand as he raised his body up. He walked out of the sea and onto a jagged black blade of ancient stone. His hands gripped and pulled his body as he climbed up to the top of the massive structure. Wiping the blood out of his eyes, he was finally able to look out and see the world that he was thrust into. What he saw brought both a horrifying realization and a comforting sigh of relief.

A red glow pierced through black clouds as acid rain washed the blood away from Azrael's body. He looked on from the edge of the monolithic cliff that rose out from the ocean beneath him. What he saw was a land marred by the wars and worship of ancient gods and goddesses. Temples and ruins littered the landscape. In the distance, he saw creatures, similar to those of mortal men, with skin grayed and their bodies frail with ghastly features as they roamed freely about. There were no cries for help, no whimpers for mercy, and, most importantly, no screams of battle. He found himself staring off into a world untouched by Seraphim hands. Behind him, he heard the rustling of wind and the swaying of leaves. He turned around to see what other secrets this new world had to offer.

Ahead of him, he could see a great and twisted forest. Its leaves were gray and its branches black as the midnight sky. The orange and red glow from the three suns above lit the landscape as if it were a world on the brink of Seraphim cleansing. There was no sign of threat from above, though. Whatever horrors presented themselves on this world had been here long before the Seraphim had time to arrive. Without hesitation, he jumped his way off of the angled jagged rock and onto the beach below. With no armor or clothing to call his own, he was as a newborn born into a world of harsh realities. It was not fear that overtook him, but a new will and determination to find out why he was sent to this place. Why Sophia's blood had chosen this world as its destination? Ahead of him, he saw hundreds of bodies litter the landscape. Some were still armored while others were stripped nude. He would take what he could salvage. The sight was a portent warning to those foolish enough to venture forth. Caution, though, was the enemy of progress. He stepped one foot forward and placed his path into the dense forest ahead.

IV. In Strange Company

Though he saw no immediate threat, Azrael's situation was no less dangerous than when he found himself to be a killer for his former lord and master Daemos or came face to face with a self-proclaimed god. No matter the creatures, no matter the places, and no matter the times, there was always something that hungered for life.

He wandered from the black stone beach and through the charred forest around him and thought of the countless worlds he had left in a state similar to this world. At times, it crossed his mind if he had once been to these lands. The smell of burnt foliage, the bones beneath his feet, and the sullen emptiness of this world seemed all too familiar to him. All he could do was venture on and hope that someone, or something, would point him to where he needed to go. For now, he simply let his eyes examine the world as it lay before him.

Countless behemoth rock formations littered the landscape. Amongst them lay the ancient fruits of the forest. Trees towered and swayed in the wind, their scent carried across the open air. Small grassy trails led to stone caverns that sat atop graven fields. Their hollowed echoes rang out from the emptiness inside the caves.

Azrael ventured further into the heart of the silent woods and listened closely to the hum and hiss of the creatures that called it home. What he could not see, he felt with pure instinct. Something was following him. Something was watching him.

Eyes tempered in the red-hot wastes of oblivion set their gaze upon the lone warrior. They watched as he hurried across the forest floor. Corpse after corpse he would stop, robbing them of their garments. With bloodied greaves and weathered boots, he covered his naked and bruised flesh. Along the treetops, curious eyes followed and studied him. When he stopped for rest, so too did they. When he stopped to strip a fallen body of its armor, so too did they. They were now his shadows trailing behind in a bloodthirsty wake.

Azrael felt his heart pound with each footstep. He knew he was being hunted. But by what and why was beyond him. This land was foreign to him, its rules as alien as the nightmares he's endured. His only option at this point would be to continue on and hope that whatever lurked in the shadows grow tired of its game. Luck, as he would have it, was not on his side.

With each passing moment, the wind grew stronger, and the trees bellowed forth their rustling growls. Rivers of clear molten plasma raced down the surrounding rock formations as the sky opened up into its rearing gaze. The indigenous creatures of the necro forest ceased their chatter. Only the silenced echoes of a nearing death knell pierced the air. Azrael kept his eyes to his side and walked at a steady pace. Now armed with the blood-stained mantle of the fallen, he was ready to face whatever pursued him.

No sooner than the stirring of an echo did the threat of battle race across Azrael's vision. It moved around him atop the apex of the tree line at a speed he had never seen before. It circled and played with his senses. Flashes of red and black trails scarred the clarity of his vision. For a moment, it seemed to stop. He reared his stance and locked his eyes toward a spot beyond the trees ahead. All too late did he realize that he had made a mistake. The pounding of cloven hooves crashed behind him, sending up dormant foliage formerly resting on the ground. On his back, he felt the fiery breath of a beast fueled by a raging inferno. Using pure instinct, Azrael shot his body forward and dodged the head of a bloodthirsty war ax. The beast stood there, revving its black lungs like the charred pistons of a man-made war machine. As Azrael landed back on his feet, he turned his body around to face his attacker. It stood roughly eight feet tall on a pair of overpowered hind legs. Its torso resembled that of a man, yet its muscle structure more defined and complex. Light gray was the color of this creature's skin except for the dark brown fur that covered its legs from the thighs down. The arms of the beast rippled with pure muscular tyranny as it gripped a bone-tipped spear nearing the length of its entire stance. Most interesting was the face that lay

upon its wide-brimmed neck. The beast carried with it the head of a

goat. Bloodshot eyes rested inside an elongated skull that lead to a

pair of razor-sharp teeth. Upon its brow sat a pair of crescent-shaped

horns. Horns that were chipped and stained over centuries of

bloodletting.

In all the worlds that Azrael has laid to waste, never has he seen a creature as threatening to his survival as the one that stood before him. Tensing his muscles, Azrael clenched his fists and ran head first at the beast. Screams of war bellowed out from his lungs as tendril-like hair whipped around like it had a life of its own. The beast reared back and swung its ax-topped spear over Azrael's head, missing by mere inches. With a quick jerk of his body, Azrael turned back to the creature and sent a fist thrusting up to its gullet, sending blood to spurt out from between the beast's clenched teeth. Azrael swung again but missed as the beast broke free at a blinding speed. The two of them switched off between offensive strike and defensive step. Azrael threw blind punches and kicks mere moments after the creature used its speed to dodge out of his way. All the while, Azrael ducked, jumped, and rolled away from the pendulum swings of the beast's ungodly war ax. Not able to keep up with the creature's speed, Azrael was finally taken by surprise. He felt its heavy cloven hooves crush into the small of his back. Muscle snapped, tendons ripped and bone cracked as the beast sent down the sharpened end of its ax into Azrael's abdomen. A torrent of energy overtook Azrael as he flipped himself over and grabbed the creature's weapon still dug into his side. He kicked the creature off and pulled the ax out of his wound, sending forth a war cry that opened the skies above. Fueled by the ancient code of destruction, Azrael broke the ax in two and tore away any excess flesh that hung from his side, and threw it to the ground.

"You think that can stop me?" Azrael yelled at the beast. His eyes widened and strained under the subconscious change happening from within. The dark pits of his soul overtook the entirety of his eyes, leaving them a pair of obsidian orbs set inside his skull. The beast did no more than break half a smile.

The ground, now stained in the blood of pure rivalry, rumbled with the quickening sprint of the two foes. More crimson nectar flung into the air as the two foes clashed their battle-hardened bodies against each other. Punches were thrown and dodged. Jabs connected and sent bits of flesh out to feed the insects that spectated this grand event. Like a well-choreographed dance, the two warriors fed off the pure rage of the other. Where one would attack and connect, the other would dodge and counter. The beast lunged its knee up into Azrael's face, sending the world-destroyer to the ground. Before Azrael allowed himself to fall, he caught his balance and flipped himself up, sending a full-forced kick into the side of the beast's face. The beast jolted back and ripped its claws into Azrael's stomach, exposing layers of sweet and succulent meat. With each pounding beat of Azrael's heart, blood was expelled from his body. It fell down his flesh and stained the already cursed armor that he used to decorate his form. Never before has any creature been able to cause such a release of pure instinct and survival. For that, Azrael both admired and loathed it.

Ignoring his wounds, Azrael continued on. Their black silhouettes climbed up over the surrounding rocks and stayed as shadows in front of the setting suns. No longer bothered by the self-gratification of victory, they now fought to simply prove to the other that each had no limit. Their arms and legs acted as violent ritualistic extensions with each bone-crushing blow. Fatigue never seemed to set in, even after their features lay unrecognizable. Only the pure heat of battle raged on as they pummeled each other into the surrounding landscape. Soon enough, the beast's speed began to wane as Azrael's rage began to satiate. The two of them realized that there would be no end to this. At one point, that notion did not matter. But as the afternoon sky gave way to rising dusk, their determination faltered. The beast looked at his bloodied and bruised opponent and stared him in the eyes. Azrael watched the creases of its mouth move as it began to speak.

"You are nothing like her," the beast said.

Confused, Azrael lowered his stance and addressed the now calmed creature. "What are you talking about?"

"The other one like you. The other one that came through the crimson sea years ago. She came alone, scarred and plagued by any breath left behind by her innocence. Only I was never able to lay a hand on her. She was a much better fighter than you," the beast said as it laughed lightheartedly while spitting up its own blood.

Azrael let out a small groan and shook his head at the beast. "What meaning is this?" he asked.

"You mark the coming of the Abyss. The Abyss that was spawned by father Chaos before time was time itself."

"I break cycles. I leave nothing more than death in my wake."

"But do you not see? Death and destruction give way to new life. The Seraphim exist in stronger numbers because you rid the universe of their enemies. Their tyranny and absolute reign are your doing. Or did you think that you were purifying those worlds for your Seraphim king?"

Azrael grew cold with the final words that the beast injected into his ears. If it was, in fact, true, then he had killed billions all in the name of lies. "What are you? How do you know all of this?" Azrael asked.

"Consider me a relative lost to time."

* * *

Echoes bounced through the tepid halls of Elysium as the Seraphim gathered towards the antechamber. They numbered in the hundreds. Countless bodies used as living vessels for beings made of pure starlight situated themselves in the gallery surrounding the speaking altar. Hidden within the core of Elysium, the room acted more as a small planet all on its own, existing independent of any known forms of physical reality.

A meeting of this size had its significance in its rarity. Only when the very nature of existence is an issue will the Seraphim embark to hear the proposals of another. Daemos, in this case, was the speaker of such a proposal.

With nearly half of the Seraphim race in attendance, Daemos made his entrance and headed to the center of the globe-like room. He let his eyes wander around to witness the chattering hum of his people. Behind him, Moloch and Gabriel followed. Unlike the rest of their peers, who were dressed in no more than simple white robes, they were adorned in the blood-stained armor of the world they had just left. They marched in confident strides behind the cracked and pale visage of their brother. With tendrils spread out in their golden luminescence, the serpents of the old world looked down upon the self-proclaimed ruler and his two guardians. Daemos stopped in the center of the room and let the cracks that plagued his callous flesh open and release their nectar. Blood fell to the glowing white floor below and raised the dead voices of the world's past to join his own.

"Our tombs are not permanent," Daemos said, with all eyes piercing down upon him. He continued, "We transcend the physical. Are we not the progenitors of life itself? What use is there for us if not to govern the existence of all? I have spent countless ages amongst those endowed by the ways of the flesh. Seen their habits and grown to their customs. They are not unlike us in that they seek to preserve their species. Yet when they become a threat, we set out and destroy them. How is this the way of all life?" Daemos looked around the room and awaited an answer from his peers.

"We do not exterminate our own. That is the difference. Those bound by flesh deserve the outcome of their fate," a fellow Seraph said from high above.

"Those you have ruled and lorded over, Daemos, are not worthy of our light, our gifts. I fail to see why you protect them so," another said.

Daemos interjected with his own reasons back to his peers. "Without our guidance, they will grow and overwhelm us. We must keep them at arm's reach. We must..."

A voice from behind the echoes of the antechamber interrupted the flaccid reasons strewn about by the fledgling god. "You keep your agendas to yourself." His voice was loud and thunderous. It held the history of tens of thousands of years of conflict and battle deep within its growling tone. "We are not gathered here to listen to your defenses. The humans and creatures of Abaddon you lord over are a scapegoat, and we know this. We gave you liege to lay waste to those worlds that were a threat to us. We cared not how you accomplished this. But it seems that the weapon you chose has become the issue at hand."

"What is your point, Samael?" Daemos asked his Seraphim brother.

"You were tasked with eliminating the one threat to our species. The race of creatures that were expunged from the vile depths of the abyss. They are the sole reason for your duties," Samael reminded Daemos.

"And that is exactly what I have done. I have cleansed every known world to harbor those vile creatures."

"It is not a matter of your conviction that bothers us. It is your method."

"What method?"

Samael stood up and stared down at his brother. Unlike his peers, Samael did not choose a pure human host body to inhabit. He instead kept himself within an amalgamation of strewn flesh pieced together by his own sick fetishes. His large almond-shaped eyes glowed red with the fury of war itself, while his face was no more than a skinless mass of muscle and bone, made from the skull of some ancient alien warrior. He decorated his body with the bones and flesh of countless victims that, at one point, lay beneath his feet. In his hands, he held a large scythe used to reap souls and feed his own lust. He was in every essence death itself.

Daemos let his brother stand in attendance. Samael did little to intimidate him, as their lineage was one and the same.

"What method you ask? Why not enlighten us with the fact that you used a descendant of the Abyss to hunt its own kind without it knowing so?" Samael questioned.

"Is this true Daemos?" one of his brothers asked.

"Yes, it is," Answered Daemos.

The crowd grew in an uproar. As the Seraphim began to grow in outrage, they tore away their host bodies, sending scores of human flesh to the ground below. Daemos felt the blood rain down upon him as his brothers grew in anger.

"There was no other way. If you all might well remember, the last time we fought with the Abyss, it took nearly a dozen of us to take a single one of them. I had neither the time nor resources to hunt our enemy down. There is no better way to kill the Abyss than with the Abyss itself," Daemos shouted at the top of his rotted lungs. "I did what you asked of me and used what method I could."

Samael took in a deep breath and let out a blood-curdling yell. "Silence," he growled at the top of his voice. "Where is this creature? This man you called Azrael."

"He is slain. Moloch destroyed him and his guardian."

"Slain? What of Uriel? As I understand, this Azrael of yours has killed one of ours. And who is this guardian you speak of?"

"Yes, Azrael did kill Uriel."

The crowd of unleashed Seraphim gasped and cowered down in fear at Daemos' words.

Daemos continued, "He killed him in retaliation for his attack against my consort, Sophia. She was Azrael's guardian."

"Why did a creature born from the darkest pits of chaos need a guardian?" Samael continued with his interrogation.

"I do not know. She was sent from elsewhere. Azrael was unruly and wild. He was a crazed killer. She seemed to calm him. He was easier to control with her in attendance."

"Then Azrael was not the threat. She was."

Moloch walked up in front of Daemos, his armored boots splashing at the blood beneath his feet. "They are no longer an issue. She died by my blade. Daemos saw to it personally to slit that other vile creature's throat as well," he said.

"Moloch, you are a fool," Samael said. "You did not kill anyone. Neither did your disillusioned master. You have sent them to a world beyond their knowledge. You failed to follow them into the abyss and finish them. If Azrael has reached Baphomet, then he will know the truth. He will know what he is and he will know what we truly are. Most of all, he will know about you, Daemos, and he will know how to kill us all."

* * *

The blackness grew larger in Azrael's heart. A void that hungered for answers, yet only fed upon morsels of half-truths. The beast at his side led him along as they headed away from the bloody shores of perdition and into the heart of this new world. The open red sky above threw down its crimson acromance upon their vision. Azrael knew he was being led to yet another set of truths, but to what end, he did not know.

"Where are you taking me?" Azrael asked the beast.

"You wish to see the undoing of the Seraphim, as do I. For that, you will need answers that only she can give," the beast said.

"And who is she?"

The beast stopped in his tracks and looked out upon the horizon. Azrael walked up next to the creature and peered over the edge of a cliff down towards a large valley hidden by ancient ruins and battle-worn statues. Ruins that were guarded by a set of monstrous gates that seemed to reach to the heavens. Beyond the gates, he could see the faint remnants of a civilization lost to time. In this city lie the answers that Azrael so wished to hear. And in those overwhelming thoughts, the creature said a single name; Baphomet.

V. The Guardians Of Dis

White-hot light spread apart its clandestine symmetry to form a pair of tendril-wrapped wings made of pure unadulterated energy as rigid palms clasped onto their scorched blade and readied themselves for war. The flame-treated armor of the Seraphim covered Moloch's body as he stood at the edge of reality. He released himself into the cold reaches of space and followed the scent left behind by the long-dead corpses of the Abyss. He would do this to find Azrael, on whatever world he was hiding, and kill him once and for all.

* * *

The gates to the ancient city were a sight to behold. They towered over Azrael and his beastly friend. Bodies torn and strewn created the glue that held these giant doors together. They were a pair of glossed black monoliths that threatened the innocent eyes of anyone wishing to get a glimpse of what lie behind them. With a life all on its own, the bodies that made up these doors skewered, teased, fornicated, and tortured each other to no end. Azrael was all but ignored as they refused to open at even the slightest command.

"What is beyond this?" Azrael asked.

"A great city. An ancient city known as Dis. It is the sixth of the great cities built on this world, and Baphomet is its guardian," the beast said.

"How do we pass?"

"Simple. Walk through the doors."

"I have no time for idiocy."

The beast walked up to the door and held out his hand. The charred, blackened hand of some poor maiden reached out and grabbed at the beast. She moaned and sighed as she tried to pull him through. The beast pulled his hand away before she could take him in. Azrael realized the trickery in the grand entrance. To enter the city meant to become a living vessel used to create the city. It thrived on life and allowed only those willing to sacrifice themselves for the greater good to enter.

"To enter this place, you must become part of it. That is Baphomet's will."

"So I must pass through this debauchery in order to get the answers this Baphomet seems to have?"

Azrael lowered his head and took a few deep breaths. He felt hot air fill his lungs as he readied himself to partake in whatever madness this living city had to offer. It took him less than five seconds for him to rear his head, open his eyes, and ready his fists. The beast half expected this to be Azrael's reaction, so he, in turn, prepared for battle.

"I hope you realize what you are doing, my friend," the beast said.

"I know exactly what…" With those words, Azrael was cut-off mid-thought by a thunderous roar.

Between the two giant doors, a torrent of bodies swirled about. They opened up and revealed a pair of blood-red eyes. Then another pair. And another. Sharpened claws peered from the torrential storm of corpses that flooded the doors. They slammed their canine foot on the ground at Azrael's feet. Soon, another giant paw came ripping through. As Azrael looked up at the door, he saw a head peer out with those crimson eyes set in place. Its jaws could swallow a man whole. What followed were two more heads attached to the same set of rock-hard, bony shoulders. This new creature finally stepped its entire body through the living gate of burnt flesh. Its shape was that of a wolf, though upon it sat three heads. It hungered for flesh and snarled at Azrael and his friend. Its size was comparable to a demigod. It was not the hound that kept Azrael's gaze, but the puppeteer controlling it.

She emerged from the gate as well, riding on the hound's back. Her eyes were as blue as a clear sky with hair golden white like that of a newborn star. Her movement captivated Azrael. She showed no fear, nor any other sign of a threatening gesture. She was dressed in a black corset made from the skin of some great beast, leather gauntlets, and fire-tempered boots lined with leather and steel. With every movement she made, the living doors behind her moaned and writhed in a dance macabre of pleasure and pain. In Azrael's eyes, she was a warrior ready for the heat of confrontation.

"Elizabeth. I welcome the guardian to the gates of Dis," the beast said.

"Who else would it be, Belial?" Elizabeth asked the beast. She looked over at Azrael and fell silent for a moment. She shook her head and spoke, "I see you brought my Cerberus a snack."

"Move aside. I have no time for this," Azrael demanded.

Elizabeth pulled at Cerberus's chain. The tri-headed creature howled and frothed at the jaws. Its eyes widened and fixed their gaze on Azrael. Belial crept over to Azrael and whispered into his ear, "Remember the other warrior I mentioned?"

"Yes," Azrael answered.

"That would be her."

Azrael bolted out at the sultry warrior and her pet. "I will not take unfounded threats from either man, woman, or beast. If it is blood you wish to spill, then let us get this over with. I have other matters to attend to."

"You are so quick to raise your arms in battle. Is that all you know?" Elizabeth addressed to Azrael.

Azrael kept his mouth silent. He knew there was something different about her. His tirades about world conquest, endless tortures and single-handedly destroying entire armies would do nothing to amuse her. He stared into her blue-gray eyes and lost himself in another world.

"Nothing to say? You had better go back to where you came from. Come back when you are ready." Elizabeth then turned her attention to Belial. "Next time, bring someone who will actually give me some excitement."

With those words, Azrael's senses widened. He felt something familiar approach. Something divine. Something threatening. In that instant, the earth around them trembled. The gates grew still, and the air felt heavy. Elizabeth looked over Azrael's shoulder and saw a flash of light in the sky. Without warning, that same light fell to the earth and exploded with the force of creation. Dirt and rock were sent up through the air. Azrael and Elizabeth were thrown against each other and into the edge of the gates of Dis. Azrael lifted himself off of Elizabeth and ran to the source of the crash. Smoke filled his lungs as he pushed his body to its limits. The closer he got, the less he could see. The dust was too thick. Out of nowhere, he felt the heat of divine retribution knock him back. Moloch had arrived.

Azrael picked himself up and threw his body into the cloud of dust without hesitation. Again, he was knocked back.

"You never learn, do you?" Moloch laughed.

Azrael swung blindly into the air with no avail. Moloch sent him to the ground time and time again. Finally, Azrael ran back to Elizabeth and Belial.

"Leave now. Go back into the city. Stay there," Azrael told Elizabeth.

"I think not," Elizabeth answered.

From beyond the smoke, Moloch made his appearance. His skin was still glowing white from the explosive landing, with trails of flame following behind each footstep.

Elizabeth loosened her grip on Cerberus and sent forth the flesh-hungry beast. Moloch raised his sword and ran towards them. Belial lunged out from the shadows and knocked down the Seraphim assassin. Elizabeth kept with her a serpentine whip, a weapon with a spiked handle that connected chain to twine and tipped with shards of molded bone. She released it from around her waist and struck the Seraphim in the chest. Belial and Elizabeth exchanged blows while Azrael carefully made his way behind Moloch. Cerberus reared his body up and crushed Moloch beneath his paws. The Seraphim threw the three-headed dog off of him and sent it flying off into Elizabeth and Belial.

"I have no time for this. Show yourself, Azrael," Moloch yelled out.

Azrael grabbed Moloch's throat from behind and pulled him in close. He dug his claws into Moloch's jugular and squeezed tight.

"Does this seem familiar to you?" Azrael asked.

With those words, Azrael ripped Moloch's throat out, sending a torrential downpour of divine nectar to the ground below. Moloch's life faded from his eyes as his neck spewed forth Seraphim flavored human blood. Before completely passing, Moloch closed his eyes and ripped open his chest. A flash of pure white light shot out from the newly formed cavity. For a split second, Azrael saw something in the light. He saw a creature with large black eyes stare back at him. Its skin was pale and gray. Tendrils took the place of wings and an exposed rib cage covered a heart made of thunder and ice. He saw the true form of the Seraphim. Within seconds, it rose to the skies above and disappeared from sight.

Azrael looked to the skies and breathed deep the final moments of his most recent victory, for he knew that complacency was a gesture only found in those brief moments between the letting of blood and pure unfounded solitude. Moloch would return and with him, an army of Seraphim would follow, ready to heed his every command.

"It seems your presence has attracted more than a simple query from the ever-watchful eyes of the gods," Elizabeth said to Azrael.

"They know I am here," Azrael said aloud. He walked up to Elizabeth, who was clutching onto the reigns of Cerberus' collar as well as the tendrilesque weapon she possessed. "This is but a taste of the threat that will follow if you continue to halt my way towards this Baphomet."

"I have done nothing to stop you, but I will not stand by as you threaten the lifeblood of Dis by attempting to smash down its doors of judgment," Elizabeth said.

"I have no time for this. I am not going to become part of some flesh-consuming cityscape."

Elizabeth reared her weapon and commanded Cerberus to lie at rest. She saw the fear and confusion in Azrael's eyes as he spoke to her. "You are mistaken. If you are worthy and your intentions pure, then the gates will let you pass. It is only if you wish to do harm to Dis or Baphomet that you will be consumed. This I cannot change. I guard these gates and enforce their will. I do not create it," Elizabeth said to Azrael.

With his nerves tensed and his muscles burning from a thousand years of war driven by betrayal, Azrael clenched his fists and lowered his head. He kept his eyes forward as he took in breath after breath. Never before has he felt fear more so than at this moment. No amount of bloodshed or sacrifice could amount to the possibility of his intentions not becoming rendered as pure in the eyes of this living gateway. Their blackened gaze pierced deep into his mind as he marched up to the monolithic effigy. All the while Elizabeth, Cerberus and Belial watched and waited to see what judgment would be handed to Azrael as he passed.

The charred and crimson cracked hand of some poor maiden reached out to Azrael. Soon after, a hundred more hands reached for his flesh. When Azrael reached his hand out, the living wall of burnt and lacquered corpses retracted in fear. Their flesh peeled back, exposing rotted muscle tissue and frayed nerve endings. As Azrael got closer, the wall of now glistening red meat had further subsided into a portal made of blood and bone. With a single touch of his finger, bones cracked and collapsed, allowing Azrael to pass. Elizabeth looked on in shock and wonder as Azrael walked through the gates of Dis unabated. His very presence had caused even the tormented souls that made up the horror of these gates to collapse in on themselves with fear. Elizabeth knew at that moment that maybe he was meant to find Baphomet and perhaps even free Dis from its bondage.

* * *

Disappointment is a term seldom used by the Seraphim. In the case of Moloch's return, it will be a term that they will have to regretfully grow accustomed. With the shell of his flesh expelled, Moloch returned not as a bearer of conquest but of defeat. The cold sins of regret flowed through the veins of the Seraphim crusader as he headed back to the nightmare dreamscape he called his home. While he pieced back together a new earthly body made of blood and stone, Samael awaited Moloch's visit.

With his headstrong confidence renewed by the taste of flesh, Moloch set foot into Samael's domain, the scent of death itself invading his senses. Rusted chains hung from giant gears fueled by the fires of war and divinity. Pillars made of the living damned acted as the skeletal frame for Samael's chamber of endless tortures. In this mansion of earthly delights did Samael weave his workings, as the judge of all things attuned to death. Seeing himself as the scale of justice in a universe gone mad with procreation, Samael took it upon himself to carry the mantle of 'Reaper.' Not to be undone by the very nature of mortality did Samael build his house of sacred remains on the edge of the universe; a towering mausoleum hidden away from the virgin eyes of the living and the divine alike. Perhaps it was out of sheer servitude or a grand culmination of seniority and severance that Samael was allowed to don the black shroud of judgment.

Moloch stared up at the gateway to the forbidden, hoping his brother would grant him sanctuary. The steps beneath his feet seemed to float upon the very stars that gave birth to his kind. The fortress did not sit upon rock nor stone but instead stayed adrift among the crushed bones and innards of whom Samael deemed to be guilty of sin. Moment by moment, the undead foundation to this house of horrors grew as death here kept itself hidden well from the rest of reality. Samael made sure that nary a man, god, or any other such beast could reach his soul asylum. Moloch knew that by looking up at the entrance to the afterlife that his brother meant that he had been invited. For had he not been, he would have already joined his long-dead brothers in the place where sleep has no name.

"Samael, brother, what sort of madness have you wrought upon yourself?" Moloch whispered to himself.

"The sort of madness that allows the very threads of existence to continue to unravel their tidings against the very nature of our father," Samael said to Moloch. He made his black silhouette appearance from between the cracks of escaped light in the halls of the recently deceased.

Samael stepped out of the light and took the steps down to Moloch. His Seraphim form had been completely erased by some other grim effigy. He wore upon him a layer of black tar expulsion made from the rancid bile of the diseased. His face had been seared away, leaving no more than a few strands of muscle tissue pieced together from various forms of creature. On his back sat a pair of sanguine wings, charred and blackened to perfection. A towering ax had replaced his Seraphim staff of ceremony with a crescent blade that he used to cut the life force from those whose time had come.

"By the words of our father, what have you become? I meant not to question your appearance at the last gathering, but this is against all we stand for," Moloch said to his death ruling brother.

"And what is it that we stand for, brother? Justice? The welfare of life? The welfare of our species? I have taken up the mantle that none have been so brave to even consider. I have become Death itself. I am not a tool, nor am I its instigator. I simply harvest those that do not fit within the cycle of life and rebirth. You of all should know about that, Moloch. With each physical body you inhabit, I must steer their soul to their destiny," Samael said.

"But these humans are nothing. They have no meaning. They are not eternal as we are."

"Eternal? Why would one ask for such a curse? The fact that you are even using a fleshly name is proof in itself that you have lost touch with what you are. All of you have lost what it means to be a Seraph. Daemos especially."

Moloch's rage grew inside as he heard the blasphemies spewed forth by his brother's tainted tongue. "It is unfortunate that we must use fleshly vessels to spread our doctrine, but name or not, I have not forgotten who or what I am. I am a Seraphim warrior and I will be the instrument for vengeance against the death of our brothers."

"Now that sounds more like the brother I know," Samael said with a cracked, maggot-dripping grin.

Samael turned around and headed back inside his black dimension of archaic ministries. Moloch followed suit while staying locked in shock and awe at the various oceans of grotesque harmonies. He followed his brother into the very realm of death itself.

"There was something you said before, brother, about Azrael learning of ways to extinguish us. If you remember, he did best Uriel with a single swipe to the neck. I am sure Azrael knows of other ways to kill us," Moloch said to Samael.

"Is that so?" Samael asked.

"What I do not understand is why, if he was able to kill Uriel so swiftly, I was so easily spared?"

Samael stopped in his tracks as the two brothers entered the house that death ruled over. Moloch saw in his brother's eyes that there was something being kept from him.

"Your answers lie not with me, but with one who might better explain your predicament," Samael said.

"Who?" Moloch asked.

"Why, Uriel, of course," Samael said as he laughed.

* * *

None so vile had the city of Dis, the city of ancient sights and prophecies, been accustomed to than that of a hunter stalking his prey. An alien more so to this world than the language that drifted across his tongue did Azrael feel as he stepped his feet across the carcass landscape so many called home. Almost as if he had been called by some romantic notion of revenge, did he keep his head up high. Vultures circled above his vision, clawing and feeding at the remains of those left dead by their previous assailants. They gnawed and tugged at bright red flesh while still attached to bodies that hung from mile-high broken and rusted gates. Upon the outskirts of Dis were the barren wastelands infected with the still-beating drums of war. The dead speak volumes not in their posture but in the emptiness of their carcasses. Dis had become no more than a city of rubble piled in and atop itself. The city still rustled with life, but not the kind of life that thrives on industry. The life of Dis had been replaced with the chattering hum of scavengers and vermin ready to pick and pull at anything worth being called a meal.

"To think someone may call this home is almost heresy," Belial said.

Elizabeth walked with Cerberus and scoured the all too familiar landscape. "It was not always like this. You know that, Belial. You, in fact, once called this place home," Elizabeth said.

"That was long ago. To think that this is what had become of Dis is unimaginable."

Azrael looked around and almost felt a tinge of guilt for perhaps being responsible for the endless sea of destruction. "What happened here?" he asked.

"Life happened. Too much life. The only outcome is the inevitability of war. There were those who embraced Baphomet. Then there were those who, well, I think it is quite obvious," Elizabeth said.

"Why is Baphomet so important? I have never heard this name before and now it is almost sacred on the tongues of those I hear it from," Azrael wondered.

"Some say that she, or he, is an empath gifted with the knowledge of the gods. If one seeks guidance, then it is Baphomet that they should seek to find," Belial vaguely answered.

"Is the entire city burned like this?" Azrael asked.

"No, just the outskirts near the gates of judgment. A few more hours and we should reach the heart of Dis. There is where we will find civilization," Elizabeth answered.

"What better way to keep the outsiders out than to keep the remnants of a dead city to surround that which still thrives," Belial said.

For hours, they walked down the road to perdition. On either side lay the remnants of a once great city, now only a pile of rubble. As the sun set in the distance, so too did their eager and battle-ready awareness, for the eyes of the enemy watched close their every movement. Soon, all light would drift to further shores as they ventured deeper into the still-beating heart of Dis.

VI. The Dead City

The old city was a graveyard. Horrific warnings of stale flesh and bone paved the way on the long trek into the heart of Dis. The gates were but a simple prerequisite to deem one worthy, as the road into Dis was the real test. One that any who wish to enter must overcome if they are truly to be a permanent force within the ancient landscape.

From around every tattered corpse, every fog-enshrouded vista, and every pack of feeding carrion, did the eyes of a malevolent flock watch Azrael. The others were of no concern to the hungry parasites waiting to sink their teeth into the grand prize of their master's calling. This was the will of the land and the machinations from which it beckoned its cycle of life and decay. Blood spilled from the flailing body of a descendant of the Abyss was more precious than the secrets of creation. Only the black acromance of Baphomet's gifts made stable the scavengers that plagued the stale and barren city of Dis. The scavengers, a leftover race of mortal men pieced together by famine and malnourished meat hanging from brittle bone, watched Azrael pass with eyes blood-filled and sunken. They licked at the cracks across their dried lips while grinding their protruded fingers into their close-to-nonexistent loins. Their need for consumption outlived any other notion of self-preservation.

Elizabeth slowed her stride as Cerberus sniffed out a potential battle line from the still-unknown threat. Above them, the sky cracked and growled, splitting apart the calm of the air while giving birth to a blackened whirlpool. The earth shook as thunder and untainted malevolence rushed down from above. Azrael looked up at the newly formed clouds and closed his eyes as the hot sting of acid rain hit his face. Cerberus shook his body as if to temporarily dry his fur while Elizabeth and Belial looked to the skies with concern. Ahead of them, the landscape became a blurred shroud of fog and rain. Azrael, still concentrated on the storm above, laughed and sighed while the others watched in despair.

"What could you possibly find so amusing?" Elizabeth asked.

Azrael brought his head back down and gave one knee to the wet and muddled ground below. He grasped a handful of mud while staring at the torrential downfall that lay in their path.

Elizabeth, confused as to what he meant, knew that there was more to his gesture than he let on. She saw the look of sadness and hopelessness that his body language so freely gave away. "What do you know?" she asked with genuine concern.

"Water will be traded for blood," Azrael said.

"You know something. What is it that you are not telling us?" Elizabeth asked.

"Just be ready," Azrael said.

Belial watched as Cerberus growled and reared his teeth at the surrounding landscape. Remnants of civilization lie in ruin all around them. What was once a sprawling metropolis of gothic beauty now acted as a den for flesh-hungry scavengers.

"Azrael is right. We are walking into a trap," Belial said, wiping the warm rain from his obsidian eyes.

"That is nonsense. I have lived amongst these ruins my entire life. The vermin that infect these parts are no more dangerous than rabid children," Elizabeth said with cocky self-assurance. She removed herself from Azrael's side and continued to trek along with Cerberus as her guide.

Belial walked up to Azrael and looked at him with strange intents as he spoke.

"She is a strange one. I can see, though, that you are not put off by her stubbornness. She is a lot like you," Belial said to Azrael.

"No one is like me," Azrael said as he walked away.

"Time will tell, my friend," Belial said as he picked up his pace.

With the ground becoming less stable, the scavengers began to sniff out their prey. From atop the battered roofs of the surrounding decay, they watched Azrael move with his companions. The beasts snarled and hissed while they reared and chomped their rotted teeth at each other. Armed with no more than their callous flesh and eroded nails, they moved along the broken skyline, following their potential meal. The beating rain hid the sound of their movement while they jumped and scurried from rooftop to rooftop, their vague human form helping them to blend in with the corpses already set in place. They hid amongst the vessels of the dead while using stone and rock to travel and follow.

The rain began to fall louder and harder, further hindering the path to Baphomet. Cerberus reeled back his growls into slight whimpers. Elizabeth drew her body back into Azrael's hold without a conscious effort. She silently stood next to him, hoping that her gestures alone would be enough to convey a need for temporary protection. Azrael knew this and locked himself into an all too familiar motion.

Belial sniffed at the stale wetness of the air and smelt the stench of an impending threat. "We are outnumbered," He said.

Elizabeth bumped her body against Azrael's and, for the first time, showed a hint of fear.

"I can smell their hunger," Azrael said.

At this point, Azrael had only to decide whether he would be the first to strike. Broken and destroyed temples of stone and brick lie on either side of the road they were traveling. Behind them stood the gates from which they could escape back. Ahead of them lay the path to Baphomet, the path to curious revelations.

Without warning, a blaze of tattered flesh swept across Azrael's liquefied vision. There was no rhyme or reason to the nature of the attack, just a base primal surge of violence. Elizabeth twisted her body and screamed out as she lunged forward and decapitated the attacking beast with her razor-sharp whips. Another jumped down from the cracked walls around them and bit into Elizabeth's arm. A splash of warm nectar hit Azrael in the face as he was reminded of the outcome of each and every world he had a hand in destroying. Azrael ripped the beast from Elizabeth's grasp and tore his hands into its gut. With its entrails spilled to the soaked ground below, the thing convulsed and choked on its discord.

"Tell me that you did not bring this upon us," Elizabeth said to Azrael.

"This is your land, remember? Your world. Whatever hunts us is your doing!" Azrael yelled at Elizabeth.

Elizabeth stood up and faced the enraged Azrael. "So, that is your game? You care only for your own life and damned are we to fend for ourselves."

"You are already dead. I have neither the choice nor the luxury of such an escape. Be glad that you are free of such a curse," Azrael said as he watched the newly formed threat race across the war-torn cityscape.

"My only curse is waking up in this godforsaken world," Elizabeth said aloud.

With Elizabeth's blood still running down his face mixed with the salt of his sweat, and the rain above, he tasted something he had almost forgotten about. Sophia. Elizabeth's blood tasted a striking resemblance to hers. Azrael turned his head and watched Elizabeth slay creature after creature without a hint of apathy or regret. She flung her body over and under each scavenger as they fell from the ruins above. He watched her spill their blood and separate their limbs from bone. She moved the way he did before the downfall of some doomed civilization. He had found what he was looking for.

Belial purged his claws from the belly of an attacking scavenger while Elizabeth tore away at its throat from behind. By the time they had killed one, ten more had seemingly arrived to pounce upon them. Cerberus ripped and tore his hungry jaws at every opportunity, while Elizabeth and Belial kept the horde at bay. Azrael watched as the beasts circled around their position. They singled him out and focused their frenzy on the others. He knew what they were doing. The others were of no concern to the beasts. It was his flesh they were saving for last.

With Elizabeth, Belial, and Cerberus at their last stand of survival, they huddled together and prayed that the end came quick. The beasts numbered in the hundreds. Their hot breath penetrated the ever-flowing current of rain that never seemed to let up. For a moment, though, the rain did seem to stop. Like a crazed madman, Azrael came crashing through while digging his fists into the backs of a legion of beasts. He screamed and growled as Elizabeth looked on in sheer wonder.

"It is my blood they want, and it is my blood they will have," Azrael growled out.

"You are a madman," Elizabeth said.

Azrael shook his head while he tore his claws into the skull of an unsuspecting scavenger at his feet.

The storm grew louder as the bloodletting continued. Both the sky and surrounding fog turned a pale gray with a hint of black rapture to further deepen all senses of despair. Belial slashed away at the creatures with some archaic weapon he had found stuck in a pile of rubble. The rigid edge of its stone blade ripped and snagged on the flesh of those he murdered.

Elizabeth and Cerberus went back and forth between juggling the scavenger's brittle anatomy up into the air, pausing only for falling rivers of blood to vacate their vision.

Azrael looked on as the swarm grew larger. With a majestic beauty, they clawed and toppled over each other. Their intelligence lies in their determination. They followed the fumes of chaos back to Azrael and sent sharp swipes of pain across his body.

With their main target now in thrall, they all but ignored the others. Elizabeth, Belial, and Cerberus were kept at bay while the beasts ravaged Azrael's flesh to a meaty supper. Elizabeth focused her gaze on one of the humanoid creatures as it stared back at her from atop Azrael's torn-open chest. It smiled at her and sent its teeth back into his exposed tissue. There was nothing she, nor the others, could do as the swarm grew larger until the moment when all they could see was a wall of broken bodies amassed over a helpless world destroyer. Somewhere in the distance, Elizabeth heard the sound of angelic laughter.

* * *

Rising bellows of fog and dust swirled from beneath the bloodied rocks of the dead city. A stark silence grew as the rain came to a halting closure. Content with their meal, the scavengers crawled away like cowards, leaving no more than a trail of famine and malevolence in their wake. Belial and Cerberus saw a look of regret sweep across Elizabeth's face. The two of them kept their silence and gave her the ground to walk on her own accord.

Elizabeth dropped her weapons and took ease when approaching the Azrael's tattered body. His chest still filled with air as each breath drew him further from consciousness. Barely noticeable were the slight adjustments in his movement. If there was life left in Azrael, there was not much to spare. With one eyeball torn from its socket, Azrael used the other, halfway covered by a blackened lid, to look up at Elizabeth. She fell to her knees and tried to come up with the nerve to speak and say, 'I'm sorry.' Before she could break the silence of her voice, she heard the heavy clanking of footsteps approach.

Heavy-plated boots trotted along with thick chains bound by the glory of some avatar of justice. The creature stood a rough seven feet high and kept itself covered in a black and red cloak. Upon its head, it wore a crown tipped in balance with the scales of Hades. The judge Minos had made his appearance. He walked up to Elizabeth and put his hand on her shoulder while looking over her and onto Azrael's barely living corpse.

"You have no idea who this man is and yet you weep for him," The judge Minos said to Elizabeth. "The black taint of his soul is what enticed those loathsome creatures to so greedily feast upon his flesh. You may not know it, and he certainly does not know it, but the one you cry for is not entirely human, if even at all."

Elizabeth stood up and looked Minos in his hideously disfigured face. "Of course he is not human. You think I am a fool? He is an immortal sent by the gods to free us of the Seraphim," Elizabeth shouted.

Minos laughed as kept looking at Azrael's vacant stare. "You are half right. He is to free us of the Seraphim but he is not an immortal. He is of the Abyss," Minos said.

"How do you know this?" Elizabeth asked.

"Come now Elizabeth. You know better than to question a Judge of Baphomet. The gears have turned and my place is here. Azrael has spoken to Leviathan in the dead flesh sea of Kingu. Or have you forgotten your history? He has bested Belial, the beast of the earth. And here he lays dead but dreaming, breathing in the air of his own martyrdom. All that remains is a trial by fire before he can be announced by any title from the lips of our holy mother. You do remember the trials of Baphomet, do you not? Oh, of course you would forget," Minos said to a confused Elizabeth.

Elizabeth held her head in a complacent state of sadness while she muttered her broken phrases. "It was because of him that those loathsome creatures attacked us, was it not?" she asked.

"Yes, it was his ancient blood that fueled their dormant hunger. Are you not listening? What is your point?" Minos rebutted.

"It means that he is more important to us than you can imagine," Elizabeth answered.

* * *

The judge Minos led Elizabeth, Belial, and Cerberus across the barren wasteland of Dis. Held together by ancient chains, Cerberus dragged Azrael's half-living body behind upon his beaten and mangled back. The beast howled for the near-fallen warrior as Minos kept the party on the track to Acheron, the city in which Baphomet resided. Dis was now no more than a recent memory as the group set foot into the lake of blood and fire that Acheron was named after. Step after step, they traveled through the infected swamp, each press of their feet letting off a geyser of molten plasma. The suns in the distance blended their red glow with the fiery liquid that defied the horizon.

The shores of Acheron hissed and enveloped every living thing that dared to wreak havoc within its sanctum. As Minos drew closer to the open roads ahead, time seemed to stop for no one. Elizabeth walked ahead of Minos and stared off into the distant lights of the thriving city, now only mere footsteps away. Cerberus dragged his claws from out of the gooey blood swamp and onto a cold road made of brick and stone. The night-sprung creatures of Dis had spread their journey across the land as well. Acheron was no stranger to the vermin that now plagued all of this world.

"A city within a city. Acheron is a true sight of beauty," Minos exclaimed.

"If not for the barricade that Dis has been forcefully chosen as, your precious Acheron would not even exist. This is a city of conspiracy. It is any wonder why Baphomet would decide to abandon Dis and settle here," Belial said with a stark glare at the judge Minos.

"Jealousy is hard to swallow. Is it not earth dweller? Dis is old. Acheron is the new flesh. Soon all of this world will be judged according to our ways," Minos answered.

Elizabeth walked up with Cerberus and pushed her way past Minos and Belial. She had grown tired of the petty squabbling between the people that had invaded her city. "Let us just get Azrael to Baphomet and be done with this. I grow tired of the Seraphim and their threats," she said with a hint of anger in her tone.

"Oh, do not worry. There will be plenty of time for threats," Minos said under his breath.

Down the stone path they walked, deeper into the city of Acheron. On either side of them, people watched from beyond their homes. Men, women, and children hid themselves behind barricaded windows and locked doors. The towering vistas lined up and around a central town plaza where many meetings were conducted for all to see. Minos led them through the residential paths and towards Acheron's central heart.

As the group got closer to the platform in the center of the rustling city, Cerberus slowed his stride. He stuck his trio of noses into the air and sniffed out a familiar scent. It was a scent of burnt bone and immediate danger. Elizabeth walked up and reassured him that there was nothing to fear.

With the center of town in view, Cerberus dropped Azrael's body onto a round slab of concrete and raised stone. Minos walked up to the world-destroyer and snarled his black-toothed grin.

"Where is Baphomet?" Elizabeth demanded.

"Oh, yes Baphomet. Your goat-headed mother whore. She, I am sorry...It...will not be joining us," Minos said with a sickening smile upon his face.

"What are you going on about? Azrael is a creature of prophecy. It is only within Baphomet to awaken him and save us from the Seraphim," Belial interrupted.

As Elizabeth looked around and saw every window and door sealed, she knew that they had made a grave mistake in following and trusting Minos. Cerberus growled and barked at a distant road from which a shadowy figure gave its entrance. His form grew brighter and his presence ever more daunting. The sound of clanking metal accompanied his stride along with the smell of burnt flesh and molten steel. It was a scent that Cerberus knew was unmistakable. He smelt the rotting carcass of a Seraphim vessel.

Minos walked up to the Seraph and greeted him. "Apollyon, how pleasant to see you here. I believe that this is the creature you asked for?" Minos gloated as he looked over at Azrael.

"What have you done? You led them right to us," Elizabeth said in shock.

"We cannot fight the divine majesty of our creators. The Seraphim will give us paradise, in return all they ask is a sacrifice. The last of the living Abyss," Minos said.

Apollyon stepped up to Elizabeth and put his hand on her chest. "I can feel your connection to that pitiful creature. You remind him of someone he once cared for. That was, until I stuck her like the animal she was," Apollyon said to Elizabeth.

Belial and Cerberus slowly moved around the Seraphim and planned to charge their newfound threat. Before they could get in a single move, the sky lit up like the breath of a fiery inferno. Clouds and wind cracked as thousands of pure-form Seraphim came rushing to the ground below. Apollyon raised his head and welcomed his brothers to the new land on which he stood.

"Our world has come to an end," Belial said to both Elizabeth and Cerberus.

Apollyon walked over to Azrael and lifted his body off the ground. With a single gesture, a pillar of rock and chain shot up from underneath the round slab Azrael just moments ago rested upon. Apollyon placed the comatose Azrael against the pillar and chained his flesh to its surface. Minos walked over to Azrael and looked up at the world-destroyer in his final moments while Apollyon spoke in his ear.

"I remember your face. More so, I remember your blood and that of hers as I spilled it in my father's name. Did you think a creature such as yourself could best a son of creation? I only regret that Moloch is not here to witness the murder of the last of the Abyss," Apollyon said to Azrael.

Elizabeth began to feel her heart beat faster with each passing second. She knew that Baphomet held the secrets to prophesy and that this moment had been part of her planned destiny. As Apollyon's cracked and clawed hand move closer to Azrael's chest, she knew the nature of what was to come. She waited for Apollyon to dig his fingers in and clutch the heart of the world-destroyer. In that instant, the Seraphim fell into his vanity of a premature victory. Using Belial's primitive weapon, she lunged forward and ripped and slashed at the hand holding onto Azrael's heart. Apollyon slapped Elizabeth away while the brittle bone of the vessel he was using broke in two. Apollyon grabbed onto his flesh and pulled away his arm. The severed forearm stayed locked within Azrael's chest, its fingers still clutching his heart. Apollyon tried to reach for the forearm, which still burned with the pure inferno of Seraphim light, but before he could reach it, flames overtook the appendage. The forearm had gone up in a blaze, and Azrael's body caught fire with it.

Minos took a few steps away from Azrael's body while he muttered prophetic nonsense to himself. "No. The Seraphim were to save us from the Abyss. What have you done?" Minos asked in anger at Elizabeth.

"I have given him the trial by fire, as you so elegantly explained," Elizabeth said to Minos.

The blazing inferno grew larger and larger. Black smoke rose to the sky as distant cries of creatures born in darkness gave forth their wailing call. Azrael could hear the voice of the Abyss as he felt his body die. With no blood destination set, there was no other reason to be reborn into a new body made from the blood sea. The plumes of flame and smoke gave away their shadowy intents as Azrael's body burned with the heat of a thousand suns. His flesh melted and seared while his bones were charred a permanent black. His human form had twisted and contorted itself into a nightmarish creature of diabolical design. With the sweet aroma of death, did he breathe in the circling winds of Dis. And now, with the fire of a crippled Seraphim, was he able to find true life and complete his nature. As the flames whipped and pulled across Azrael's flesh, somewhere in the dark recesses of retribution, the ancient gods gave their blessing. A new devil was born.

VII. Nemesis

Chaos. The Abyss. The weights of their meaning multiplied as the shrieking call of those charred and eyeless creatures found respite in the knowledge that they had been reborn. In the middle of a city called Dis, one of their own had found its way to a chamber of rebirth. The fires of retribution rose higher than mortal eyes could see. Its unnatural burn halted the advances of the Seraphim legion from preying down upon the city and its inhabitants.

With passing moments of calm indemnity, Minos waited for Azrael to awaken. Apollyon stared at the towering inferno in genuine fear. After a few minutes had passed, Minos began to laugh.

Belial walked up to Elizabeth and put a sympathetic hand on her shoulder. "You did what you could. He is no more than a…" Belial was interrupted by the sound of cracking bone and tearing flesh.

With the flames at their apex, a roar of thunder shook the ground. Demonic wings made of burnt flesh and translucent skin spread from beneath the flames. They shot up to the sky with a trail of tail-like fire to guide their way back. The beast twisted and turned in the air before it came crashing back down. Its face resembled that of Azrael's, with added horns protruding from above his brow. Where his nose once was, lay only two simple slots for taking in breath. Carnivorous teeth hid behind a pair of wet and slithery lips while three forked tongues peeked out from behind. His skin was dark gray and highlighted by areas of charred flesh. His hair had become a series of whip-like tendrils that moved and lived of their own accord. He spread his wings again and flexed his blackened claws, hissing and growling. From beyond his backside whipped a tail that was lined with quills, sharpened to a razor's touch. Azrael had been reborn. He was now the product of his ancestry. No longer was he to be held permanently captive by his human form under a Seraphim curse. He was the Abyss.

Not completely transformed, he still partly resembled his human form. His muscle structure and anatomy still lay intact while hind legs, sprawling wings, a whip-like tail, and infernal visage made him stand out from his human and Abyssal brethren.

Elizabeth looked up at the devil and uttered a single word as he growled into the still of the air. "Beautiful."

With his nerves finally calmed, Azrael took a still posture and stared his black eyes into Apollyon's soul. Apollyon shed his human vessel as fast as he could to make a quick escape. Before he was able to fully make his leave, he felt something no Seraphim had truly felt in a thousand years; pain. Azrael dug his claws deep into Apollyon's spine and tore out the Seraph's still-beating heart from behind. Apollyon's body fell back to the ground as pools of liquid light gushed out from the newly formed cavity. His angelic tentacle-made wings struggled to move as he crawled away. Azrael floated back down and turned Apollyon over to face him. He shoved the Seraph's heart into his demonic mouth and swallowed it whole. Apollyon looked in disbelief and faded out of reality. Azrael grabbed the dying Seraph and whispered into his aura, "Consider this your final death."

A slave to the ravenous lure of violence had Azrael become. In every true intent was he a product of the Abyss. As dawn played its strings against the horizon, the fires of retribution laid low to give way to their son. His image stayed burned in the minds of the surrounding Seraphim as they witnessed the birth of a new creature. The hunters had become the hunted. Ancient prophecies reeled their leathery tongues as would-be saviors grew in tirades enveloped by rabid fear. No such palpable offerings could hold over the angelic choir before they would soon be turned into a meal for the newborn demon. And as a demon, he hungered.

Legions of Seraphim warriors swarmed the skies above. They rained down with a torrent of violent fury as Azrael looked up at the glowing mass of his next meal. One by one they flew down and struck at his flesh, causing little to no damage to the newborn spawn of the Abyss. With each strike, he grabbed at their mortal form and ripped them apart at the seams to expose their glowing flesh. After murdering a score of the would-be Seraphim assassins, Azrael took to the skies and hunted his prey in the same air they occupied.

Minos looked on in horror as the demon of prophecy laid out his plan of barbaric carnage. "We are all doomed. The gates of oblivion will open and he will lead us into a world of fire and eternal suffering. The world destroyer will consume us all," Minos said in pure terror.

"You are as big a fool as you are a liar. It is within your Seraphim saviors that the world will burn. They care nothing for any life besides their own," Elizabeth said back to Minos.

"How can you be so sure? Look at him. He is pure evil," Minos said as he watched Azrael tear the Seraphim limb from limb in the bloodied skies above.

Belial walked up to Elizabeth and the judge Minos and watched on with an equal amount of amazement. "It depends on where you stand. From what I can see, Azrael is ridding this world of a plague. Were our gods not made immortal because of their sacrifice to the ones before them? The Abyss are a race of survivors. They live in the dark and the dark will always be there, no matter the invading source of light thrust upon it. For light will eventually fade and the darkness will still be," Belial said to Minos.

"For all of our sake, I hope you to be right," Minos said back.

With each slain Seraph, Azrael watched as their bodies were set ablaze by the imploding blast of their own waning life force. Masses of fiery corpses fell down to the ground below. The city of Acheron burned, engulfed by the consequence of the battle ensuing overhead. The fires of war continued to rise as the Seraphim continued their strikes against Azrael. Neither he nor the Seraphim knew when to quit the onslaught. Even with their fallen brothers numbering in the hundreds, the Seraphim still rushed against Azrael. People below left their burning homes and tried desperately to find safety. Some ran to the outskirts of the city walls, while others lay trapped under a charred grave. Azrael saw this and halted his movements. His warmongering had spilled into the streets of those not touched by either the Abyss or Seraph. He had brought war to those undeserving of the act. Before he had the chance to stop his engagement, though, he saw the Seraphim concentrate their havoc on the innocent. Knowing that they had little to no chance of stopping Azrael, they instead focused their efforts on slaughtering the people of Acheron and in turn planned on using their fresh corpses as vessels for future Seraphim consorts.

Elizabeth ran and dodged each swipe of the ancient blade as she sprinted to a Seraph holding the corpse of a small child. Before the creature was able to secure his breath within the child's body, she thrust her blade into the Seraph's back and skewered its electric heart. "Let the dead die in peace, you foul creature," Elizabeth said to the slain Seraph.

Belial looked at Cerberus and, with a single animalistic gesture, told the three-headed hound to get those still living to safety. Cerberus ran off and snatched up those that still had enough breath to cry out in pain. He carried them upon the fur of his back and headed for the edge of the city, dodging and weaving between the falling inferno of Seraphim dead.

"Do you see? Azrael is sending the burnt bodies of his slain down upon the innocent people of this city. He will do this to us all. You must trust the Seraphim," Minos cried out.

"No. He is simply fighting with his truest intentions. Any aftermath is of no consequence. Now keep quiet," Belial said as he struck Minos down.

Minos, enraged, grabbed Apollyon's fallen weapon and used its power to pull at the earth beneath Belial's feet, trapping the satyr in a coffin of rock and stone. Minos picked himself up and laughed as he gloated over his newfound prisoner. "May the beast of the earth stay encased within the earth," Minos said to the trapped Belial.

With Elizabeth and Azrael busy fending off the Seraphim horde, Minos called out to any ally that might be within earshot. "Go and find that other wretched beast. Do not slay the dog, but take him for the slave he will become," Minos shouted out.

"No. What has that fool of a judge done?" Elizabeth asked herself as she watched Minos and a party of Seraphim brethren drag away the encased Belial. The harder she tried to run towards the traitor judge, the more she found herself surrounded and outnumbered. One of the overzealous killers decided to speak to her.

"Submit and you will find paradise. There is nothing to fear," it said to her.

Elizabeth stabbed the Seraph in the chest and watched as its heart exploded in a blaze of liquid light. "I already knew paradise before you arrived," she said back.

Seeing the young warrior girl surrounded, Azrael reared his body and flew down toward her. He crashed into the ground and sent a dozen Seraphim up into the air. Without even a pause in his stride, he charged forward and carved a bloody path to the trapped Elizabeth. Her attackers turned around and saw the oncoming meat grinder as it made its way closer. With claw, tail, and serrated wing, Azrael mutilated the unsuspecting Seraphim all around him. The sky above was a canvas of blood-painted carnage.

The dance macabre played out like a ballet of virulent gore-painted discharge as Azrael moved with the speed of a bolt of lightning. Elizabeth grabbed and pulled at any and all limbs within reach. She sent scores of Seraphim victims into Azrael's unstoppable rampage, the two of them working in tandem off of each other's actions. Elizabeth would lead her targets, and Azrael would take the kill.

With the surrounding area now in ruins, there was no further need to wage war. The remaining Seraphim took to the skies and left behind their wounded and dead. Azrael landed his feet on the bloody ground below and stood by Elizabeth's side. They watched as the Seraphim took retreated back to the safety of the wailing heavens. When all was done, they were the only living creatures to stand in the now charred center of Acheron.

Elizabeth stared at the beast by her side and watched as Azrael's bones began to twist and crack. He growled in pain as his demonic Abyssal form retreated forcefully back into that of a man. Azrael fell to his knees and held his face deep in the bloodied palms of his hands. His skin had gone from the hardened gray rock-like shell back to the soft white and pink flesh he was born with. Elizabeth picked up the battle-worn fatigues of a dead vessel once inhabited by a Seraphim killer and handed them to Azrael. Unable to move, he stayed balled up against the cold chill of the ground. Elizabeth made subtle gestures across his naked flesh as she covered his worn and beaten body with the dead man's armor.

"You are the creature of prophecy," Elizabeth said to the shivering Azrael. "I am sorry. I did what I thought had to be done. I only…"

Azrael interrupted Elizabeth. "You did this," He said.

Elizabeth picked up the wounded Azrael and carried him to the outskirts of the battlefield. Together, they made their way across the city of Acheron and continued their search for the one called Baphomet.

* * *

Moloch paced back and forth across the chambers of solitude as he watched Samael work his black magic.

Samael grabbed and pulled at fresh souls from beyond the shadowed cells of time, their energies swirling about and screaming for paradise, instead left only with a need for consumption. He let loose his tyrannical prose onto those misguided and lost souls. Those that he had not yet used to whet his appetite were cast into the all too luminescent vortex above his cathedral.

"You have spent too much time writhing within the prison of your mortal shell. You even subjugate the pure fabric of our species by choosing to be addressed by a mortal name. I see the sick sense of irony in all of this," Samael said as a legion of burning spirits attached themselves to his backside.

Moloch followed his brother's movements, followed the weightless drift of Samael's wings, made of the souls of the recently damned.

"And what of you, Samael, our self-proclaimed angel of the dead? What history do you recognize behind the choosing of your name?" Moloch replied.

"We have changed. The Seraphim of the old way has died," Samael said as walked over to a table in the middle of the all too ornate mockery of a dining hall they occupied. The surrounding pillars twisted and turned as he passed by. It was as if some unseen force possessed them. "We must learn to adapt to the ever-changing universe around us, brother. There are those that now worship us as beings of divinity. There are those that will hunt us for no sound purpose. There are those that will fear us for the gifts we may bestow. If we are to survive, we must demonize the creatures of the Abyss. Call them by the monstrosity they are. We must take up our labels proud. We must show the coming of this new age that we are more than a single thread on the wheel of fate. We are many. We are legion," He continued.

"And we do this with our names? Names given to us by the sickly mortal men of Abaddon?" Moloch asked Samael.

"Yes. Names given by those who worship and sacrifice for their allegiances to us. Let them give their lives to feed us," Samael answered.

"What of Apollyon and the coward Minos?" asked Moloch.

"Insignificant."

Samael took a long and overdrawn stare deep into the living gears that powered his necropolis. He stared past and out through an open window and watched as rays of bright green light pierced through darkening clouds. All around the tower swirled a thin layer of soul-veiled fog. "The essence. They come at constant and from different worlds. Before I built this place, this haven, they would end up as food for the Abyss, if not taken by the ferryman first. Now the dead may rest amongst the inner space of paradise. This place is hidden even from other Seraphim. Soon though, all will know of it. It will be the place where all are judged," Samael said.

Moloch stared at his brother. He looked at the Seraphim he once knew now adorned in the chewed and torn garments of flesh taken from the living dead. The patchwork alien mask that sat upon Samael's head seemed more like a war ornament taken from a creature of the Abyss than for something so noble as a Seraphim.

"And by what name will your warden possess in this prison palace of heavenly delights?" Moloch asked.

Samael turned his gaze back to his brother and walked up to Moloch. He stared his mask of requiem made terrors into Moloch's onyx black eyes and kept his posture still. Samael had seemingly become permanently bonded with the physical body of his amalgamated human host. For all Moloch knew, it was his brother's Seraphim blood that allowed him to exist in all dimensions of reality while keeping the face of death upon his brow. Moloch knew this and feared sharing the same fate. It was what Samael said next that reassured Moloch of the coming storm.

Samael spoke, "Creation will begin anew and we will be at the forefront. When the world of men is reborn, so shall we be as well. When the light burns once more, we will be called Lord."

VIII. The River Styx

Death.

Destruction.

Domination.

None of it seemed to matter anymore. Azrael dreamt of blackened skies and seas overflowing with the blood of his enemies. The routine of death and bloodletting had claimed its stake as the natural order of things. He tried to find the means to care for such meaningless prose, but could not. Life to him had only one meaning; that it ends.

Elizabeth kept him propped up against her body while they trekked along the barren landscape. They slid over pockets of rising smoke and past barren fields covered in black soot. The ground below rippled with the blackened mud of volcanic ash while the skies above roared their graying thunder. Aside from the few trails of blood that they came across, all color had left their vision.

Hours had passed since they left any traces of civilization. Not even the wasteland scavengers of Dis dared to venture out past the prying eyes of Acheron.

"Where are we?" Azrael muttered as Elizabeth carried him over one shoulder.

"I do not know. This is the only way Minos could have gone," Elizabeth said.

"Baphomet?" Azrael asked.

"I…do not know that either. Minos must have planned this. I can feel it," Elizabeth answered.

With a steady stride, they plodded along. The flat and barren wastes soon blended their surface with flesh-hungry jagged rock formations that reached up like ravenous teeth. Elizabeth pushed and pulled at Azrael as they climbed up and over the sharp stones. Over black hills and under fog-shrouded caverns they traveled, their goal becoming bleaker with each step they took.

Not a sound was heard for miles. The flames of creation had done more than purify the landscape ahead; they had rendered it barren of all forms of life.

Azrael fell to the ground and suffered deep to catch his breath. Elizabeth followed and sat by his side. She pulled his body up to her chest and held him as his heart slowed to a crawl. Pain and fear left Azrael's body as he slowly stumbled into oblivion. Elizabeth kept her hand upon his head while she awaited the same fate. Hunger and fatigue had done all they could to beat them down.

Azrael clutched onto Elizabeth's arm and spoke, "I did not mean for this."

"This world has always been like this. I have heard tales of worlds where the oceans run clear and the sky glows with life. Where the dead do not walk and the blood stays within. I was born here. This is the only home I have. I was proud to guard its gates," Elizabeth answered back.

"What happened?" Azrael asked.

Elizabeth closed her eyes and thought of the past told to her through the eyes of the slain. "I know not of the time before my birth. Man and beast alike have always shared these lands. We have had alliances and wars over the meaning of our past. My first memory is from years ago. I remember voices and a covering blackness. I remember floating and wiping blood from my eyes. I swam for miles before I reached something to pull my body to shore. I was naked with fright. That was when I met Belial. I felt him following me through the forest's edge. He jumped out from behind the trees and attacked me. He was able to get in a few cuts, but I eventually won. I fought by reflex. I did not know how, but I did. He then said to me, 'good, you may survive the onslaught yet'," Elizabeth said. She opened her eyes and looked down at the fading Azrael. He slipped out of consciousness and grew silent. "Or maybe we are cursed to damnation," she said to herself.

The two of them fell asleep beneath a large claw-like rock structure while the clouds hissed and cracked against each other. Plumes of black and gray ash shot down below from the fiery rain in the skies above. If not for a passing stranger, they would have perished beneath a blanket of hot ash.

Cold flesh wrapped around tempered bone crept along the surface of the threatening landscape, its black cloak flowing behind like a ripple of liquid smoke caught in a raging tempest. The creature kept its footing between the cracks and creases of the jagged rocks. It tilted its head as it caught the scene of Azrael resting upon Elizabeth's fatigued body. Its partially sewn mouth pulled apart to form a smile guided by charred muscle underneath. A sigh of relief swept across its face while a bony hand reached out and touched the girl on the shoulder.

Elizabeth's eyes twitched as they struggled to open. She took in a deep breath and coughed out a plume of black smoke from between her cracked lips.

"Do not breathe too hard, my dear, for you inhale poison. I am sure you did know that though," the creature said as it laughed.

Elizabeth moved slowly and cumbersome as she held onto Azrael. "Who are you?" she asked the creature.

"I am Charon. I am but a servant of her majesty Baphomet. You keep with you a creature of prophecy. She knew you would be led astray, so I was sent to find you," He said.

"How do I know you are what you say?" Elizabeth asked the creature.

"If I am what I say, then you will live long enough to see if I am, in fact, what I say I am. If I am not whom I say, then you will perish before you have the chance to dispute my claim. It is quite simple, really," Charon answered.

Elizabeth propped herself up and pulled Azrael to his feet. Charon climbed down and helped Elizabeth carry Azrael out of the makeshift tomb they had made for themselves.

"If you are lying…," Elizabeth paused to stop and look into Charon's empty eye sockets. Charon looked back at her and shifted his gaze to Azrael. "…I will kill you," she finished.

"I would expect nothing less," Charon said back.

Charon and Elizabeth carried the unconscious Azrael into a thick mist that blocked all light from entering their vision. The sound of waves and lightning hitting against burning rock filled their ears. The gates of the underworld had been pried open and the vessels of the dead made their welcome known.

"Ah yes, all is well upon the river of creation," Charon muttered.

"I cannot see anything. It sounds like war has come," Elizabeth shouted.

"No, no, my dear. The souls are screaming in delight. They too know of Azrael's role in the salvation of this world. They are excited," Charon said.

Elizabeth wiped away the black muck from her eyes and stared out into a red mist hovering above an ocean of blood and souls. They danced and splashed around while black clouds threw forth jets of concentrated flame to the ocean's surface. "What has this world become?" she asked herself.

"That is not the question you should ask, my dear. It is what this world will become once the Seraphim are purged from existence. Their white light and sacrificial rapture will be a thing of the past. Now, let us get to my vessel," Charon said.

With the mist receding, Elizabeth was able to see clearer towards the horizon. She felt the waves rumble and growl. The lightning grew stronger and a thousand voices carried the names of the damned across the winds. Black rot and calcified bone were the laid-out architecture of the vessel, void of a sail. Blood splashed and cracked against the boat's hull as it pushed closer to the edge of the gray sand beach. Elizabeth set Azrael down on the soft sand and took in the wonder of the necrotic-formed behemoth that approached.

The front of the ship was adorned with charred carcasses of dead creatures unknown to most except the ferryman. Their burnt wings lined the edge of the ship while their skulls and rib cages made for a sanguine and ornamental front side decoration. It had neither ore nor engine placement, as it was fueled alone by the sheer will of Charon. By this design, only he was able to pilot the ghost ship.

"This is the Choronzon, my ship. And I welcome you and your unconscious friend aboard," Charon said with an accompanying bow.

"It is...magnificent. And terrifying," Elizabeth said.

"Then we will be off and you, and Azrael, will have your meetings with the great mother, Baphomet," Charon said.

With the ship docked upon the beach, a long ramp, made of flesh stretched across sturdy bone, folded out from beneath a newly opened doorway on the lower hull. Elizabeth picked up Azrael once more and drug him along inside the boat. Charon followed and closed the door behind them while the ship hissed and growled as it pulled away from the beach. The Choronzon reared its gallows and ventured back out into the celestial blood river Styx.

Elizabeth took her leave from Azrael's side as he lay still against the edge of the ship. She walked from mast to mast and took in the intricate carvings of another language that littered the surface of the boat. She slid her fingertips across the charred wood and followed along the shapes of the ancient runes.

"Enochian. The language that drives the engines of this vessel. I speak it to command my will and they allow me to bring the dead to their resting place," Charon said.

"Why are we able to travel with you? Are we, Azrael and I, dead?" Elizabeth asked.

Charon walked over to the slumbering Azrael and gazed at the warrior. A breath of morose relief escaped from his bony lips. He stared at the man who caused the deaths of billions, a creature far too unnatural to exist within any sort of logical reality.

"Dead? No. Neither of you are dead. You, however, have visited me countless times. As for him, he has sent you to me countless times," Charon said.

Elizabeth walked up to Charon with a disturbed look on her face. She feared the explanation he might give, yet needed to know for herself what the meaning held. "I have never met you nor the world-destroyer before," Elizabeth said.

"Yes, you have. I am a ferryman. But I am one of many. I exist on every world that holds the gift of life. It has always been this way. Every world has its own river Styx that the dead travel to reach their own form of paradise. They are given a choice when I carry them across. Some choose to move on and become the dust of the cosmos or the fuel to keep the stars burning. Others feel unfulfilled and return to the land of the living. You, my dear, have been resurrected more times than even the gods can count," Charon laughed.

Elizabeth held onto the edge of the ship and looked down at the passing current. She witnessed the driving of skeletal souls against the lower hull. They pushed the Choronzon along the river Styx and over the bloody waves of resurrection. "Why do I keep coming back?" she asked.

Charon touched Elizabeth on the shoulder and turned her towards Azrael. He guided her down to Azrael's level and removed his hand. He stood behind her while she kept her stare on the unconscious world destroyer's face.

"It is because of him. Never before has a creature like him existed. With each world he visits, the rivers would overflow with the blood of the dead and their souls would crowd my vessels. You have been on more than a thousand worlds that he has seen destroyed. Yet, each time I gave you the choice to pass on, you refused and decided to resurrect. For ten thousand years you have done this," Charon told Elizabeth.

Elizabeth balled her fists and ground her teeth. She felt her blood rage as a new hatred began to develop for the murderous destroyer of worlds. "Revenge," she said.

"Not...exactly," Charon replied.

Elizabeth turned her head and looked up at Charon. She stared back at him with a look of confusion.

"Think about it, my dear. How can he, even with his insurmountable strength, engulf an entire world in flames? The will for fire is not a power of the Abyss." Charon leaned down and crept his words carefully into Elizabeth's ear. "Only the Seraphim can purge a world into a blazing inferno. Azrael is not the true destroyer of worlds. That job is held exclusively for a Seraph with the means to burn all. A creature with a sword sheathed in the living flame of retribution," Charon said.

Elizabeth felt a cold shrill overtake her body as she realized whom Charon was speaking of. She stared up at the darkened sky above and realized now that Azrael was no more than a pawn being used by creatures claiming to be mankind's angelic saviors. Elizabeth uttered the name, "Moloch."

"Azrael was sent as a scout. For what reason I do not know. Hidden from even him, though, Moloch would watch from the skies above and wait until Azrael could no longer wield a blade. Once Azrael had killed thousands, Moloch finished by killing billions. With each fallen world, I guided you back to another, to be reborn and endure life's journey once more. Not once have I ever met Azrael, though I knew of his existence through the whispers of the dead. This is the first time I have met him in the flesh," Charon answered.

"That is how you knew to find us. You had his scent, and mine," Elizabeth said.

Charon left Elizabeth's side and walked to the middle of the deck. Above them, the sky opened up and the red glow of resurrection had shifted to a cold and chilling grayish blue. The river Styx slowed to a crawl while the blood turned into a coagulated black sludge. The souls that had once guided the ship backed off and returned to the warm springs of their eternal crimson nectar. Charon returned to Elizabeth and helped her back up to her feet.

"We have arrived, my dear. Baphomet is but a day's travel from the shores of Limbo. There you will find answers to the questions that elude even my knowledge. I may know the what, when and the how, but she knows the why," Charon said.

"Can Baphomet help us stop the Seraphim from destroying this world?" Elizabeth asked.

"I can only pray."

Elizabeth walked over to Azrael and put his arm around her shoulder. She ran her fingertips down his face and watched as his eyes cracked just enough to let a small amount of light in. "We are here," she told him. She carried him over to the same ramp that they used to board the ship and stepped off and onto the shores of Limbo. Elizabeth looked back at Charon. "Thank you for not ever allowing me to choose the path to paradise," she said to Charon.

"Paradise is to each their own, my dear. Now go to Baphomet and find out why," he answered back.

Elizabeth, with Azrael propped in her arms, stepped off and into the lightly fog-laced landscape. Ahead of them lay a dark wood lit by candles that held living flame. The candles seemed to grow directly out of the twisted and contorted trees that held them. The dark blue sky above gave off a further glow that added to the chill of the dead forest. Here, night was eternal and only the crackling of fire and slithering hiss of the mist that slid across the dirt below broke the sound of silence. She took a deep breath and set out on a path that would lead her to answers both expected and, more so, unexpected.

* * *

Moloch stood out upon the balcony and watched the bright green light of Elysium set across the horizon. The putrid stench of fresh souls circled around him in this place of everlasting resurrection. This was to be the archetype of their home. A kingdom built from the ashes of an old dynasty to span the grand lapse of an entire galaxy. All of this would be done for a single purpose; to ensure their own survival.

"You think too hard, brother," Samael said as he approached Moloch from behind.

"It must be Daemos. He must be the one to bear the burden of creation. He is the oldest of us and he must be the new creator," Moloch said.

"I agree," said Samael.

"I will go back to Abaddon and meet with our brother. I will tell him of your work. He will follow the new construct. We must destroy the form of man and recreate it in our image. This heaven, this paradise, it will be our feeding ground. At least that much we have in common with the Abyss," Moloch spoke.

"And what of your role in this?" Samael asked.

Moloch gripped the hilt of his blade and closed his eyes. His mind twisted itself into a frenzy of zealous retribution. His self-righteous indignation fueled the delusional dreams of a just and holy crusade. "I am a warrior. I will protect my lord with my life. I will give no quarter to our adversaries. I will be feared by those without salvation in their hearts. I will become to war in what raptures are given to sin," Moloch said.

"You always were the high and mighty one, Moloch," Samael said.

"And by what title will you go?" Moloch asked.

Samael lowered his head and felt the heat of a raging inferno burn behind the black ribs in his chest. He savored the sweet taste of mortal souls as much as the Abyss craved the still-beating heart of a Seraphim. His hands clenched and cracked as he felt the serpentine slither of a living spinal cord wrap around his arm. It dropped from his grasp and straightened before it hit the ground. The spine formed a horned skull atop its crown and a large crescent-shaped blade slid out from behind its jaws. A pair of black leathered wings unfolded from behind the scythe's skull. Samael grasped his living weapon and gave the name by which the world of man will know him. A name that struck the cold strings of inevitability. "Death."

IX. Baphomet

Flames were all that remained as the world of Abaddon came to its final calling. Daemos stood out on the balcony of his once-great citadel and took in the scent of burning cinders and cooked flesh. There was neither a tinge of joy nor sadness as he came to expect the tide of inevitability. He watched the skies above as Moloch rained down plumes of fire from above. With each swipe of his sword, a new gust of murderous flame was sent down. Daemos could see Moloch's eyes light up as he brought Armageddon to yet another world. Moloch smiled while his white-hot tentacle wings pushed and pulled his body across the smoke-filled air. He did this without consequence or remorse. By the midpoint of his rampage, he merely added flame to flame, as life had ceased to be for the days passing.

"When I return, Azrael, the world you chose to call home will share the same fate," Moloch said to himself.

With his senses coming to a calmed state, Moloch flew to Daemos and accompanied him to the now-engulfed citadel. Daemos struggled to walk as his host body was falling victim to the wear and tear of Seraphim possession. "Enjoying yourself, are we?" Daemos asked Moloch.

"Before, I would have done this out of duty alone. I have spent enough time in this fleshly shell to enjoy being an instrument of retribution. I have learned to regrow my host body, to live between our world, the world of the living, and the world of the divine," Moloch said.

"How is that possible? Not even the Abyss have such strength," Daemos questioned.

"Ah, brother, Samael has constructed a new place for us. A shining tower where he reaps fresh souls. He feeds upon them and uses them to hold his fortress afloat. You should see it. Its emerald skyline, made from the light of Elysium, is a wondrous sight to behold. There is where we will form anew, away from the prying eyes of Baphomet, the Abyss, and all the other false gods of darkness."

Daemos limped along through the now-cracked halls of his domain and made his way to his throne room. Moloch followed as the sound of burning stone and crumbling rock filled the air. Daemos slipped along the edge of the throne room, clutching the wall, and felt its surface as new cracks tore up through the foundation. He could feel heat radiate from the fires below, slipping through the cracks. He knew that his options, at this point, were at their limits.

"When I made Azrael my personal weapon, I intended for him to rid only the Abyss from existence. I never intended for harm to come to others. That was the point of having a single assassin. You, Moloch, would kill millions to extinguish yet a single threat. That makes us no better than the creatures we hunt," Daemos said.

Moloch spoke "Brother, I…" before he was cut off by Daemos.

"No, you will listen to me. I have contemplated whether or not to tell Azrael of his past lineage. To tell him that I was sending him to hunt his own kind. Only because he was born as a creature of mortal flesh was he able to be kept a secret. How or why a creature such as Azrael existed was beyond me. I now know that I made a mistake. A terrible mistake. He carries the blood of the Abyss. I thought by using his ignorance against him, I could rid the universe of their dark plague. Now he has returned to his birthplace. He is back on the world where I found him. When you seemingly killed him and Sophia, you opened up the void and sent him reeling through." Daemos leaned back on his throne and looked up to the sky above through a fire-blasted hole in the ceiling. "It is only a matter of time before he finds his creator and she grants him the power of his full potential," Daemos told Moloch.

"What does Sophia have to do with this?" Moloch asked.

Daemos brought his gaze back down and gripped tight the broken skull armrests of his throne. "She was his guardian. She kept him from rampaging in much the way you do. More importantly, she was also from his world. She was once a servant of Baphomet. It is her blood that will guide Azrael back to the beast," Daemos answered.

With that information, Moloch grew stiff and cold. His Seraphim heart slowed to a crawl as he realized that any new threat to arise from Azrael's meeting with Baphomet would be a fault of his own. Moloch dropped his sword and fell to one knee. "What have I done?" he asked himself.

"Why do you think I sent legions of our kind to kidnap those from his world? I needed living vessels to bring him back. I needed a guardian to keep him sedated. You burned all in his path. He believed he was the world-destroyer. He grew far too confident. His victories changed him. What I need to know is why he grew reluctant. He began to question the perfect lie we made for him. I need to know whom he met or what he found during his time cleansing our sins," Daemos said.

Moloch picked himself up and walked up to Daemos.
"Samael has a plan, brother. We must leave this place and visit him. I cannot speak anymore of this, for we may have jealous spies amongst us. Just know this. His citadel works as a new source of eternal feasts. We can be the source of a new light of creation."

Daemos rose from his crumbling throne and held his brittle body together for as long as he could. With a final mortal breath, he clenched his fists and ruptured the weak internal organs within. His host's eyes popped in a gush of blood and pus. His skin tore itself away as each strand of muscle broke free, letting out streams of hot blood. From beneath the surface, a white light broke through. With his physical body gone, Daemos floated in front of Moloch in his true Seraphim form. From his backside shot out six glowing tentacles that flowed as if they were submerged in liquid. A seventh tentacle acted as a balancing tail. His face had no discernible features aside from a pair of large black eyes that contrasted the white glow of his mouthless, human-shaped skull. His legs were replaced by a series of winged tendrils that waved about to keep him afloat. He reached his elongated claw-tipped arms and welcomed the light of the stars above.

"I will take you to Samael, brother, and we will create for you a new body and a new world to call your own," Moloch said. With those words, he spread his tendrils and took to the skies and beyond. They left behind the world of Abaddon to burn until its end.

* * *

Ever so lightly did Elizabeth travel with Azrael by her side. She crept along the candlelit forest path as she watched the sky and surrounding darkness for any sort of threat. It was strange to her, to have lived on this world for so long but to have never ventured beyond the safety of Dis. Elizabeth felt alien on her own world.

A cool breeze swept over them as they made their way deeper into the dark wood. She breathed in the fresh air and watched the organic tree-made candles flicker in the wind. No matter how hard or soft the air thrust itself, the flames never grew nor died. They were indeed controlled by a life of their own. The permanent dark blue of the sky above, and snow-kissed winds, gave off just enough light to keep these lands sedated in a frost-laden winter chill. Only the orange glow of the flames gave her any sense of warmth.

From beyond the fog, she was able to make out what looked like a shadow. She stopped and waited for it to get closer before making any sort of action. Soon, the single shadow was accompanied by another, and then another. There were six in all. She stood there, still holding Azrael, as the cloaked figures approached. They hid their faces under the guise of a simple black cloak, wearing nothing more, nothing less.

One of them came up to her and spoke, "We serve Baphomet. You are here by design, not coincidence. You will follow us." Elizabeth knew that her words would serve as no more than a pointless stall. She nodded her head and followed the cloaked wraith figures deeper into the forest.

They walked for what seemed the passing of a full night, yet the darkness never subsided. Eventually, the fog cleared, and the creatures stopped. She found herself standing before a large gate that had the same written inscriptions as those found on Charon's boat, the Choronzon. The six creatures gave off a growling hum as the symbols glowed with a bright blue light. The gates opened, and the chanting ended. When the creatures began to walk once more,

Elizabeth followed.

She looked around at the surrounding architecture and noticed that it resembled the spired design of the buildings in Acheron. Bridges and gallows connected the midpoints of various buildings while their roofs were adorned with tall citadel and cathedral-like spires. This was no city, though. Its only inhabitants resembled the cloaked monks that led her down the path to Baphomet. She realized that this was a holy city. A place of power. It was then that she knew that Baphomet never resided in Acheron, that Minos bluffed about kidnapping the god. It was Acheron that was modeled after this place. Baphomet had always been here, and no one except for the servant priests knew of it.

Once Elizabeth regained her attention on the road ahead of her, she saw the great temple. It sat atop a towering stair structure that was lined with statues of the Abyss. The temple itself had three towers. The largest one sat in the middle, while two smaller towers lay by its sides. All three towers were topped with a spiked spire that pointed to the evening sky.

She continued to follow the monks two hundred paces up the stairs to the temple. When they reached the top, three of the monks took their leave and entered the tower on the right, while the other three entered the tower on the left.

Azrael and Elizabeth were alone in front of a large doorway littered with Enochian symbols. Elizabeth felt that speaking any other language would cast her out of Baphomet's presence. She stood and waited while trying to think of the words that Charon and the monks spoke. Elizabeth realized that it was not in speaking the words that commanded the symbols, but in sheer will alone that their power resided. It was with that thought that the doors opened and she was able to carry Azrael in with her.

When she entered the temple, she saw a small pool of water, clear and blue, in the center of a large antechamber. She set Azrael down in front of it and rested herself as well. In front of her was nothing but a shroud of darkness. She could not see beyond the center pool. When she stood up, the ground gave off a slight shake and a thousand whispering voices could be heard in the distance. Slowly, the darkness was taken back by the self-lighting of several living candles. Behind the flame, she finally saw the creature she had spent her entire life giving praise to. The creature that Azrael was destined to meet and receive his final blessing. She gazed into the eyes of a living god. Baphomet.

She sat upon a throne of blood-born tyranny and morose apathy. 'She' being a very loose term to describe this godly creature. Baphomet was neither male nor female, yet had no semblance to the hermaphroditic form. Its organs sexless, yet apparent, defied the physical design nature intended. Strands of torn, blackened muscle lay upon her chest while a distant cousin to the female anatomy sat, surrounded by eager tentacles, between her thighs. It was the mother and father of its own race of bastard children. The jackals that guarded her were direct in lineage to her oversexed womb. When the time came yet to procreate, she subjugated her slick opening to the surrounding tentacles in an orgy of pleasure and self-gratification. At times, it seemed more as if it were a preconceived mutual rape on her part. A mother goddess she is, and a ruling god, so is he.

The god stared back at Elizabeth with black eyes set upon a goat-like head. Without moving its mouth, it spoke softly, in a slow undulating tongue, "A scent familiar to me has made its ground inside this temple. My children have returned as I have longed to see them so. It is a sadness that rules the house of your fates. Soon you will know retribution."

Elizabeth stood in awe, as it was more beautiful and more terrifying than she could ever have imagined. She watched Baphomet's tentacles slide in and out of her glossy external opening. Each tendril would take turns in the act of impregnation when the one before it climaxed. Elizabeth knew not how to react. She feared undergoing some sort of ritualistic fate unknown to her.

"I have been laid barren. Try as I may without result, my time of creation has ended. What pleasure have I felt once has turned to pain," Baphomet said as she began to cry tears of blood.

It was then that Elizabeth realized that the god acted out her perverse situation out of desperation. It was not an act of pleasure that she was witnessing, but an act of punishment. "I am sorry. I know not if I should speak, but I feel that I must. It was the Seraphim that did this to you, was it not?" Elizabeth asked.

"Indirectly, they have stopped my cycle of creation. I am no more a god than I am mother witnessed to the death of her family," Baphomet said.

Elizabeth leaned down at Azrael's side while keeping her gaze on the god. "What happened?" Elizabeth asked.

"Before the inception of light, our father came unto me. He asked that I watch over our race of serpentine beauty, to uphold the dark passages of eternity. Their black-clawed wings to soar across the seas. A tail for their inundated guidance. Teeth and claws to consume without end. Skin laced in the color of night. A thing of beauty," Baphomet said.

"What of the Seraphim? Who is their god?" Elizabeth asked.

"Seraphim blood begets Seraphim blood," Baphomet said.

"How do we stop them?" Elizabeth asked.

"Sacrifice," Baphomet said as the winding slither of several tentacles made their way toward Azrael.

Elizabeth looked at Azrael and knew what Baphomet would have to do to him. She thought about what Charon told her. That at some point, they were entwined into each other's existence. Now, after finding and helping him to his destiny, she was about to lose him to a vengeful god. "You cannot take him. I will not let you."

Baphomet reared her head and grew silent. From behind her stepped out four men. Each one had the head of a jackal and was dressed in black and gold armor. They made their way to Azrael and dug their claws into his flesh. Elizabeth tried to fight them off, but she was held in place by a guard that crept up behind her.

"No, you cannot do this," Elizabeth screamed out.

The jackals placed Azrael in the pool of water and retreated to Baphomet's side. Elizabeth was let go by the guard holding her and she lunged forward at Baphomet.

"My poor child, these intentions are not in destruction but salvation. Azrael is to carry on the bloodline of our race," Baphomet said.

"But Azrael is not a god," Elizabeth said back.

Baphomet drew in closer and cut a wound into her arm with the claws of her left hand. As the blood dripped into the pool, the water surrounding Azrael began to hiss and churn. It started to boil, turning his flesh from a soft pink to a scolding red. Still unconscious, he made not a single movement as his flesh was seared and cooked. Elizabeth watched in horror as Azrael suddenly convulsed and screamed in torment. Before the moment of death, he made his transformation. The waters thrashed about as clawed wings shot from behind his back. His tail whipped about and he reared his horns high above his vision. His skin turned back into the charred gray color of the beast within.

"Azrael is more than a god. He is our savior," Baphomet said. With those words, she sent forth a pair of tendrils to penetrate deep into Azrael's chest. She drained out enough blood to still sustain his life. The tentacles then pulled away and made their way to Elizabeth. They wrapped around her neck and forced their way down her throat. She could taste his demonic blood as it ran through her body. "Now you will see what he has seen," Baphomet finished.

Elizabeth's mind raced as countless lives were taken in a split second. She felt the hunger and bloodlust that Azrael felt. A creature unguided and thirsty for war. Within a few moments, a millennium had gone by. The stars had shifted their routine and Azrael had redefined his tactics. Each world was different from the last. Some were no more equipped than with swords and shields, others had turned their steel into cities with weapons that fired streams of pure light. While the men of some worlds rode across the backs of ancient beasts, others used winged machines to flood the skies. On each world, she saw his life, death, and resurrection. Not too long into the journey of his past did she see herself. She felt the cold whispers of death fade away within Azrael's thoughts of her. She felt their first meeting, on a world far away from all she has ever known. She saw as he put down his sword and renounced his destruction. At that moment, she felt flames. They purged her flesh and ripped at her cortex. It was his punishment for exploring her purity. She saw as the Seraphim lied and used him to hunt his kind. From his eyes, she saw her countless deaths and the pain he went through.

The tentacles slid out of Elizabeth's mouth and dropped her to the floor. She grabbed at her chest and struggled to breathe. She now knew what Azrael had gone through and understood more than ever why the Seraphim were a threat to every living thing in existence.

"With this baptism, do I grant thee new life. Save our race," Baphomet told the newborn Azrael.

The beast that Azrael had become turned and stared at Elizabeth with its sharpened black eyes. His face, adorned with Abyssal horns, told a story of punishment. Grayed muscles pulled and tore their way across his hardened shell as his whip-like tail thrashed and cut through the water he was standing in. He spread his wings and growled out while rearing the pointed tips of his claws.

"My children have seen the creation of a new life. Through baptism, you are complete. Change your form at will. Rid us of the Seraphim plague," Baphomet told Azrael.

"Why have I lived a thousand lives yet have no memory of this?" Elizabeth demanded.

"Countless lives have you lived. On countless worlds have you met Azrael. Forgetting each time after you burned with destruction. To have lived, loved, lost, and fallen with each life. A mind torn by confusion. Time will be your guide," Baphomet answered.

Elizabeth walked up to the transformed Azrael and touched his demon skin. He moved his vision slowly across the form of her body. He saw the very threads of her blood as it pumped throughout, and the secrets kept buried deep within her flesh. His bones cracked and contorted back into their human form as his skin retracted and turned from an ash-gray back to its milk-white color. Once again, he was human.

With her job done, Baphomet subdued the candles surrounding her throne and reverted back into the darkness. Azrael held onto Elizabeth's hand while his human eyes caught merely a split-second glimpse of the god that gave him back the true strength of the Abyss. No longer would he have to wait for ritual cleansing by fire to become the beast.

"I fought and killed to meet with her. To get answers. Now she is gone," Azrael said.

"She is still here, resting, waiting for peace to reach these shores. And we have answers. More than you can imagine," Elizabeth said.

* * *

Daemos closed his wings as he approached Samael's citadel. He made no gesture for a light entrance, nor did he wait for Moloch to give any sort of grand tour. His feet landed on the stone walkway while a torrent of fresh souls weaved about their presence. Daemos kept his composure as he made his way toward the black gates of the floating monstrosity. Before he was able to reach the doors, they had opened. Samael stood at the entrance and waited to greet his brother.

"Daemos, I see Moloch has convinced you of our cause," Samael said.

Daemos reached his hand out and grabbed one of the passing souls by its ethereal throat. He dug his Seraphim claws into its neck and tore away at its existence. Streams of molten necroplasm fell to the floor as Daemos ingested the soul and transformed his body into the form of a mortal man. With a new temporary physical body, he spoke to Samael in the language of the flesh.

"My world burns while you two play out mockeries of creation and death," Daemos growled.

Moloch approached from behind and stormed in with an angered fury. "Was it not you, dear brother, that suggested and led the attack against our creator? We sucked dry the marrow of our god so that we may attain glorious power," Moloch yelled out.

"And it was you, Moloch, that kept his power in your blade. No weapon should burn with the eternal fire of a god. What you carry is in all forms heresy," Daemos shouted.

"Heresy? I would leave that accusation to the one that planned our lord's execution. You are the heretic Daemos," Moloch yelled back.

"Heretic? Our great lord Jehovah was on a warpath against the Abyss, and any in his way. How long until Jehovah deemed his own kin a threat as well?" Daemos lashed out.

Samael grabbed his scythe and crashed it onto the floor. The ground shook and, for a moment, everything, including the lost and rippling souls, seemed to stop. "Enough. We are all heretics. It has come down to us now. Moloch, as always, will be the warrior archangel to rid the Abyss and all things we deem unholy from existence. You, Daemos, will take the throne of paradise and oversee its rule. I will guide the souls worthy of consumption past the gates and to our brethren so that our species may survive. This is where our strength stands. It is by this design that our kingdom will prevail. We will create man in the image so fitting for mortal life. We will take from him his mortal soul. In life, it will grow. In death, upon it, we will feed. They must learn to fear us, to put their faith in us. They must never learn of our true intents, for if they do, we will starve," Samael said.

Daemos calmed himself, and Moloch followed suit. The three of them walked across the emerald hallway and through the newly formed white pillars of judgment. They made their way to the back of the citadel, where they were able to watch the clouds, above and below, twist and twirl as this new dimension still worked hard to form its own set of natural laws.

"If this is to be paradise, then where is there to be punishment?" Daemos asked.

"The world that Azrael is on. It is a world covered in blood and ash. No more than a thousand millennia have gone by since the ancient ones claimed it as their battleground. He has most likely met with Baphomet by now. If so, then he has reverted into a full-blooded creature of the Abyss," Moloch said.

"Then we use that to our advantage," Samael said.

"How so?" Daemos asked.

"We demonize him as we have been doing. Amongst every world, he will be known as a world destroyer. He will have no place to go. He will be stuck in the world he is on. We will rid the oceans of blood and create a new landscape. Fill its lands with the infection of mankind. Make them believe in our holy powers. Make them worship the light while fearing the dark. In death, they will come to us while leaving dry the boats of Charon," Samael said.

Daemos looked at his brother and felt a tinge of uneasiness cover his divine flesh. "To think that a being of light could plan a scheme as ruthless as yours is surprising even to me," Daemos said to Samael. "Humans have worshiped us before, but this is beyond a mere guise of prophetic salvation," He continued.

"Oh, Azrael will not live amongst the world of men. We must keep him trapped, sedated under our ever-watchful eye. We will create a place away from Tartarus, exclusive to him and those who will undoubtedly follow him. It will be a place of eternal suffering and anguish. Only the scourging heat of a blistering sun and the frozen sting of the harshest winter will be his companions," Samael said.

"You are not merely collecting souls, you are creating a foundation. Oh, you must be careful when playing with creation. You are building a prison. And by what name will this new prison world be called?" Daemos asked.

Samael answered, "By many a name, it will leave a mark. It will be the great inferno. The realm of sin. The pit of suffering. A place by which mortal man will call damnation."

With those words, the three brothers looked out and toward the landscape of their future. While their new order gained a newfound potency, the names of the ancient gods would soon be buried in myth.

X. Love And Death

A haze of black ash rose upon the horizon. Prophecies of creation and destruction came upon their final calling as gods and servants entwined their fates. As roles shifted from villain to savior, a new sense of hope infected the air of Tartarus. Creatures once thought to be slaves of damnation were now seen in the dark light of salvation.

There were some that would refuse to see the coming of a dark age of reason. From upon the top of his infernal desert tower, Minos paced back and forth, awaiting to hear news spilled from the lips of his fellow conspirator. Impatience set in as he made his way across the arched walkway that connected his tower of judgment to his other, less inviting, tower of punishment. Through mid-stride, he saw the pillars that lined the walkway light up with the fury of a thousand suns. The red floor beneath his feet shined bright in the otherworldly glow and the night sky around him turned to day for mere moments. His impatience finally satiated as he spoke, "Time may be of no importance to you, but I have a schedule to keep."

Moloch approached Minos from behind and walked around to face the self-proclaimed judge. "There are plans taking shape which call to my attention," Moloch said.

"Oh, and what plans might they be?" Minos asked.

"They are of no concern to you. Your role in this is to secure Azrael," Moloch answered.

Minos looked over his Seraphim master with disgust as his blood began to boil from mental exhaustion. He grew tired of the games that they seemed to play without end. "If Azrael is of this much importance to you, then why do you not simply kill him yourself?"

"If the task were so simple, it would have been done long ago, you fool," Moloch shouted at the subservient judge. "Our plan is not one of murder, but entrapment. We know that Azrael is at the temple of Baphomet. Find what he holds onto and take it. Leave a trail and bring him here to us," Moloch demanded.

"I believe I have already taken all that he holds onto, as have you. What more could that beast wish to save?" Minos asked.

"You have forgotten the most basic laws of survival, Minos. A pet and a few companions from past battles are not what drives a species forward. At his core, he is looking to continue his bloodline. Capture Baphomet and bring the beast here to follow," Moloch said.

"And if we are too late?" Minos asked.

Moloch lowered his head to the blood-red floor below and latched onto the sound of a legion of Abyss screaming their impending doom. Those memories put a smile on the Seraphim general's face. "Then rip the child from its unholy womb," he said.

* * *

The blue glow of the moon set itself upon Azrael's naked flesh as he stood looking up through the opened ceiling of Baphomet's baptismal chamber. He stood mid-leg in a pool of clear blue water while Elizabeth paced around him. The blood had dissipated from the pool since his rebirth as an Abyssal beast, no less than a few moments ago.

Elizabeth closed her eyes and tried to sort through a barrage of newfound memories that plagued the deepest parts of her mind. Her next heartbeat sent her mind speeding through a thousand lifetimes of pain and endless war. "I remember you," she whispered.

Azrael kept his eyes closed as he felt Elizabeth put her arm across his chest. He opened his eyes at her touch and thought of the countless worlds he had seen her on. Each one ended in the fires of destruction, her body always shifting from a vision of beauty to a charred mass of blackened flesh and bone. "I have never forgotten you," he said.

"So much pain," Elizabeth said back.

Azrael kept silent and thought only of the thousands of years of fire and horror he had endured. When Elizabeth came back into his vision, she had already disrobed. She walked around and pressed her body against his, the two of them standing in Baphomet's pool of life and rebirth. Azrael moved his hands down her body as she explored flesh forgotten but familiar to her senses. As their lips met, a taste of thousands of years of death passed between their tongues. She grabbed onto his demon skin and pulled him in closer. In her eyes, he saw death. The black soul of the Abyss swam inside her as well, though without her knowledge. The two of them fell onto each other and began to defy the gods with their own acts of creation. They clawed and gripped each other's nude flesh as if it were the first and last time they would be able to do so. The water moved and twisted as it reflected itself onto Elizabeth's perfect form. She swayed and rode herself atop Azrael while he leaned in and dug his claws into her backside. She thrust his cock deep inside her to the point where she felt as if her innards could come ripping through. Their lovemaking splashed the clear pool of water into a murky white as their bodies released fluid upon fluid. Azrael held his grip as she swayed her hips to a grind against his loins.

A whole day passed while the suns of Tartarus beamed through the open domed roof above. Time, for them, stopped though as they fornicated like a pair of rabid animals, their shrieks of sex and lust spilling into the echoed chambers. Again and again, Azrael released himself inside of her, and still, it was not enough to make up for watching her burn for the last few millennia. Elizabeth stayed latched onto his flesh and not once ever thought of letting go.

By the next turn of the night, the two of them had finally ended their plague of lust and fell silent under the moon's watchful gaze. They held onto each other as sleep infected their weary bodies, the two of them lying on the floor next to the now-tainted pool. From beyond the shadows, Baphomet was finally able to put her own forced lust to rest. She closed her eyes as she knew that the Abyss might have a new chance at life.

* * *

The stirring echo of prophecy surrounded the temple as domesticated jackals marched their routine. The nocturnal sounds of insects and the crackling of living flame were all that the children of Baphomet seemed to drown their senses in. Only the whispered howl of the night air filled their fawning ears. It came without warning to them that their chests were torn open by Seraphim blades in the still of darkness. The Seraphim moved within the shadows and killed each child of Baphomet in silence. One by one, their bodies fell as tightly gripped spears were set free from dying hands. The loyal jackals of Baphomet caught but a glimpse of their killers as black and hollow eyes stared back at their latest victims.

With swords and spears in hand, the Seraphim assassins surrounded the now unguarded temple. Elizabeth and Azrael were ripe for the picking.

The large double doors to the temple slowly creaked open as three of the assassins made their entrance. They made their way around the slumbering Azrael and stared in awe as he held his arms upon Elizabeth.

"This is not Baphomet," one of the Seraphim assassins said aloud.

The three intruders looked at each other to come to some sort of meaningful conclusion as to what they were seeing. As one of the Seraphim assassins took a closer examination of Elizabeth, he drew a puzzled look across his host's possessed face. "I have seen her before," he said.

Within that split-second of breath that the Seraphim used to exhale his words, so too was his life cut short. Azrael had spread his wings, impaling the two that stood behind him, while piercing the heart of the onlooker with his now extended spine-like tail. While the three failed assassins fell, Azrael and Elizabeth arose.

"There will be more outside," Azrael said to Elizabeth. He sniffed the air around him and looked at the dead bodies at his feet. He took a second to catch his composure while his vision shifted around the chamber room. "A lot more," he finished.

Elizabeth gathered whatever clothes she could find not tainted with blood, while Azrael wore no more than a pair of tattered leg greaves. "Then we kill them," Elizabeth said.

"Let us feast," Azrael growled.

Over a hundred Seraphim stay perched outside the temple in various arms of foliage while the rest of the jackals below slept unaware. They waited for their brothers to exit with the bodies of Azrael and Baphomet. The doors to the temple re opened in the distance. In their vision, they could see one of their brothers rise into the air, yet his tentacle wings gave no sign of life. As they looked closer, his body was flung across the courtyard while Azrael expelled his tail from the dead Seraph's midsection. Azrael screamed, waking up the jackals, thus giving the Seraphim a reason to expose their whereabouts. The Seraphim horde flooded the skies and rained fire down upon the temple and all surrounding living quarters. The jackals in turn raised their spears and sent them flying through the air.

"We must help them. These jackals are Belial's people," Elizabeth said to Azrael.

"Go to them," Azrael said, as he looked at the bloodied sky above. In mere seconds, his body cracked and reshaped itself into its Abyssal form. "I will take out as many of these parasites as I can."

Elizabeth smiled at her lover and ran off with one of the dead Seraph's weapons in her hands. Azrael watched her as she attacked the horde in a bloodied frenzy. With a deep breath, he spread his wings and took flight. His body moved through the air with such fluid motion it almost looked as if he were submerged in liquid. With each Seraph he flew by, a torrent of blood and a flash of extinguished divine light followed. He killed with ease. It took almost no effort to rip, flay, and mangle their soft, white, glowing flesh. Once he ripped the physical host apart, he dug his claws into their true form and crushed their hearts. Somehow this time was different. He hunted and murdered them for what seemed an eternity, though they were not retreating. And he knew why.

One after another they swarmed Azrael, their claws digging and scratching into his Abyssal flesh. He dodged, chased, and hunted down each of his attackers. Some were slain by the swipe of his massive wings, others skewered by his serpentine tail. They tumbled and swirled throughout the violet skyline as each act of violence was beset by another.

With each wounded Seraph that fell, Elizabeth ran to catch it mid-air to slice away at its flesh. Azrael and Elizabeth played this game of bait and switch with their jackal allies. Whatever creature Azrael did not kill, he would send down to the ground below for his lover and the jackals to finish off. As the bodies piled up, so too did the red that filled the sky.

Elizabeth fought as hard as she could while she watched the children of Baphomet fall in front of her. There were too many opponents to fight off. She looked up at Azrael, her face covered in human blood infected with the Seraphim curse, and moved her lips for Azrael to read, "Find me."

Azrael saw her gesture and allowed one of the Seraphim to strike a blade into his chest. He fell to the ground as a comet would, spiraling down in a trail of fire and black smoke. Elizabeth and a few remaining jackals were knocked back at the initial impact. Above him, a swarm of Seraphim followed. They fell to their feet and surrounded him. As quickly as smoke filled the crater, so too did it dissipate. Once the smoke cleared, Azrael, now back in his human shape, said his seemingly final words. "I will…never surrender. You will never know…the Abyss."

The surrounding Seraphim looked down at their fallen enemy and contemplated his words. Elizabeth held onto her breath as she waited for the killing strike, knowing that Azrael would return no matter how deep the cut. She thought of him returning once more. He would bring his brothers of the Abyss to put an end to the Seraphim nightmare. The moment was shattered when she looked at the open doors to the temple of Baphomet. One of the Seraphim assassins that Azrael impaled stood at the doorway. With a heavy chest, he spoke out, "It was not Baphomet. He lay with her," He shouted, pointing to Elizabeth before falling to his death.

The Seraphim looked at Azrael and then over to Elizabeth. "Grab her," One of them said aloud.

"NO!" Azrael yelled out.

Elizabeth was held down by five of them while one held a blade to her neck. Another forced her head up to watch Azrael's execution.

"Why do you lay with her? She is not of the Abyss. What has Baphomet told you?" one Seraph asked Azrael.

Azrael sat silently with the sword in his chest, watching as the blood kept running without end. He feared that he would not have enough time to heal himself and strike before the Seraphim drove their blade into Elizabeth's neck.

"End it," Azrael demanded.

"What?" another Seraph questioned.

"Do it. And do not stop at my throat. Take my head. Give it to Moloch in exchange for her," Azrael said back.

Elizabeth shed a tear as she looked at Azrael, who was willing to give up his life for her. She shook her head lightly as if to say 'No.'

"You will do this willingly? No tricks, no unnatural healing?" the Seraph asked.

"Cut my head off before I cut your heart out," Azrael answered, with his teeth clenched.

With a single swipe, the blade cut through Azrael's neck and severed his head from his spine. Elizabeth cried out as the executioner lifted Azrael's head while his body slumped down into a massive pool of his own blood.

Elizabeth struggled to go free, but the Seraphim holding her only gripped tighter.

"Bring her with us. Find out why she was of such interest to this demon," the executioner said to his brothers.

Elizabeth gave out one final cry before being taken to the skies by her Seraphim captors.

* * *

Moloch stood outside on the balcony, high above, within the judgment tower of Minos. His eyes scanned the twilight skies as he awaited his brother's return. Minos approached from behind and gave Moloch's vacancy some unwanted company.

"They have been gone for quite some time. Do you really think your…brothers could succeed where you have failed?" Minos asked Moloch.

Moloch tilted his head and gave a slight smile to himself. His hands found their way to Minos' throat as he rushed the judge against the pillar behind him.

"And by what degree have you to slip your tongue within my actions? Azrael was not my plaything. I am cleaning up my brother's mess. Just pray for your sake, Minos, that my legion has taken care of Azrael and his whore Baphomet," Moloch said as his voice trembled with thunder.

"My information is trustworthy. I have told you where the temple is. Now let me go," Minos coughed.

Moloch loosened his grasp on Minos as the judge twisted his head and swallowed in a deep breath.

"There is no need to overreact. My loyalties lie with the Seraphim," Minos said.

"You are a creature of flesh and bone. Your loyalties lie only with yourself," Moloch said as he took his gaze back to the now-blackened sky.

The end of an era of false prophecy came closer to fruition as Moloch watched his Seraphim brother's approach. They flew with urgency. Moloch could sense that his worth would finally be put to the test once the bodies of Azrael and Baphomet were delivered to his feet.

One by one, they poured into the tower in a storm of tendril-winged light. One approached Moloch from above. He landed on the terrace and retracted his tentacles as he gave his brother welcome. In the Seraph's hand was the mangled and bloodied head of a man. He placed it on a table in the room that Moloch and Minos occupied. Moloch walked up to the head and knelt before it.

"Raphael, you have done what so many have failed. Oh, how the mighty have fallen," Moloch said to Azrael's decapitated head. "And what of Baphomet, the mother-whore of the Abyss?" Moloch asked his brother.

"Azrael did not lay with her," Raphael answered.

"What?" Moloch asked in shock. "Why would a creature of the Abyss not lay with another creature of the Abyss when given the opportunity?"

"Maybe…Baphomet is not what you thought she was," Minos interjected.

"Do not speak out of turn, human," Raphael said.

Moloch made his way back to the balcony and looked out upon the landscape. His mind twisted and wandered in every direction. Raphael followed his brother in his thoughts.

"We have been stuck like this for too long, brother. Have you seen how we now use fleshly names to call one another? We are becoming more like these flesh creatures every day," Moloch whispered to Raphael.

"It is true that Azrael did not lay with Baphomet. But there was another. A mortal the same as those we inhabit," Raphael said.

Moloch's eyes widened as he felt his possessed flesh turn cold. For the first time, he felt something that he thought he would never feel; fear. "Bring her to me. I need to see the creature that Azrael chose over one of his own race."

"She is already here," Raphael said.

The doors behind them flew open as Elizabeth was thrown into the room. Her Seraphim captors gave a final stare before walking away back into the bowels of the tower. Moloch and Raphael gave a nod to them as they left.

"Who are you?" Moloch asked Elizabeth as he walked over to her. He knelt in front of her as she backed away, trapping herself into a corner.

"You are no god," Elizabeth said.

"I never presumed to be," Moloch answered back.

Elizabeth stood up and stared Moloch in the eyes. What she saw was a creature no more gripped in fear than a slave under the whip of his master. She saw the confusion and disbelief in his eyes as he stared back at her.

"Azrael chose you over Baphomet. Why?" Moloch asked.

Thoughts of uncounted lifetimes ended in flame, and screams tore through Elizabeth's thoughts. She remembered the smell of charred flesh serving as a prerequisite to the time of each of her deaths, her memories torn away and reconstructed with each new resurrection. "I have fewer tentacles," Elizabeth said with a smirk.

Minos laughed at Elizabeth's rebellion. Raphael struck her down as Moloch clenched his fists and gripped her throat.

"You are meat. Nothing more than a lowly mortal with a body built for mortal lust. Tell us why he chose you over his own kind," Moloch said.

Minos walked up and interjected his own thoughts. "You may be asking the wrong question, my lord. Maybe she is a creature of the Abyss herself," Minos said as Moloch gave him a crooked glance.

"That is absurd!" Elizabeth shouted back.

"Wait," Moloch said as he turned his head back to Elizabeth. "For once, Minos, you might actually have merit in one of your theories." Moloch walked up to Elizabeth and grabbed her by the throat. He held her up against the wall behind him as he smelt her flesh. It was not like the bitter scent of the Abyss, nor did it hold within it the sweet nectar that other mortals have. She was different.

Elizabeth fell to the floor as Moloch let her go. She took in several deep breaths as she uttered her threats to the Seraphim in her company. "Do not think for a moment that you will ever again see the light of day. Azrael will find you, and he will kill you!" she shouted.

Moloch turned to Raphael and walked out. "Lock her away for now," he said as he passed his brother. Moloch then focused and looked at Azrael's decapitated head sitting atop the table in the middle of the room. "And burn that godforsaken thing before it has a chance to blink."

"What shall I do, my lord?" Minos asked.

"Nothing. It is what you humans do best," Moloch answered.

As Raphael grabbed Elizabeth, she looked at Azrael's decapitated head sitting on the center table. She stared into his dead-opened eyes and knew that somehow, somewhere; he was waiting, plotting a way to return as he had done before. She just hoped that it would be before another death yet again.

XI. Dead Memories

Azrael felt his body reeling through time and space as his mind was ripped apart from the seams. Like a bolt of lightning, he crashed into a shell of once-dead flesh and jolted himself awake. His body ached and cracked while the scent of a world burning through retribution filled his head. His brain pounded away against his skull as he forced his eyes to take in his surroundings. Little by little did the scene become all too familiar. Above him was a ceiling destroyed by some unknown force. Stained glass windows and statues of men were either cracked or scorched black. He set his hand down to gain his balance and felt that the ground was wet and cold. He looked at his hand and saw that it lay in a puddle of blood. Then his mind came rushing back into his body as he realized where he was.

"Sophia," Azrael said, as he saw her body lying next to him on the floor. Somehow, he had returned to Abaddon, to the place where he and Sophia had been killed. He looked at her with a sullen gaze of sadness as blood still poured from her throat. Within a split second, she let out a small gasp.

"Sophia? You live?" Azrael asked in desperation.

Sophia tried her hardest to open her eyes and look at Azrael. With a faint whisper of breath, she spoke, "Did you find her? Did you find whom you had lost so long ago?"

"Yes, I found her. Daemos and Moloch, they did this. Why am I here, though?"

Sophia faded in and out of consciousness, but held on for long enough to speak. "I brought you here. My blood always brought you here. My blood is your blood. As is our brothers."

"The Abyss?" Azrael asked.

"No. Our brother. Follow his blood," Sophia said before she took her final breath and died in Azrael's arms.

Azrael held her until the blood on his hands dried and cracked. He carried her to the altar, where Daemos once conducted sermons of peace and longevity and placed her body upon it. With one final glance, he grabbed a piece of burning wood and introduced the flame to her body. Through the passing of the years, Azrael knew he had a connection to Sophia, but never understood why. Why it was always her that was able to calm him, why she looked after him as if he was one and the same? It was only through her death that he was able to learn the truth. The night sky filled with flames as the once-feared destroyer of worlds watched as his sister burned before him. He wondered too if his brother had shared the same fate.

* * *

Samael stood out upon the terrace of his celestial fortress and haven for lost souls. The cosmos stretched far beyond the reaches of his imagination, and he wondered how much of it could be taken for his kingdom. It was not his kingdom, though; it was the kingdom of a god. He knew not the name by which a god would call itself, only that he would play the architect to the highest bidder to the throne.

"Azrael is dead," Moloch said as he approached Samael from behind. "What is interesting, though, is his choice of a mate. It was not Baphomet, as we so fervently thought. It is a mortal woman, yet I do not think she is native to the world we found her on. Her scent was…off."

"Abaddon," Samael answered.

"No, I do not believe she was from that mistake of a world. Perhaps another infected by mortal men."

"I was not asking about her. Abaddon burns and here we stand gloating over the death of the Abyss and his woman," Samael said. He turned to Moloch with his scythe in hand and walked past him, down the marble corridor. Moloch followed.

"Is this not what we wanted, brother? We can reshape the world below, infest it with mortals, bring them through our gates and sustain our life," Moloch exclaimed.

Samael stopped and turned to Moloch. The ornate skull that sat upon his face hid his expression. "Yet, something does not sit right," Samael said.

Hearing the clamor of victory, Daemos joined his brothers and looked at Moloch with the hope of hearing an answer that did not involve mass destruction on a planetary scale.

"You bring news, Moloch?" Daemos asked.

"Yes, Azrael is dead," Samael answered in Moloch's place.

Daemos turned his attention to Samael. "Is that so? How?"

"We found him and his female at the temple of Baphomet, as we predicted. Raphael was so fortunate to remove his head from his body," Moloch answered.

"Decapitated. Lovely. Bring his head to me. I must ensure that he stays dead and cannot resurrect," Daemos said, as he walked away.

Moloch looked at Samael, then back at Daemos, now in full stride. "There is no need brother, his flesh, both head and corpse, burn as we speak," Moloch said with a grin.

Daemos stopped in his tracks as his eyes spread wide open. His flesh began to sear and smoke as the white-hot light of his true Seraphim form began to scorch away his mortal host's body. He turned around and walked back to Moloch, the look of death and fear across his face. "His flesh burns?" Daemos yelled as he reared his claws and slashed Moloch across the face, exposing the Seraphim light underneath his skin. "Do you know nothing of resurrection? Have you forgotten why I sent you to burn every world Azrael so thoroughly purified? Only through flame tearing away at dead flesh can one rebuild himself as he so sees fit. All Azrael needs is blood and a destination, a world on which to breathe life and a body in which to inhabit and tear itself out from. He already shares Sophia's blood. Who knows who else he shares his blood with and what world they inhabit? You just gave him the chance he needs."

Moloch stood there and said not a word as Daemos walked away, smoke still rising from his now burning mortal shell. Samael looked at Moloch and saw a tinge of hatred sweep across his face.

"I suggest that you go back to the world below and question the woman. Azrael will no doubt come back for her. Be ready when he does," Samael ordered.

Moloch stared off in the direction that Daemos left and held his blade tight. "Yes…brother," he answered.

* * *

A shiver swept up Elizabeth's spine as she lay naked on the cold stone floor. It was her own personal dungeon, set aside to revel in past thoughts. Her hands and feet lay sore from the shackles set in place by the Seraphim. She kept her body curled in a ball to try to keep any warmth that she could while her mind wandered off into oblivion. With nothing more than the darkness in front of her to focus on, she thought of the first time she met Azrael, the once-feared destroyer of worlds.

Her memories brought her to a world where they had their first encounter.

A gray fog lingered upon the edge of the horizon. Men prayed to their gods while others cursed those same gods. The end of an era was fast approaching, and the beating of war drums and clashing of steel was how life would meet its end. There were no innocents in the final days. Men, women, and children shared equal payment in the distribution of blood. What was once a bright blue sky had turned to ash while the ground slowly rose with the piling of corpses.

This was the world she knew, a world leftover from a time of mystics and religious warring factions. Now all that was left was for the last remnants of life to cause their own extinction.

Across forests and rivers, over desert sands and endless dunes, through dead cities covered in snow, she traveled. From town to town, she avoided the murderers and rapists that now held sway in the new landscape. A few times she met them face to face and each time they died by her hand. She was born of violence through necessity. She had killed would-be rapists with the snap of a neck, disemboweled highway robbers, and sliced the throats of children that acted as bait for their cannibal parents. The lands have shown her no mercy and she, in return, would show none as well.

The same gods that she cursed were the same gods that, unknown to her, had set her path in motion. They watched as she stopped to rest on the edge of a cliff, against a pile of rocks. The fire she started marked her camp and signaled her presence. Where there was no blood, there would be plenty to allow the flow of a river.

As the sun began to set on a certain fateful eve, she witnessed a battle from atop the cliff side. She had seen men wage war in the past, but there was a change in the air with this onslaught. One by one, men fell by the chance meeting of a blade swiped across or sent through their soft flesh. Blood flew in every direction as they killed each other off. As the hours passed, only a handful survived, but they too would meet their end. Hundreds of men lay dead as a single man finished off the last survivors.

He stood amongst the dead, covered in blood from head to toe. His hair was caked with red plasma and his armor was barely visible under the liquid sacrifice. She watched as he climbed over the dead, taking from them what he could. He killed off the stragglers as he took new bits of armor, any weapon that was still of use, and whatever he could grab as a meal. For a moment, she saw as he stopped and sniffed the surrounding air. Her eyes caught his gaze as he turned and looked up at the hillside and directly at her. She quickly hid behind the rocks, hoping he would ignore her stare. When she peeked back to look at him again, he had gone. Before she was able to catch her breath and move on, she felt a tinge of hot air move across the back of her neck. When she turned around, she saw the bloodied warrior standing no more than a foot away from her. He grabbed her by the throat and held her up in the air and over the edge of the cliff. She grabbed onto his arm and dug her nails deep into his flesh while she gasped for air. He failed to flinch or show any sign of pain. With one final desperate attempt to flee, she pulled a knife from her side and plunged it deep into his neck. He let go of his grip on her as they both lost their balance and fell over the edge of the cliff and onto a pile of fresh corpses.

Elizabeth tried to get up from the fall but instead began to fade out of consciousness. The last thing she saw was the man she had just stabbed get up and pull the knife from his throat before her vision faded to black.

* * *

Screams echoed from every direction. The world had been plunged into chaos. There was no sense of light or dark, up or down, real or unreal. It seemed as if the borders of consciousness and slumber had been fighting for supremacy. This was in every sense a lost world.

In his final moments holding Sophia's lifeless body, Azrael was pulled back into that dark abyss. His attendance was required by a god he had become all too familiar with. It was never the destination that riled his flesh, but the journey. His return to Abaddon was as real as it was an illusion. Sophia had been taken into the god of the Abyss long before Azrael had arrived. Though, through her blood, dead memories were made reality. With the veil lifted, he found himself within the void once more.

Azrael clawed his way out of a pile of flesh. His skin was still wet and red from the blood of the body he had just torn his way out from. His hands and feet clawed away at the surface below. It was warm and soft, yet rough beneath the jellied gore. When his eyes were able to fully take in his surroundings, he saw that his hands gripped at a floor made of meat and bone.

"And so you return as quickly as you left, my odd little creature of habit," a voice said from the distance. The presence of oft-held omnipotence made itself known before Azrael.

"Leviathan. Are you here to berate me once again?" Azrael asked.

"So you do know the tongue by which I am called? Your brothers have missed you. It seems that the monotony of your existence has finally come to an end. Shall you pass that end to the Seraphim as well?"

"I intend to," Azrael said as he pulled himself closer to the monstrous, towering god. With each step, he saw more clearly the true form of the beast that spoke. The living darkness that hid the god before had faded away. He saw as its form rose above an endless ocean. Closer did Azrael come to the god and further into the water did he submerge himself until he was waist deep, leaving the bloodied stench of the corpses he crawled out of behind.

"The elements bring you here, only one part of a whole. Four souls joined by a common task. To rid the Seraphim from existence," Leviathan said to Azrael.

"Who?" Azrael asked.

"Follow your dark prophecies and all will be revealed. You have been tasked with this endeavor and you shall fulfill our destiny," Leviathan spoke. "You must find your mate and reunite your blood. Only then can we join as the Abyss."

"Reunite my blood?" Azrael asked.

"There are carvings upon the walls of creation that you must venture and seek for your own."

"And Elizabeth? She has been in my shadow for all of my life."

"No Azrael, you have been in her shadow. You were born to join with her."

"She is my birthright? If I am truly one of the Abyss, why then do I suffer as a man, a mortal only to die and rebirth at the whim of some self-proclaimed god?"

Leviathan released a thousand arms guided by insect-like tentacles towards Azrael. Each one pulled and grabbed at him as they circled his body. Like a prisoner held in thrall he was risen up to the eye of Leviathan, a massive black orb tenfold the size of a mortal man with a green center pupil that stared directly at Azrael.

Leviathan then spoke, "Because Azrael, you were not born as the Abyss. You, like your siblings, were born as something unnatural."

XII. Resurrected

"Enough of these games. Send me back and be done with this," Azrael shouted to Leviathan, the towering god of the blood seas.

"Yes, Azrael, you will be sent back to seek your grievances. But you will not stop there. For all lives you have taken in the name of the Seraphim, you will fulfill our revenge. You will not simply destroy the Seraphim, you will murder and erase them from history," Leviathan said to Azrael.

The towering god of the dead sea let go of his grip on Azrael and dropped him to the black and red waters below. Under the surface waited legions of hungry Abyss, ready to tear Azrael's flesh apart and send him off to fulfill his command. He swam deep into the blackness of the sea and allowed for his brothers to render his flesh useless so that he may reborn on another world. A world where his enemies lay siege. One by one, they tore at him. Skin ripped from fat as muscle separated from tendon and bone. He aided them by tearing away at his flesh. Once death set in, he tore back into the bloodied seas of creation.

Leviathan took in the cloud created by Azrael's blood and drank it deep. He tasted the sweet nectar of the Abyss as he examined the memories of his blood. He saw the world that he and Baphomet once called home, a world now ruined by the greedy hand of the Seraphim. "Go now, Azrael, and purge the Seraphim from existence."

Black sails sewn together by threads of flesh and skin warped and shifted in the fog-shrouded distance. Crimson waves cracked against the celestial storm as the ferrymen of the dead approached closer. Leviathan turned his hulking form around as he looked down at Charon's ship. It paled in size compared to the towering god.

"One day, Azrael will find out what you really are. When that day comes, I pray that the stars are extinguished," Charon said. With those words, Charon turned his ship and left the false god to his domain.

"When that day comes, all of creation will come undone," Leviathan said to itself.

* * *

With no other memories to give her comfort, Elizabeth continued the journey of her first meeting with Azrael in her own broken mind. She remembered his callous grasp, her swift attack, and the fall. Never before did she feel pain, fear, hatred, and curiosity all at once.

Her next waking memory was one of confusion. She lay broken and in pain as her attacker wiped clean the blood that covered his naked flesh. He would occasionally stare back at her, to what purpose she did not know. With neither hands nor feet tied, she was free to move, but her curiosity kept her from doing so.

"Are you going to kill me?" Elizabeth asked him.

He paced around the newly formed bonfire as he made a habit of switching his gaze from her to the star-filled sky above. He sat next to her for a moment and stared into her eyes before sniffing her skin and taking in her scent. Elizabeth backed away in confusion, yet stayed perched up against the stone wall. She knew that fleeing would be pointless as she had seen this man kill hundreds before her eyes. All she could do was await a response if, in fact, any were to be given.

"If you choose to stay silent, then just kill me now and end this. I will not wait here while you contemplate my death," Elizabeth said.

With his back turned to her, the man spoke. "Azrael. My name is Azrael. Everywhere I go is the same. Men fight, they die, more fight, more die. Always for nothing. No matter the time, no matter the place, you are all the same," Azrael said. He turned around and faced her as he saw her body tremble in fear. "It has been so long since I was able to...share words. I only remember blood. Never my own, though. Not until you stuck me with your blade. I had almost forgotten that I was capable of bleeding."

Elizabeth moved closer to Azrael as he fell to his knees and stared into the fire. She watched as the flames sent their shimmering reflection off of his face and back into the inferno. "We all bleed, some more than others. What has kept you from spilling your own blood for so long?" Elizabeth asked.

Azrael kept his gaze deep into the whipping flames. His mind twisted and turned as he thought about the countless worlds he had rendered lifeless and seen burn before him. Each time he would burn as well, only to be ripped from the clutches of reality and sent into the flesh of some poor girl strapped down by rusted chains and hooks. Each time, he would rip his way through virgin flesh and walk down the stone corridors of Daemos' castle, back to his room, where he would wait to leave yet again to another world in need of divine cleansing. "I have never had the choice to bleed. It was always made for me," Azrael answered.

"And who has made that choice for you? Are they here now, listening to us?" Elizabeth asked.

"No, but soon this world will be lost to memory like all others before it," Azrael said.

"All life will eventually become a memory," Elizabeth told Azrael.

"Not mine," Azrael said, as he closed his eyes.

Elizabeth saw that there was something different about him, aside from the wanton bloodlust that he so fervently relished. It was apparent to her from the beginning that he was not of this world. She knew that in his current state, she could find the chance to leave and never look back. Curiosity, though, played a dangerous game and kept her seated, staring into the fire.

* * *

"This situation is becoming more trouble than it is worth," Samael said to the enraged Daemos.

"Moloch is losing his grasp on reality. He is bending and weaving the rules as if they are his own. I now regret ever letting him convince our lord to create that godforsaken weapon of his. It was never my intention to have him follow Azrael and burn everything in his path. I want that sword destroyed," Daemos shouted aloud. He ripped away the burning mortal flesh from his Seraphim form and grabbed another hapless victim hanging from a hook amidst hundreds of other vessels.

"You must calm your nerves, brother. Neither Moloch nor I have found the need to change our flesh since Abaddon lay in flame. I do regret you having to lose that world as I saw how you so adored it," Samael said.

Daemos, in his Seraphim form, floated by Samael and stared at him with his large black eyes, eyes that sat in contrast to his glowing white form propelled by six tendrils that protruded from his back. Only when the Seraphim wear the flesh of mortals, can they speak the language of mortals. Daemos found a suitable host in the form of a middle-aged man with long, sharp features and a worn look of experience on his face.

Samael followed Daemos as he set himself inside his new host body. They made their way out of the factory of mortal flesh and further down the catacombs of their still-unfinished home. Its luminescence would burn the cornea of any living creature, but this was a celestial flesh locker for the Seraphim to try out different hosts of mortal skin. With the corpse now possessed, Daemos was free to speak.

"Why do you always choose the worn and frigid?" Samael asked.

"Their age brings wisdom," Daemos answered. "Only through their human memories can we ever hope to understand them better."

"Why would we ever need to understand that which we consume?" Samael asked.

"Because dear brother…" Daemos paused for a moment as he walked up to a corpse hanging with the others that lined the bloodied and chain-ridden walls. It twitched and moaned as it had seemingly found a spark of consciousness. "Through their memories of us, we can learn more about ourselves than you can imagine."

* * *

Azrael found himself washed up on the same bloody shores as before. He had returned to the world where Elizabeth, Belial, and Cerberus lay hostage. The same world once ruled by the goddess Baphomet, who now lay tormented in her own temple, unable to spawn anymore of her kind.

Inch by inch, he crawled his way back onto the beach, blackened by the ashes of inferno, away from the ocean of molten blood behind him. With just moments to grasp for air, he turned on his back and stared at the endless starry sky above. It was infinite in its darkness, yet the stars gave way to the empty space that surrounded his mind. Whatever world he was on, he thought, was no world where life had originated.

Behind him, in the thick of the trees and plants, amongst broken and ancient ruins, he heard a scatter of steps and heavy breath. He lifted himself up and clenched his muscles, the heat of his blood ripping through his veins. His bones cracked and reshaped themselves, and his skin hardened and turned a cold dead gray while his demonic wings, tail, and horns broke through his flesh. His eyes stayed fixed and his claws strained. One by one they came at him, the scavengers from the ruined city of Dis. Before they had intended to make a meal out of him, this was simply now an act of revenge. Arms and legs were severed from their torsos as Azrael tore away at his attackers. His fists crushed into his enemies' skulls with his tail slicing open their soft bellies and his wings cutting them in half from the groin up.

They seemed an endless lot. For every ten he killed, twenty more jumped out of the darkness. Yet even in their superior numbers, he did not falter. As a demon of the Abyss, he moved flawlessly. He was as a living shadow, leaving only a trail of blood and carnage to signify his presence. Even during their retreat, Azrael followed, killing and feeding on each one he came across. His eyes widened and his chest burned harder with each kill. His only goal for these scavengers now was extinction.

Rage had set in as he pursued the scavengers back to the gates of Dis, back to where he had met Cerberus and Elizabeth. His mind flashed with images of his battle with Belial and his eventual defeat by these same scavenger beasts. There was no remorse to be had with him. He flew over walls that surrounded Dis and across the boneyard ruins and immaculate wasteland.

Thousands were waiting for his arrival. Their jaws snapped at his flesh while their bony hands reached for his grasp. He saw them for what they were; once mortal men and women now lost to the disease and plague of the Seraphim promise. They were kept alive in a cruel sense. They were not allowed to pass to the realm of death for Charon to ferry, instead trapped in a state of un-death, left to hunger for any and everything that passed their way. The flesh of the Abyss sent a frenzy of wanton feasting amongst their numbers. Azrael, however, would show them a hunger of his own. He spread his wings and took to the air circling the ravenous crowd. Not wanting to keep his guests waiting, he aimed himself straight down and sent his body into the masses. The force of his impact sent countless bodies flying through the air. He swiped and clawed at the rest, who were foolish enough to defy his attack. Their blood flew up and came down like rain. Within minutes, the skin and tattered clothes of all those around Azrael were plastered red. His clawed hands found their way into the intestines of many, ripping and throwing their gore to the ground. Hearts, lungs, and stomachs exploded from impact. Skulls were split apart and cracked bone was further shattered by his monstrous tail. He gripped their necks with his teeth and tore away their throats from their flesh. The sound of skin breaking under the pressure of his fangs and muscle being torn from its holding invaded his ears. One after another, he tore away and pulled their flesh from their bones. The idea of mercy was a foreign concept at this point. This was a bloodbath.

Slowly, the vermin of the wasteland fell to his unrepentant mercy. He was created as a beast and so a beast he shall be.

By the passing of the suns, the crying and howls did cease, for no life was left within the wastelands of Dis. He stayed perched against a ruined fixture that once housed a great and noble palace. No more than petrified bone and stone rubble now lay in its place. Gorged on the flesh of his enemies, Azrael found a moment of peace to accompany his fulfilled hunger.

The wind that swirled around him changed. The scent of blood and sweat left the air and was replaced instead with the stench of a long passed and lingering death. He heard a thousand voices approach from every direction while a glaze of fog began to creep its way on the stained ground below. From beyond the gray mist, he was able to make out a figure. Its form was tall and shallow. Bony hands gripped a tattered cloak while the skeletal remains of a human face peeked out from beneath a worn cowl.

"I see that even a beast may turn back into a man at will," Charon said as he approached Azrael.

Azrael picked himself up and shrugged off his sick state, trying to ignore the overabundance of vermin meat in his belly. Although never having formerly met the ferryman, Azrael did know of his deeds. "You take with you the dead and willing. I am neither dead nor willing," Azrael responded.

"Neither were you the last time we met. Oh, but your mind was not with you, if I recall. And you are welcome for the passage to Baphomet."

"Why are you here, Charon? You have already taken me to the mother goddess. What more is there for you to give aid to me?" Azrael asked.

"My reasons are my own. We both wish to rid the Seraphim of their existence. The souls I once ferried to start anew are now being consumed by these monsters. Life begets life and when there is no life left, well, I believe you get the point," Charon answered.

Azrael walked up to the ferryman and stared into his empty, hollow eye sockets. "What am I, Charon? What am I really? I am sure you of all creatures know this," Azrael asked.

"I think you know exactly what you are. Is it reaffirmation that you seek or are you really infected with forgetfulness?" Charon asked as he prodded his bony finger against Azrael's forehead.

"I thought you might say that. I was a fool to expect a straight answer from you, one who cares only for the dead."

"And it is the dead that speak volumes above the living. You should know, Leviathan has delivered you back to Daemos ten thousandfold. Back each time to do the Seraphim bidding."

"Leviathan claims to have never known of my existence."

"Oh, does he now? Well, I am sure Leviathan has no reason to lie. Or any other selfish motive. You trust the word of a god?"

Azrael thought to himself about the countless worlds he allowed to be laid to waste. "The blood rituals. They used my own blood to find me," Azrael said to himself.

"No Azrael, not your blood."

"Sophia. It was her. She was always at my side when I returned," Azrael realized.

"Now you are beginning to see. Sophia has passed. I have seen to it she was not to be lured in by the Seraphim lie of paradise. Your brother may not be so fortunate," Charon said.

Azrael turned his head and glared at Charon. He thought for a few moments of who else he might have unknowingly lost. The secrets that were kept from him began to take their toll and now he demanded answers. Azrael walked calmly up to Charon and placed his hands upon the ferryman's shroud as he clenched his fists with white knuckles and protruding veins. "You are going to tell me everything you know," Azrael said, as he tried his hardest to prevent a violent outburst.

Charon put his hands on Azrael's wrists and set himself free. He walked out into the open air of the swirling fog and looked up at the stars above. "What fate worse than what I could pass? Azrael, I do not know the fate of your family. I am not entirely sure you ever had an actual family. What I do know is that you share the same blood with another. He is lost to me, as you are lost to him."

"Lost how?" Azrael asked.

"I am a harbinger of the dead. Never have I interfered with the dealings of creation and destruction. I simply act as a guide."

"Get to the point ferryman."

Charon turned his attention toward the concern in Azrael's voice. "I fear that your brother may be a creature beyond my reach."

"And what sort of creatures are beyond your vast reach?"

"Only those that surpass death and control it at their very whim. The only beings that I have seen that are capable of this are the Abyss."

Azrael began to walk off as he readied himself to set his wings free. Charon stopped Azrael in his tracks with his next set of words.

Charon took a deep breath and let slip a secret he wished never to reveal. "And the Seraphim," he said with a heavy tone.

XIII. Secrets In Flesh

Samael paced like a beast in torment within the confines of his cellar. His thoughts were filled with schemes and conspiracy. He watched as Daemos got comfortable in his new skin. The burning heat from their Seraphim form molded the host's living tissue to their own. It was as if each living creature were made to fit their abductors, no matter their physical size. Daemos stretched and cracked his bones, making the stolen physical body fit his own celestial likening.

"What now, brother?" asked Samael.

"I must find a way to stop Moloch before he undoes all we have come to accomplish," Daemos answered.

"You speak of heresy and treason," Samael said.

"No, it was Moloch who has committed heresy and treason when he burned my world in his needless crusade. I was rooting out the Abyss with Azrael. Moloch's impatience will cost us. Azrael is not so easily dispatched."

"And why is that, oh brother?" Samael asked.

Daemos looked down at his clenched fists with closed eyes while a myriad of placated histories and falsified truths swam across his mind. Thoughts of the truth about Azrael's conception, the lies hidden from his birth, and the consequences of his actions sent up a shiver of guilt and doubt. He opened his host's human eyes and turned around to look at Samael. "I made Azrael what he is. Moloch has become what he is in reaction to Azrael."

Samael walked up to his brother and spoke into his ear, "Then help Moloch murder Azrael and be rid of this guilt."

"No. Azrael must know the truth. About who and what he is," Daemos answered.

Samael watched as Daemos walked out of the antechamber and into the entry hall of his celestial fortress. He walked down a newly placed floor, its surface made of the lacquered blood of the dead. Its red shine was in contrast to the white and gray walls made of hardened and petrified bone. Daemos marched down the crimson aisle, and between the giant bone spires that led up to a ceiling made of the skulls and rib cages collected from those willing to sacrifice their flesh for the building of this heavenly cathedral.

Daemos made his way to the end and stopped at a pair of giant ornate doors that pulsated with life and longing. They opened at his command to the entirety of the stars and heavens below. Brilliant swirls of gas and living clouds held the fortress in place. With each second, the souls of the dead added to its magnificence. Daemos watched as history formed its foundations before his very eyes. Soon a second fortress would be built and not too long after, a third, and so on and so forth. And until there were no more souls to come to the heavens would these grand designs of salvation grow. From one there would be many until the Seraphim could call, what was once a single fortified structure, a kingdom. And in this kingdom, their lord shall reign.

Darkness fell upon the face of the deep as Daemos knew what must be done. He closed his eyes and let his tendrils burn through his host's soft, fragile flesh. With his tentacle-laden wings spread, he readied for his descent back into the realm of the living.

Samael approached from behind and dug his soul reaping scythe into the steps where Daemos stood. "On hallowed ground do we tread. Be sure your decision is one of honor and grace, for no one of the Seraphim will tolerate any further blasphemy."

"Do not worry brother, for I will bring with me rapture. And when the time comes, you shall ride once more." With those words, Daemos flung himself off the fortress steps and fell into the stars. As he disappeared from Samael's sight, a new light was seen in the darkness of space.

* * *

Azrael kept a violent gaze in Charon's direction. He tried, for what seemed an eternity, to grasp the concept of his own flesh and blood being one of the creatures he was sworn to kill. "How is this possible?" Azrael asked.

Charon took a seat on a nearby pile of rubble and looked deep inside himself to come up with a viable truth.

"You and your siblings were an oddity even for me to comprehend. I have seen your corpses more than any other in all of creation, yet you seem to defy the nature of death. Only through your many deaths was I able to piece together what you are, or what I think you are."

"And what would that be?" Azrael asked further.

"You are a mistake. So is your brother as well as your sister. She allowed herself to pass after growing tired of watching you destroy yourself. She begged me to send her to you. I gave her the chance of immortal bond by holding her soul upon my vessel until she was claimed by your god. When that was not enough, the Seraphim again returned and executed you, as well as her, and took Daemos back with them."

"She was not of my blood. She was not of the Abyss. Now tell me the truth," Azrael demanded, as he yelled out to Charon.

Charon got up from his perch and stormed at Azrael like an unhinged beast. For the first time in the ferryman's existence, he felt the emotion of anger sweep across him. "I have told you the truth. You fail to see what you really are. You are no creature of the Abyss. You never were. I do not know what you are. What Daemos did to you, why you are able to change into an Abyss, is beyond my knowledge. I speak what the dead see. I have seen you die more times than I could count the stars threefold. It was never I that brought you back. Had it been my choice, I would have allowed you to pass on to a true death. I still fail to see what Elizabeth sees in you as well. As long as she lives, maybe it will keep you from flooding my shores with more needless corpses," Charon said back to Azrael with a stern and angered tone.

"Where is Sophia?" Azrael asked.

"She is gone. She held on just long enough for you to return to her, even if in dream. I guided her through to the void, as I said, with the promise that she will soon see you again. You, on the other hand, are too stubborn to die," Charon answered.

"And which of the Seraphim is my brother?" Azrael asked.

Charon looked down at the bloodied ground beneath him and, though he was not sure of the truth, behind his mind, thoughts of something ancient told him that his theory was more than perfectly accurate. "I am not entirely sure, but not too long ago, I began losing souls to send along their way. There is a single Seraph that has begun luring mortal souls away from beyond my reach for reasons unknown to me. I believe that he may be your brother, not a Seraphim by nature but by choice, to hide in plain sight. How he is able to walk amongst them unnoticed, again, is beyond my knowledge. His mortal name is unknown to me."

As Charon ended his confession of knowledge, the sky cracked with a loud thunder that scarred the ears of everyone within its reach. Azrael and Charon looked up and watched as the red twilight sky turned a blinding white. The flash of heat and explosive force left them temporarily blinded. When they came to, they saw a star shoot across the sky and fall directly toward them. It moved with precision as it aimed itself directly at Azrael and Charon. The two of them began to run for cover, but not before the star fell to the ground, sending up an explosion that covered the sky in ash and dirt. Before the smoke could clear, Azrael picked himself up and knew what had just landed.

Azrael muttered a single word to himself, "Moloch." He clenched his fists and forced his body to crack and break itself out of its mortal form. Shards of onyx bone ripped their way through his shoulder blades as they transformed into his Abyssal wings. His eyes glossed over in a black haze while his brow gave way to his majestic horns. The dark gray color of his skin matched the falling ash. Teeth turned razor sharp and his legs broke to reform into their superior hind counterpart. As he began to charge at the rising cloud of smoke, his tail let loose and whipped about, scarring the ground and anything else it hit.

Not one to make the same mistake twice, Azrael ran directly towards the light glowing at the center of the crater and jumped over it before the Seraphim could get up to strike. Azrael landed behind the fallen one and cracked his tail against its body, knocking the Seraph back a few feet. The Seraph spread its wings and lunged back at Azrael. Hardened claws grabbed the Seraphim by the throat and threw him across the air and into a hard stone surface. As the Seraph hit the wall, Azrael came charging through. He dug his horns into the Seraph's chest and ripped his claws across its face. The Seraphim brought its arm close and flung them back out, throwing Azrael off its body. Azrael readied himself again and proceeded to swipe his claws again and again at the Seraphim invader. They exchanged hits and slashes to each other's flesh. Bones broke and blood flew about in what was a horrifying display of violence.

Charon made his way through the smoke and ash to find Azrael locked in combat with the Seraph. He watched as the Seraph made no attempt to inflict a fatal wound on Azrael, instead only acting in self-defense. Azrael pushed forward with each strike meant to be a killing blow. Charon knew that something was not right. "Azrael, stop this. Look at whom you draw blood," Charon shouted.

Azrael took Charon's words to heart and backed off for a moment. He saw that it was not Moloch who lay in a blood-covered mess, but a shell of a man that resembled his former lord, Daemos. Azrael lowered his stance and felt his bones break and crack back into their mortal human form. He walked up to Daemos and grabbed him by the throat, raising his beaten body up to eye level. "What are you doing here?" he growled at his former master.

Daemos coughed up some of his own blood before saying, "I am here…" Daemos coughed and proceeded to continue, "to help you save Elizabeth…and kill Moloch."

Azrael let go of his tightened grip as Daemos fell to the ground, holding his hand against his throat. Charon walked between Azrael and Daemos and interjected some sense of his own. "Perhaps we should let the man speak," Charon said.

"Now you refer to this creature as a man? How fitting," Azrael said with a scowl across his face.

Azrael walked away from the ferryman of dead souls, and the now-professed traitor to the Seraphim, as he closed his eyes and kept a single thought to himself. "Elizabeth," he said under his breath.

* * *

Further down the throes of imprisonment lay Elizabeth's cold and shivering body in some unknown barbaric torture chamber. Still, she continued the journey of her first meeting with Azrael as she awaited her executioners.

She remembered him standing by the fire, looking up at the stars. Not concentrating on their beauty, but watching for the unknown threats they hold.

"If you knew what watched you in the dark of the night, you would never find rest," Azrael told her.

Elizabeth rose up and placed her hand on Azrael's back as she leaned in and whispered into his ear, "Perhaps you should watch me, then." She held a knife up to his throat while he barely flinched, still fixated on the stars.

Azrael turned around and looked into her dark blue eyes as he saw in her what humanity had left him so long ago. "What are you?" he asked her.

Elizabeth lowered her blade and looked deep into the fire as she let her mind wander off into oblivion. "I was born here," she said. She walked around in front of Azrael and looked up at the same stars that he seemed so concentrated upon. "But I do not belong here."

The fire began to die out as the two of them stared up at the stars. With the scent of ash and blood now fading, Azrael opened his senses to a new lingering aroma. He had smelled it before but could not pinpoint the origin. He approached Elizabeth from behind and placed his face near her neck while she closed her eyes and took in a slow breath. Azrael's eyes opened and turned a deep midnight black, as he had now recognized the scent. Her blood carried with it the sweet aroma of the Abyss.

"This is not possible," he said to Elizabeth. He backed away and reared his teeth, ready to strike. In all the thousands of worlds that Azrael was sent to purge, not once had he ever found that which Daemos sent him to hunt. He only assumed to have rid that world of its demons through the final cleansing fire. Azrael lamented, "You are what I am sent to hunt. And kill."

Elizabeth slowly raised an arm and touched Azrael on the cheek.

"Look at me. Look. What do you see?" she asked softly.

Azrael calmed his senses and saw that she was different. Her bones neither cracked nor twisted in a frenzy. Her eyes stayed their dark blue and not once became engulfed in the black smoke of the Abyss. If she was of demonic origin, then she had no knowledge of it. Azrael now had more questions than answers. He kept a stark gaze and a deep frown placed in her direction. His knuckles cracked as she backed away slowly. With her back to the stone cliff wall behind her, she had nowhere to run. Azrael charged forward and placed his hands around her throat. Before she could scream, she found her lips locking with his. He felt the blood of the Abyss pump through his veins, as she felt the same demonic blood pump through hers as well. No longer did they follow the mortal rules of nature. They tore at each other's clothes and soon at each other's flesh. Their true animal instinct came forth. They drew blood and other sweet nectar from each other's bodies. Azrael injected himself between her thighs and she in turn pulled him inside her with lustful invitation. With each thrust, images of shadowed talons and leathered wings invaded their minds. As Azrael filled her womb, she felt the heat of her lust explode with frenzy.

With their fornication subdued, they let the stale air fall over their beaten flesh. They lay naked in the dirt, next to a dying flame, keeping the scent of blood and sweat close to their senses. It was enough distraction to ignore the cracking shrieks of lightning and thunder overhead. The sound of a coming storm ripped through the sky as neither cloud nor rain were present.

As Elizabeth lay in slumber next to Azrael, he pointed his ears to the heavens and heard not the arrival of a storm, but of a threat much worse. He knew that his time on this world was at an end, for the fiery winds of Armageddon were drawing closer with each breath. Azrael bit deep his fangs into Elizabeth's neck as she slept, and drank enough blood to wet his tongue. With his mouth glazed in her red plasma, he whispered into her, "I will find you."

Without ever having the chance to open her eyes, Elizabeth was bathed in a torrential inferno. Azrael held her close as the flames whipped and pulled at their flesh. He closed his eyes as he felt her burn to a charred mass of ash and bone, like the rest of the world around him. He heard the searing cries of maniacal laughter off in the distance as he, too, met the same fate.

Elizabeth opened her eyes and released her mind from the dreams of the past. Her hands and feet were still chained to the wall next to her. Only a faint sliver of light made its way into the cell, though its origin was unknown to her. She heard footsteps echo from beyond the cell door as they came closer and closer. With a slow creak, the door opened as her captor walked in.

Moloch greeted his prisoner and examined her naked flesh from head to toe. He pondered the excuse for such a being to be in the clutches of a demon such as Azrael. He walked up to Elizabeth and knelt down next to her. "What are you to him?" he asked her in a slow, threatening tone.

Elizabeth turned her head to Moloch and pierced her dark blue eyes into the empty black orbs that sat upon his face. She used what energy she had to sit up and wipe the muck and dirt from her face. "Salvation," she said.

Moloch leaned in closer and looked at her as if to convey a confused child. "Salvation?" Moloch asked. "You can not offer what only the gods possess. You are a mortal. You can not grant salvation."

Elizabeth made a slight smirk as she knew what her overly confident warden was alluding towards. "Not just for Azrael, but all of our kind," she continued.

Moloch picked himself up and realized the mistake he had made. "You are not a mortal." He clenched his fist and realized that Azrael was not the only creature to be afflicted with the soul of the Abyss. "Did my brother make you as he made Azrael? Did he take the corpse of a stillborn babe and give you the stench of the Abyss? Are you but another hunter hidden from both Seraphim and Abyss? Answer me!"

Elizabeth spread her smile from ear to ear as she looked up at a Seraph in full thrall to his own fears. She debated for a time whether to keep silent or instill the wrath of her built-up rage. She knew that no matter the words she chose, the Seraph would do her no harm. His curiosity had far outlasted his temperament. With that, she spoke, "Thorns shall grow over your strongholds with nettles and thistles over your fortresses. We shall bring the haunt of jackals. Wild animals shall meet with demons and you will cry to your fellow brothers. We will desecrate your resting place. We will gather, each with our mate." As Moloch turned away to leave, Elizabeth finished her tirade, "and we will devour you."

XIV. Dark Revelations

Azrael, Daemos, and Charon made their way past the rotten carcasses of Dis and deeper into the old city. The sky above them was a resilient red that illuminated the ground and surrounding ruins of pillars and once-oversized monasteries. They passed through a once-sacred place of worship where ancient men would bring offerings to appease their now-extinct gods.

"It was once a magnificent sight," Charon said aloud.

Azrael kept his silence as he stared up at the cracked stained glass windows and decapitated statues of giant monstrous gods.

"They were nothing. Mindless, oversized beasts that waged war over popularity. Their only contribution was the blood they provided to build this world," Daemos added.

Azrael stopped in front of the statue of a large serpent. He stared at the intricacy of its carving. Its scales and fangs were crafted in a way to pay homage to something greater than a mere beast.

Charon stepped next to Azrael and spoke, "You should give praise Azrael, for you look upon the image of Tiamat, the great serpent whose flesh gave part birth to this world."

"Not once in my life have I ever awoken in a sea of blood until this world. Mortal men run sparse while creatures of instinct and hunger run rampant. What is this place?" Azrael asked.

"You have died, returned, died yet again and returned…yet again, and now you ask of this world's origins?" Charon asked with a sarcastic tone.

"Excuse me if my curiosity bothers you," Azrael said back. Daemos continued to look through the ruins, as he too saw statues of great beasts; lions with human faces, men and women with wings sprouting from their shoulders and hips, and creatures with talons, claws, horns, and serpentine tentacles. He interjected into Charon's thoughts as well. "Yes, ferryman, tell us both of this world. Why, though I have never sent Azrael here, was he brought to this place?"

Charon turned to face both Azrael and Daemos. "This is where you were born, both of you, the Seraphim as well as the Abyss. You were not always enemies."

Azrael and Daemos looked around and saw the familiarity of their forms within the statues. Charon began, "I thought you knew of your past. History, it seems, has its censors." Charon pointed at the statue of the serpent and continued, "Tiamat was once beautiful, one of the first creatures in existence. She gave birth to me as well as my brothers. We watched over all of creation. One of my brothers grew tired of merely watching and wreaking havoc on our mother's creations. She thus created a monster, Kingu, to fight off her defiant son. Kingu was slain, though. His blood was spilled upon this world. In his honor, she created mortal men from his flesh."

Azrael and Daemos let their eyes follow the statues and carvings as their images matched the story that Charon told. Charon held on to his staff and looked at the carvings as well. "She gave men souls, the same energy and life force that the gods used to thrive on, only in sparing amounts. It was her decision that no other creature shall live in physical flesh forever. She wished to not repeat her mistake. I was chosen to guide the dead souls back to her realm, to the land of Sheol, where she would once again reunite the soul with the body."

"That was how you came to ferry the dead?" Azrael asked.

"Yes," Charon answered. "My defiant brother grew bored and jealous and soon killed our mother and spread her flesh throughout this world. He took her creations and exiled them to other worlds. Man no longer had a home. Those that stayed were changed. Some turned to the seas to reunite with their mother. They grew cold and their bodies deformed. They sprouted claws, their teeth sharpened, and the vast ocean of thick blood kept them from the sun. They lived and became the Abyss. Those that took to the sky flew too close to the fires of the heavens. Their eyes were blackened while their skin took on the light of creation. They became the new gods, the Seraphim. Both Seraphim and Abyss soon left this world. What you see now is a wasteland. This planet is a dumping ground for mortal slaves and other…undesirables."

"What of Baphomet and the people of Dis?" Azrael asked.

"Baphomet was one of the first Abyss born here. She stayed with her jackal children to watch over the people of Dis, the first city ever built. She knew that one day a lost child of the Abyss would return. She was waiting for you, Azrael. To show you your true form. That was why the blood of the Seraphim changed you into a beast. We all share the same blood."

Daemos looked at Charon as if he were mad. "These are all lies. How can you say that creatures like the Abyss, demons that feed on life, have relation to the Seraphim?"

"Are we so different?" Azrael asked Daemos.

"Enough time has gone by that this world has been forgotten to both of your races. The Abyss were not born in darkness and the Seraphim are not holy beings of light. You were born, flesh and blood, from a serpent that wished to carry on her legacy. As was all life on this world," Charon added.

Daemos stared at Charon with a hidden discontent as he let Azrael and the ferryman walk by. Thoughts of blasphemy and the beginnings of a grand scheme swirled about Daemos' mind like a spinning cauldron.

They continued through the ruins and headed to the east, towards the one place where they knew they would find Moloch, to the tower of Minos. Daemos stayed behind and leered at Azrael and Charon with an ever-watchful eye. So determined were they to end Moloch's existence that they kept their concentration ahead of them, failing to hear the slight creaks and scratching claws upon the ruins behind.

* * *

Pieces of rust fell from rotten steel like flakes of snow. Hour after hour of pulling and prodding had weakened the binds. It was enough for Elizabeth to pull and weave her hands-free from bondage. The chains shrieked and popped as they broke apart. She got up and looked around her cell for any sign of a quick escape. The door was a large and sturdy, oversized piece of stone and steel. The walls were built from finely cut rock and placed in such a way that no human hand could construct. Her determination outweighed the chill that shot up her nude flesh. She held her arms close to fight off the cold and watched as plumes of fog escaped from her breath.

When all hope seemed to be eclipsed, she heard more footsteps approach her cell. The guard was not a Seraph but a human working for the divine monsters. She stood against the wall next to the door so as not to be seen through the opening. As the guard entered, she emerged from the shadows and placed her hands around his chin and forehead. His neck snapped like a frail twig. Her daily meal fell to the floor, along with the heavy weight of the guard. She dragged his body into the shadows and stripped him of his clothing and armor.

She made her way out and into the halls of the great tower. Its architecture was only matched by its madness. The inner hallways resembled more of the inside of some large beast than a man-made structure. Pillars covered in carvings of snakes and demons lined the walls while the halls themselves gave the illusion of walking down a ribcage-laced atrium and outward bent bones. The only light to be seen was the flame that sat upon the ceiling, which seemed to have a life of its own.

As the sanctum began to open itself up, she soon started hearing a distant commotion. What seemed like only a few voices had turned into hundreds. Elizabeth pressed herself against a wall next to a nearby doorway and listened to the crowd. She heard screaming, cheering, and fits and laughter as she did her best to stay concealed. While she hid, she slowly peaked her face around the corner to look inside. She saw Minos, the unholy judge, sitting high atop a platform perched behind a podium made of corpses and meat. He stayed nestled on his throne of gold and bone while he laughed and slammed his gavel into the podium before him. One by one, she saw men, women, and children approach his bench and stare up in terror. They were stripped, beaten, and bruised. Each one cried and shivered as Minos yelled out his sentencing. Without hesitation, his answer was always "guilty." The crowd roared and cheered at his verdict and watched as fat, rugged, masked executioners pulled at their victims by their chains. They were dragged to a cage in the center of the courtroom and strapped down on a still-wet and bloody slab of cut rock. Their bellies were sliced open and their innards pulled out and thrown to the cannibalistic crowd. Heads rolled off bodies as dull axes made repeated slams into tense necks. Minos had no room for discrimination. He executed the young, the old, the willing, and the unwilling. "What say you, my people? Do you thirst for more?" Elizabeth heard him say to the salivating audience.

Minos continued his mockery of justice while Moloch stood beside him and watched in amusement. "You find glory in these punishments. My kind, no matter the sin, would never succumb to such barbarism. That is why you serve us, mortal," Moloch said.

"We may serve you, but you are nothing without worshipers. Now let me get back the festivities," Minos answered back.

Moloch looked down at Minos and growled under his breath. He turned and left through some unseen back door while Minos ignored him and continued to carry on with the executions.

Elizabeth watched as Moloch left and waited to pass until the next execution so as to not draw attention to herself. She held her breath and heard the heavy whimper of a child pleading for her mother. The child was barely ten years of age and was covered in slashed flesh and dark bruises. She was one of many slaves used as a physical conduit for countless Seraphim. The child had no memory of how many times she had been possessed and for what purpose. Elizabeth heard the crying grow louder as Minos laughed and pointed out mockeries to his Seraphim guards.

"It seems you have outlived your purpose, little girl. Do not worry, there is a better life waiting for you after this one. Maybe," Minos said as he chuckled and laughed.

Elizabeth gritted her teeth and stepped into the giant courtroom coliseum. Its size was comparable to that of a large cathedral built around a crater made from fire fallen from the sky. It was built by the Seraphim specifically for Minos to enact his law. The bloodied cage in the center of the room was placed far enough from Minos, but close enough to the crowd for them to smell the iron of hot blood.

Elizabeth made her way to the crying girl and pushed her aside. She looked up at Minos as he stood up and yelled out in anger. Three of his Seraphim guards readied their spears as they jumped down and surrounded Elizabeth.

"Wait," a voice yelled out. Moloch walked back into the courtroom and made his way up to Minos. "Back away," He told his fellow guard. "You are more resourceful than you seem. I am beginning to see what Azrael sees in you," Moloch said to Elizabeth. Moloch raised his hand and the three Seraph guards backed away. The girl soon grew silent as curiosity began to outweigh her fear. The low-hummed noise of marching footsteps grew louder and soon the courtroom was filled with a few dozen men. They were mortal men in service to the Seraphim. They were armed with every weapon conceivable of inflicting more damage than was necessary to win a fight. Swords, maces, axes, spears, scythes, and daggers were but a few of the toys they brought with them.

Elizabeth backed away and kept her eyes fixed upon the newfound threat. The girl hid behind her as she took her stance and readied herself to draw blood.

"What is this? Just go down and kill her," Minos said angrily to Moloch.

"I would not dare waste my efforts to murder someone so… resilient," Moloch said.

"Wait…you wish to possess her? But you do not even know what she is."

"It matters not what she is. What better way to get close to Azrael and kill him for good?" Moloch watched as his human guards drew in close to Elizabeth and the girl. "Well, men, how much longer will you keep us waiting? Attack her."

Elizabeth closed her eyes and listened to the stampede of footsteps rush towards her. She shifted her weight and listened to the crowd as pointed blades made their way closer to her flesh. She kept her body as a shield in front of the crying child as the human monsters came ever closer. Within seconds she felt their hot breath on her back. She opened her eyes and turned to face her attackers.

A streak of steel flew across her face as she backed inches away from striking distance. Without a weapon to call her own, she grabbed the arm of the attacking guard and let his body rush toward her. With her blood running on hatred and revenge, she twisted his wrist and sent his sword into the stomach of another. She flipped herself around and snapped the neck of the guard she held onto while dodging a flurry of speared attacks. Clutching the handle of her former opponent's blade, Elizabeth ripped it from the guts in which it lay and whipped the sword in front of her, sending a trail of blood into the eyes of another crazed maniac. She spun herself around to meet another soldier by her side and sent the edge of her new weapon across his throat. He clutched his gaping wound and watched as Elizabeth cut one of his brethren from crotch to sternum before turning around and sending sharp steel through his teeth and out the back of his skull. Like a possessed marionette, she danced around the men and drew blood with each strike. In one instant, the head of a mace sped towards her as she dodged, sending the spiked ball crushing against the face of another guard. Eyes popped and bone broke through skin, followed by droplets of blood and fragments of teeth and cortex. In the next instant, the length of a spear made its way across her back as she arched to avoid injury. Elizabeth spun her arm around, cutting halfway through the neck of her attacker. Blood bubbled up around the wound and eventually fell like a crimson river to the floor. The harder the guard tried to breathe, the greater the force his blood was sent gushing out. She came around for a second swipe and dislocated the gagging soldier at the base of his skull, sending his head to the ground at her feet.

More men ran into the now blood-stained room with readied weapons and orders to kill. One by one she weaved and twisted between them, slicing necks, ripping open stomachs, and eviscerating flesh. Each strike she gave was a killing strike, and they followed suit as well. The floor cracked with missed hits from heavy-bladed weapons. Walls were splintered with ill-timed strikes as dust flew with each impact, and corpses piled up with confrontations that Elizabeth put to rest.

Minos watched in horror as Elizabeth played with his toys as if they were no more than rag dolls made for her to tear apart. His mouth parted while he tried to form the words to describe his disbelief.

"Did I not tell you that she was something of an oddity? Her scent comes back to me. She shares it with Azrael. My, how many worlds have I laid in retribution while Azrael held onto her flesh? I understand now why she is special to him. She is the Abyss, the demon he was sent to find and destroy. Oh, how Daemos misjudged his pet," Moloch said.

"What nonsense do you speak?" Minos sneered at Moloch.

"Azrael had no idea the creature he lay with was the same as him. I do take fault as well. Although separated by all of existence, their blood still sought each other out. She fights to find him, as he to find her. It is almost…noble."

"This is about two mindless child beasts in lust? All of this? My men die because of such trivial nonsense?" Minos shouted at Moloch.

Moloch turned around and grabbed Minos by the throat, slamming him against the wall behind them. He lifted the judge to eye level so that he could see the black charred orbs that sat within his face. "Had you not held sway in this world, I would suck dry the meat from your bones myself. This has nothing to do with any simple mortal fallacy. This is not about the meeting of soul mates or whispers of lust. It is about survival. Love or not, Azrael will find her and they will produce offspring. That abomination will produce more unholy spawn and in time we will once again be forced to contend with the Abyss. I will not see that day come to pass."

Moloch let loose his grasp on Minos as their fears arose. The sound of the ensuing battle had ended. Only the noise of heavy drawn breaths and the whimpering of a child were left. Moloch looked down from atop the podium and saw Elizabeth standing amongst a mountain of stripped, torn, and lacerated body parts. From head to toe, she was splattered with the red nectar of her enemies. The child, still alive, let tears fall down her face while she wiped away excesses of secondhand sprays of blood. The crowd before them fell silent as they had never witnessed a single creature, let alone a human, murder so many in such little time.

"I must give you my praise for the heavens smile upon you this day. Such a noble act to save a child from a terrible fate," Moloch said. Minos scoffed in disgust at Moloch's ending words. "What now shall I do to appease you?" Moloch asked.

Elizabeth looked up at Moloch and saw his nerves break through his skin. He tried to hold back from tearing away his flesh to expose his Seraphim form and Elizabeth knew this. She looked down at the crying girl and knew that even if there was a way to set her free that this world was no place for anyone to live. "More. Send me all of your men so that I may bathe in their exposed stench. And when those are exhausted, send me the crowd, so that I may share with them your acts of murder. And when I have tired of them, send me your brothers, so that I may render the extinction of your lives."

Moloch clenched his fists and held back the feeling boiling in his gut. His mortal skin cracked and bubbled as the heat of his Seraph body rippled from underneath.

Minos stepped up to Moloch. "Just kill her. End this," Minos said.

"And have her lost to us so that Azrael may find her? No," Moloch answered.

Elizabeth stood her ground and waited for the judge and the Seraphim to give their answer.

"So be it," Moloch said. He raised his hand and looked up past the bone-laced ceiling and into the stars above. Within seconds, the courtroom-turned arena began to shake and quake with a thunderous force. The crowd screamed and panicked as pieces of stone and fixture fell and crushed those beneath. The people scattered like insects and fled out from the looming threat of danger. Only Elizabeth and the girl stayed.

Moloch closed the grip on his hand as it radiated with a pulse of white-hot light. Tendrils shot out from his back while his human shell broke and tore away, revealing the black-eyed creature beneath. His skin glowed and illuminated the room. Soon, the quaking died down and fell silent. In that instant, Elizabeth ran to the girl and held her close. They were allowed only a moment to take in the silence before a star fell from the sky and crashed through the ceiling. It hit the ground behind them and roared like a crazed beast. Two more stars fell and joined the roaring beast. When Elizabeth turned her head, she saw that Moloch had called three more of his brothers down from the heavens. They arose and showed their true Seraphim state. Each one had six tentacles that spread from their backs. Their black eyes broke through their white faces as they stared down at Elizabeth and the girl. The other three Seraphim guards shed their armor as well, exposing their true form.

"Please forgive me," Elizabeth whispered into the girl's ear. She shed a tear and held the girl close in her arms. A burst of growing laughter from the beasts that surrounded them flooded their senses. It was clear to them that they had become as a cornered animal, a whimpering mass of helpless flesh waiting to have its skin picked from its bone. The girl stopped crying and looked into Elizabeth's eyes, knowing the act that she was about to commit.

XV. Trial By Fire

Cracked fingers made their way around the stripped and rotten foundations of stone once taken in the form of worshiped gods. Men, women, and children, now infected with the blight of plague and cursed by their gods, crept along their hunting grounds. Their callous feet ran along stone pathways and weaved between the winding corridors of the ruins while they followed the scent of meat. The ashen coloring of their skin helped blend them in with the surrounding rubble, to stay hidden from their enemies. Their hunt, however, was not to go as planned.

Azrael heard the scavengers approach from behind and readied his war nerves. Daemos stopped in his tracks as he turned his head to face the threat that approached. In an instant, hundreds of crazed ash-skinned creatures lunged out from beyond the foundations and stone pillars. Their cracked nails let go their of grip as they released themselves from the giant statues of the gods.

Charon held tight the grip of his lantern-topped staff while the horde approached ever closer. One by one, they ran and jumped from wall to wall. Azrael, Daemos, and Charon prepared to fend off an impending attack. When the first crazed mutation ran by, Azrael held his fists up to block a swipe to his face. The attack never came. The infected mortal ran by and off into the distance. A dozen more followed suit and completely ignored the demon, Seraph, and ferryman. Soon, the entire horde made haste, racing past them.

Azrael lowered his stance and watched as the creatures ran off in the same direction they were traveling towards as well. "They are not here for us," Azrael said.

As Azrael watched the scavengers run past, he noticed one creep up to him. Its eyes were cracked with red vessels and yellow pupils. Its skin was pale and thin and he could see black and red veins run beneath the surface. It opened its mouth and revealed a set of dirt and bile-stained teeth while a layer of slime dripped from its callous mouth. It made a gurgling sound as it tried to form words.

"God…we want…our god. We…eat…our god. Kill…our god. We…smell…you. We…smell…another. Follow," the creature said.

Charon walked up to the creature and stared at it. He recognized it as a soul that had once crossed over after death but had somehow returned to its mortal body. "It is an undead. I have ferried all of these souls across before. Someone else has tainted the natural order and placed them back in their deceased flesh."

"Who would do such a thing? And for what purpose?" Daemos asked.

The creature slumped and scurried along the ground as it approached Daemos. It lifted its frail body and sniffed the Seraphim, taking in his scent.

"You. You…smell…you…make…us."

"That is impossible," Daemos said.

The creature turned its head and ran off to join its brothers as the crowd of the undead continued to make their way toward the tower of Minos.

"What was the meaning of that creature?" Azrael demanded.

Charon raised his head to the heavens and looked up past the stars to the point of creation. "It is one of your brothers, Daemos. You cannot create life, but you are able to pervert it. Like as one of your own has perverted himself."

"Who?" Azrael asked.

"Samael," Daemos answered. "He has become obsessed. He wears the mantle of death upon his brow."

"It is your brother, then, that is breaking the natural cycle. Nothing more than a ferryman of the dead shall be allowed the title of 'Reaper'," Charon said as he gritted his teeth.

"Samael no longer sees the natural order as viable. He has declared himself as the one veritable angel of death," Daemos answered.

"We shall see. I exist on every world, in every plane of creation. Samael is but a single being," Charon replied.

Azrael stepped between Daemos and Charon. "Enough of this. We follow the horde. They travel to the tower as well."

Azrael walked off and deeper into the frail ruins as they followed the remaining flock of infected mortals.

Charon approached Daemos with a fervent scowl draped across his face. "It is Samael. No other of your kind is capable of twisting the souls of the living as he does. He was mortal once. He was Azrael's brother. By the heavens Daemos, what have you done? How long do you think you can keep this secret before he finds out?"

"I did what must be done. I did not know that Samael would be driven to insanity, while Azrael and Sophia accepted their gifts without incident. Samael does not even know that he was once mortal," Daemos said.

"Your acts of defiance against nature will be the end of us all." Charon turned away in disgust from Daemos and kept a close stride toward Azrael. Daemos took a deep breath into his burning Seraphim lungs and followed suit.

* * *

Elizabeth held the girl as the seven Seraphim assassins gauged their movements closer. Their clawed hands gripped onto their holy instruments of war. The girl calmed her cries as she watched the beast's approach from over the view of Elizabeth's shoulder.

"Please forgive me," Elizabeth whispered into the girl's ear.

With those words, she stuck the end of her blade into the girl's gut and felt streams of warm blood run over her hands. She held the girl as the life faded out from her eyes and spilled onto the ground below. Behind her, Elizabeth could hear the Seraphim laugh and taunt. With the girl's blood on her hands, she took the knife and sliced open the palm of her other hand. She threw the mixture of her blood and the girls to the floor while raising her eyes up to Moloch, who was transfixed not ten feet away from her mid-air.

Moloch swayed his body like a sea creature submerged in liquid smoke. His tendrils whipped and cracked against the air as he floated weightlessly above Elizabeth. "Is this your failed attempt at sorcery?" he asked, mocking Elizabeth as she threw more of her blood to the already stained floor.

The Seraphim began to close in with their weapons in hand when they felt the shock of the earthquake beneath their wings. The tremor was small, but noticeable enough for them to show curiosity.

"You forget who I now share blood with," Elizabeth quipped at Moloch.

The crackling of flame and living shadow could be heard from beneath the darkness. Elizabeth raised her head to face the inevitable. She felt the beast race up from its captive prison and speed closer to her reality. With their patience drained, the Seraphim rushed in for their attack. Before they were able to reach their target, the ground beneath Elizabeth exploded in a burst of fire and black ash. Moloch and his brothers were knocked back against the corners of the room as they watched the beast rise from the fire.

Elizabeth held her hands out as the black serpent rose from a fiery pit beneath her feet. She touched its leathery flesh as it coiled itself around her body and took its protective stance. The serpent reared its razor-sharp teeth at the Seraphim and kept Elizabeth close to its quarters. Elizabeth stepped over the flaming pit and made her way around the back of the serpent.

"Abyss. She has summoned a demon of the Abyss," Moloch said to himself.

The seven Seraphim warriors picked themselves up and raised their weapons to match their composure. Before any of them were able to take flight, the dragonesque serpent had already sped its way around the room, crashing through pillars and sending chunks of rock and foundation through the air. Moloch heard one of his brothers scream as the serpent held the Seraph in its jaws. It snapped and clenched its teeth shut as white light faded from the Seraph's body. The serpent chewed and gnawed at Seraphim flesh sending streams of its victim's illuminated blood across the room.

Moloch jumped over and dodged the serpent's next charge. He swiped at its charred flesh with his sword, to no avail. The serpent kept on his path as it slithered around the room at the same speed that Moloch fled. They played this dance macabre as Elizabeth stripped away the remnants of her broken armor, leaving her upper arms, legs, and mid-torso bare. She ran to the fallen Seraph and grabbed his holy weapon while sliding under the swipe of another war ax in her path. With a well-timed duck, she avoided losing her head while grabbing tight the clutches of her new toy. She swung the sword around and pushed it through the back side of her attacker. The impaled Seraph grabbed the blade protruding from his gut and ripped it out from his flesh. His wound closed as he pursued Elizabeth across the newly created battlefield.

The six remaining Seraphim weaved in and between both Elizabeth and her serpentine pet. Each one of their movements was timed perfectly in sequence with their opponents, almost as if they were engaged in a pre-planned choreography. Only on those rare occasions where an attack was possible would blood be drawn, never enough though to constitute a kill.

* * *

Through the ashes of the wasteland, the beasts of men and undead women and children rushed to the tower of Minos. Their callous flesh pulled with each sprint and stretch toward salvation and vengeance. They snarled through black lungs infested with decay and basked in the scent of their once glorious landscape, now turned into a waste of barren ruins. Their claws gripped and clutched onto the broken walls, sandblasted stones, and weather-worn foliage. They were a frightening scene of stampede bred with thunder. A blaze of fury awaited the gods as they approached the very tower that had shunned them so many years ago.

Azrael spared not a moment longer as he shed his human flesh and exposed the beast within. His bones cracked and reformed upon themselves as his newfound wasteland scavenger pets rushed past him. With wings spread and claws and horns pointed to the sky, he took flight and discarded all notions of a stealthy approach. He followed the howls as their morbid shrieks flew like infected carrion against the wind.

Daemos and Charon made haste, as well. The confrontation they had hoped to avoid was now closer to their feared vision. They knew that this would not simply be an act of petty vengeance, but the markings of the beginning of a war. In the distance, they could already see smoke and flame rise up from the outskirts of the tower.

* * *

Blood flew from the four corners of the room as each race fought for supremacy. Elizabeth jumped and dodged each attack as the Seraphim continued their pursuit of both her and the serpent of the Abyss.

In a single moment, time seemed to stand still as Elizabeth looked up past a broken hole in the ceiling to see a familiar shadow cast upon her gaze. Her heart pounded faster each moment that she saw the shadow move closer. She recognized the expanded wings, the crown of horns, and the spinal cord-like tail.

Azrael crashed through the side of the tower and caught his claws against one of Moloch's Seraphim assassins. He dug his fingertips into the Seraph's throat and pulled away while his grip lay firm, like the jaws of perdition biting through steel. Divine blood spilled to the floor and caught the attention of the other Seraphim assassins. One by one, they jumped and flew at their demonic opponent. The first was met with a swipe of pure, concentrated pain. The attacker clutched onto Azrael's tail as it slid through its torso and continued ripping past its heart. Azrael twisted his body and flung the now-dead Seraphim to the ground. He met the second Seraph warrior with the edge of his wings. With his talons spread, the Seraph's head fell to the floor while Azrael slipped his wings across its holy throat. The fourth enemy was finished off as Azrael chased it across the room and past the Abyss serpent. Azrael pinned it against a wall with his claws as he dug his thumbs into the Seraph's eye sockets and growled while he snuffed the life from his foe.

Elizabeth looked up and smiled at Azrael as he murdered one after another in his bloodlust. Behind her, another Seraphim assassin crept along her path. He spread his illuminated tendrils and rushed with the tip of his blade aimed at Elizabeth's back. She turned around just in time to see her summoned pet crash up through the floor and engulf her attacker in its jaws. The Seraphim screamed in agony as the serpent ripped its teeth into its guts and tore at it like a rabid animal. Before the serpent could finish its meal, Moloch rushed down from his perch and sliced its head off with his sword. Elizabeth screamed for Azrael as Moloch took his stride toward her.

Before Azrael could come to her aid, Moloch heard the sounds of the earth quaking beneath his feet. He watched as hundreds upon thousands of rotten and fetid mortals crashed into the tower and ripped apart everything they came across. Behind them, Daemos and Charon approached. Moloch lowered his stance and took to the air, hovering above Azrael and Elizabeth.

"So, this is what you had in mind? Rebellion? You think even a planet full of these vermin are enough to account for all of my brothers?" Moloch asked Azrael and Elizabeth.

"No Moloch. You have grown mad with power, become the very thing you wished to extinguish. You are worse than the Abyss ever could have been," Daemos said from behind a cloud of dissipating smoke.

"Brother? Is that you?" Moloch questioned. He saw both Daemos and Charon walk into the destroyed room. With his assassins now dead, Moloch knew that he was both outnumbered and outmatched. "You conspire against me as well? Your own brother? With these…beasts?"

Daemos approached Moloch and tried to plead with him. "No brother. I wish to see you become what you once were. Noble, loyal, and empathetic. What you were before you sacrificed our father and made that ungodly weapon of yours."

Moloch's skin burned as his brother spoke. His eyes cracked and showed their true blackened form. "We all agreed that our father's way was folly and that our existence depended on strength. I gave us that strength. You were the one that chose to take in that child and raise him as a creature of darkness. And for what? So that he could have their scent? So that he could hunt them down for us? You had little faith in me, brother, but I always had faith in you. Even when your pet disobeyed, I was there to clean up his mess."

Azrael took a moment to listen to Moloch as he changed back into his mortal shell. "What is he speaking of?"

"Nothing, Azrael, mind your tongue," Daemos commanded.

"No, I am no longer your puppet. Speak your words of truth or I will unleash fury on you and all of your brothers, man, and beast alike," Azrael demanded.

"I do believe the boy deserves the truth," Charon stated.

"I found you, beaten and torn, as an infant on the brink of death. It was not on this world. Your home was destroyed long ago by the Abyss. You were one of the last mortals I found before the planet was covered in darkness. I imbued you with a dying creature of the Abyss. You were never supposed to come here, to meet Baphomet and pass through her trials. All of this was a mistake," Daemos said.

"Yes, brother, it was a mistake. And now we shall all pay for your arrogance," Moloch snarled.

Charon looked at both Azrael and Daemos and nodded his head, knowing what was going through their minds. When he turned to find Elizabeth, she was vacant from his vision. "Azrael, where is Elizabeth?"

When his words faded from their ears, he saw Elizabeth climbing the wall behind Moloch. She jumped off and lunged at his back, plunging her blade deep into his neck. Moloch screamed in bloody horror as he was caught off guard. Elizabeth yelled into his ear, "Burn in the cinders of your destruction, Seraphim parasite."

Hoping to stop the bleeding, Moloch threw Elizabeth to the ground at Azrael's feet and dropped his sword. Upon seeing the flaming blade penetrate the floor, Azrael rushed forward and grabbed the hilt, ripping the sword from the tethered stone. Moloch looked down in horror as his enemy now had his holy weapon. He shed his mortal flesh and spread his tendrils as he took to the heavens above. Streams of white, glowing blood fell upon Daemos' face as he watched his brother return to the cosmos.

"What have you done?" Daemos asked Elizabeth.

"What needed to be done. He now has no weapons to fight us with. We will take the fight to him," Elizabeth answered.

Charon stepped forward and looked at both Elizabeth and Azrael. "I hope the two of you are prepared for the fallout of your actions."

Azrael wrapped his fingers around Elizabeth's hand as he stared into the living flame of Moloch's sword. He saw visions of a thousand worlds burned by the very weapon itself. He remembered his countless deaths and watching Elizabeth burn before his eyes. "I have been prepared for this since the day I was born," Azrael said as he looked directly into Daemos' eyes.

XVI. The Temple Of Lilith

Like specs of dust wading in oceans of time, each one of us travels to their purpose. Some with a guiding direction, others simply drifting through space in the hopes that someone, or something, will find them. The stars are the everlasting, guiding light in a universe filled with darkness and decay. A cold chill and an echoing silence are all that remains to remind us that, in a million worlds filled with life, we are still truly alone. We spread our wings with the noblest of intentions. We do as our creator says. To gain approval through loyal recourse. At times, though, we must betray our thoughts for the greater good. What purpose is there to life if even those we trust end up questioning our motives? As we drift through our reality, only one thing can be certain; the end will come for us all, and his name is Death.

Moloch kept his mind busy with thoughts of justification as he floated through the stars. His Seraphim eyes waded in and out of consciousness as he swam past worlds devoid of life and other planets teeming with civilization. Had he still had his weapon, he would have traversed one of these worlds and given his divine retribution. All he could do now was look down past the clouds and watch as people waged war, made love, lived, and breathed hope and fear. He was sickened by the unholy chaos.

He cursed the day that his forefathers and all the ancient gods created his kind. He cursed the day that the mother of all creation created mortal man from the blood of her slain son. He cursed the day that the gods grew defiant and exiled man across the stars. In those moments that he thought of his gods, he cursed his own existence as well.

Consciousness began to fade from Moloch's eyes. His arms and legs grew limp while his skin began to wane in its holy luster. Nearly a world away, one of his brothers spotted him, floating above a bright blue planet inhabited with life no more intelligent than that of a common virus.

* * *

The scavengers had all but plundered and torn down the foundations from the very tower itself. Minos watched as his monolithic structure was brought crashing down to its roots one brick at a time.

"We found...in...dark…in...deep…in hide," one of the ash-covered scavengers told Azrael.

"What you find, you may keep," Azrael told the lowly mortal as it scuttled away to fight with another of its kind over a severed leg they wished to take as a meal.

Minos looked at Azrael, Elizabeth, Daemos, and Charon with a look of fear and concern across his face. He watched as Azrael and Daemos bickered like they had known each other for years.

"You think your words to be of revelation to me? I was told that I was born a mortal by another," Azrael told Daemos.

"By whom? The abomination of the blood seas, Leviathan? I wished to tell you first," Daemos exclaimed.

"Then why wait until now? If what you and Leviathan say is true, then I am no creature of the Abyss. I simply share their blood," Azrael exclaimed.

Charon stepped in and made his voice heard. "You two still do not understand. Seraphim, Abyss, mortal…you all share the same blood. We are all children of Tiamat. Each of your races was born of her divine blood. Mortal man came first from her son Kingu, then…" Charon was interrupted by Elizabeth.

"Yes, we all know, the Seraphim were born from those who took to the skies and the Abyss from those that wandered into the sea. I was told of these legends since I can remember," Elizabeth said.

"And how would you know of these things?" Charon asked.

"I just know them. I can remember the stories told to me as a child. The scholars of Baphomet would read to me and tell me to never forget who I was, what I was made for," Elizabeth answered.

"And what were you made for?" Daemos asked.

Azrael looked into Elizabeth's eyes and knew the answer all too well. "She was made to survive. Now let us drop the history lesson and move before Moloch returns."

"Agreed," Charon said.

"You do realize that my brother will return to Elysium. Once the others of our kind find out that Azrael has his sword, there will no doubt be a swift retaliation," Daemos exclaimed.

"Then we need to act quickly. We need to find Belial and Cerberus. Build with them an army," Elizabeth said.

Azrael picked Minos up by his collar and held him up to his level. "I am only going to ask this once. The three-headed hound and the jackal. Where did you have them sent?" Azrael growled at Minos.

Minos looked at Elizabeth and back at Azrael, his hands and tongue shivering in a fear he has never known. "To the east. They were sold as slaves to a witch named Lilith. She commands a harem in praise of Baphomet. If you like, I could show…"

"That is enough," Azrael said. He threw Minos to the ground and watched as the former judge crawled on his hands and feet. Azrael walked over to Minos and picked him back up. He wrapped his hands around the side of Minos' head and plunged his thumbs into the judge's eyes sockets, ripping away at his ocular cavities. Minos screamed out in pain as he tried to hold back rivers of blood with his bare hands.

"Why? Why? Why?" Minos kept repeating.

"That was to make sure you were telling the truth. If you are lying, then I will come back for the rest of your head," Azrael snarled.

Elizabeth walked up next to Azrael and looked down at the weeping mess that was Minos. "I take it you are off to seek this, Lilith?" Elizabeth asked.

"Yes. Go with Charon and Daemos and take Minos back to Baphomet. Tell her children, both the jackals and mortal men alike, of the coming danger they face," Azrael told her.

"A thousand lifetimes is preparation enough," Elizabeth said.

"We will wait a thousand more if we keep our enemies at bay," Azrael replied.

"Touching," Charon said aloud.

"Is this sort of thing common with those that you send to the afterlife?" Daemos asked.

"Only before the coming of a storm. On other occasions, when old age is not an option for death, I see men holding on to their own innards, pleading for another chance at life. Neither Azrael nor Elizabeth pleaded once in all the times I have seen their deaths. But their existence is hardly ruled by nature now, is it?" Charon asked.

"No, it certainly is not," Daemos answered.

Elizabeth let go her hold of Azrael and kicked Minos to her command. "Move, you waste of mortal flesh before I decide to finish what he started." She continued to kick and berate him as Daemos and Charon watched in shock.

"A bit harsh, are we?" Charon said to Elizabeth.

"This godless heathen deserves no less for the crimes he has committed," Elizabeth answered.

Azrael looked back as he watched Daemos, Charon, and Elizabeth escort Minos away from his now burning tower and back towards the temple of Baphomet. He took one final look up to the heavens before unleashing his demonic nature and spread his wings out across the skies. He took off to the east in search of another temple, the harem of Lilith.

* * *

The essence of creation made its way into the antechamber one sliver of light at a time. Moloch slowly began to feel his mind return to his body as his arms and legs once again tingled with the sensation of life. He was no longer floating like a corpse, lost and cold in the deep of space. One of his brothers had found and returned him. With his eyes now fully open, he was able to make out where he was. The room was a magnificent pearl white. He lifted himself off from the crescent-shaped table and gathered his strength. He recognized the room as being one of the light chambers of Elysium. It was a place for him and his brothers in times of needed rest and meditation.

"So you are awake," a voice said from beyond the room.

"My body, you have fixed the shell of my mortal host. I must give my thanks," Moloch said.

"No need, brother. The others are quite anxious to hear of your time spent on the Abyss home world. You did return to the Abyss home world, did you not?"

"Yes, I did, in fact. Come in. I wish to speak to you in the flesh."

Moloch watched as the large organic door spread apart like a set of slithering snakes uncoiling from their slumber to allow his brothers to enter. Raphael and Gabriel entered the room to meet with their newly revived brother.

"You are lucky, dear brother, as Raphael found you. He informed me of the attack and followed you during your escape," Gabriel told Moloch.

"Yes, how fortunate," Moloch said as he sneered at Raphael. He got up and walked over to a nearby mirror to see the work done on his body. His face and skin had been restored to its human form to a near-perfect semblance.

"We are all growing accustomed to keeping the permanence of our host bodies. We have even decided to take up having mortal names on more than formal occasions," Gabriel said.

"Yes, I am…filled with joy," Moloch said with a sarcastic tone.

"I looked across the stars where I found you, but could not find your sword. Do you wish me to return to the world below to retrieve it?" Raphael asked.

"No," Moloch said. "I want the two of you to call a meeting."

"With the seven?" Gabriel asked.

"NO, not just the seven. With all of our brothers…and our sisters," Moloch said.

Gabriel looked at Raphael with a gesture of puzzlement and confusion. "That has not been done for two full millennia. The sisters are not normally spoken of unless it is a great time of need to replenish our numbers. Why the sudden course of action?"

Moloch walked over to Gabriel and placed his hand on his brother's shoulder. "Azrael has the Sword of Jehovah."

Raphael and Gabriel took a step back and looked at Moloch, hoping that this was some sort of sick joke. After a few moments, they realized that their fears were true.

"Give word to all the corners of creation. All Seraphim are to meet in Elysium at once," Gabriel said to Raphael.

* * *

"Eyes, my eyes. Eyes to see, ears to hear. Will you take my ears? Will you take them as well?" Minos whimpered as Elizabeth pushed and prodded him along back to the temple of Baphomet.

"Maybe I will take your tongue as well," Elizabeth answered.

Minos shut his mouth and coughed up thick recesses of blood deep from within his gut. Charon and Daemos followed behind as they watched Elizabeth have what she would never admit to them was amusing in her mind.

"Do you wish him to fetch you a bone as well?" Daemos asked Elizabeth.

Elizabeth turned around and walked up to Daemos. She glared at him while he and Charon looked on in pity at the former judge. "This man…this…creature will pay for his crimes."

"I am sure Baphomet will be just," Daemos said, with a sarcastic tone.

Elizabeth turned back around and kicked Minos along the path once again. She turned her head to the side so that Daemos could barely make out the fact that she was smiling. "Your brothers will pay for their crimes as well," she said as she turned her head away and continued to smile.

Daemos felt a fire grow inside his chest as he let Charon walk in place in front of him.

"By all intents and purposes, she has lived a thousand more lives than you or any one of your brethren. Be glad she has not found out her full potential. Yet," Charon told Daemos.

"What is your game, ferryman? Abyss or Seraphim? What is your gain in all of this?" Daemos asked.

"That is simple; to restore the natural order that your, and Azrael's kind, have so inconsiderately disrupted. Life and death have become interchangeable. Both realms have lost their meaning. And without meaning, both are reduced to nothing," Charon explained.

"Then let us hurry this," Daemos said, as he picked up his pace behind Elizabeth.

* * *

From above the clouds, Azrael could see the intricacies of the landscape. Man-made towers and jagged mountains interweaved with one another as their forms took an almost bio-mechanical shape. Further, into the rising sun of the east he flew, and further did his gaze wander. The earth beneath him slowly turned from a charred, black, barren void to a magnificent blood-red ocean of sand and rock. Hot winds blew against his wings as the desert below thrashed upon itself like an ocean during a storm. He flew between mile-high pillars that jettisoned up from the sands and seemed to reach forever into the sky. They were lined with the same Enochian carvings that littered Charon's ship. The tall black spires seemed to twist and move amongst themselves as large serpentine stone effigies coiled their bodies against the surface. It was as if the Abyss had touched the desert and given it the very rabid life that they themselves fed upon.

A red glow peaked from above the horizon as the sun began to settle. From beyond the towering spires, Azrael could see a temple. It was a large domed structure surrounded by smaller versions of the pillars he flew through and in between. Large desert serpents danced under the sand in front of the monolithic entrance, while people, nude and vulnerable, moaned and hissed in pools of cool blue liquid that sat in contrast to the overwhelming crimson of the landscape. He had arrived at the Harem of Lilith.

The entrance was merely a short distance walk at this point. He barged forward and forced open the gateway to the harem, forfeiting any gesture of hospitality. In that instant, for the first time in a long time, Azrael's eyes widened in shock at the sights he saw.

Lilith had kept her residence stocked with the finest silks, furnishings, idols, and trinkets she could find. None were more so important than her legion. Azrael approached slowly as he watched people beg and plead for their skin to be touched and fondled. Men and women fornicated in whatever spot they could find, regardless of the danger or consequence. He witnessed as one couple was eaten alive by a captive beast when they had reached their climax with one another. As the beast's teeth bit into their flesh, streams of blood, semen, and bile erupted in a macabre palette of living art. Beside them, a woman birthed a child that screamed with new life. The sounds of creation and destruction came frothing from these unfortunate pets. These people were under Lilith's spell.

Lilith took notice of Azrael as he strode into her den of iniquities. She moved her body with a serpentine grace as she let the prodding tentacle slide in and out between her legs. Her black-tipped hands gripped the armrests made of skull and spine that kept her throne balanced upon the mound of dirt and bone and pulsating bodies that it sat upon. Hands, lips, and genitals made their way over her flesh in a shameless display of pleasure and worship. She let herself stay exposed in an act of blood and fornication for all her pets to see. With a full thrust from the prodding snake into her womb, she rose her eyes to Azrael and welcomed his entrance. "You must either be lost or sent by the gods. And you do not look lost from where I sit. So stranger, who sent you, and what is it you seek?" she asked.

Azrael wasted no time getting to his point. He pulled the bone-shard hilt of Moloch's sword from beneath his cloak and held it in front of him for Lilith to see. From it shot a bolt of living flame. His grip tightened as the flames grew around the ethereal blade. They danced and swirled as they took on a life of their own. Lilith's attitude changed from that of a smug sex fiend to a creature whose life was in danger. Azrael kept the weapon held in front of him as he spoke. "The jackal and the hound. Where are they?"

Lilith slid herself off of her throne of macabre pleasure, the phallic serpent dropping from her slick gash back to its base, and walked down to meet Azrael with her thighs still wet from her pass time. "Who are you to make demands? You tell your brothers that I am not your slave driver. You may hold your brother's sword, but I still dictate when and where…"

Azrael cut off her speech by letting his wings rip through the flesh in his back, exposing his demonic form for all to see. Lilith stumbled over her own words as she lost her balance and fell to the floor in terror. "I am no Seraphim dog. I answer to my flesh and my flesh alone. If you wish to keep your pets between your legs with your head still attached, you will tell me where the Seraphim are paying you to keep your prisoners."

Lilith was speechless as she took breath after breath, reeling in terror from the sight of the Abyss creature making demands before her. She took a moment to compose her words. "You have the sword. That must mean you have killed Moloch. His curse is lifted. Are you here to kill or free us?"

"Neither. Moloch lives." Azrael retracted the flames from Moloch's sword and took a step back from Lilith. He saw genuine fear in her eyes as her pets sat motionless as well. He realized not all was as it seemed. Curiosity got the best of him. "What is this place?"

Lilith picked herself up and grabbed a dark red cloth roughly the same color as her shoulder-length hair to cover her naked flesh. Having a demonic being like Azrael so much as lay his eyes upon her sent a shiver through her spine. "Moloch came to me. The taste of his blood treated my eternal youth." Lilith looked around at the people she had kept in chained pleasure. Her house of lust was a market for flesh that the Seraphim used to barter their trade. "We bore children for the Seraphim to use as they please. For sacrifice, for food, for war. It mattered not the cause. They spoke of you, the winged demon. The destroyer of worlds. And now here you are, in my home, asking to free the slaves I keep for them. If you do not kill me, they surely will."

"That is your choice to make. I can promise you, though, that death at my hands will not be as swift as their angelic touch."

"They were working with another of us, a man named Minos. He held his position as the judge of these lands."

"His tower burns as we speak," Azrael rebutted.

Lilith fell to her knees and began to weep. She felt the tears run through her hands and between her fingers.

Azrael grabbed her by the hair on the back of her head and clenched his teeth by her ear. "I have no time for your misery." He gripped his claws around her throat and made slight cuts into her neck with his talons. "The jackal and the beast. The next time I ask, you will be missing a vital part of your flesh."

Lilith turned her head to Azrael, shaking in terror. She could feel his grip tightening as his patience waned. The air surrounding them grew thick and stale with the stench of lust. Lilith's subjects sat silent and watched as Azrael kept his motions still, making his threat all the more real. Tired of awaiting an answer, Azrael raised his newly acquired weapon above his head and readied it to strike down upon Lilith.

XVII. Gateways To Annihilation

The Seraphim arrived at Elysium, their believed celestial birthplace, by the thousands. For so long have they flown on the winds of the cosmos that they have forgotten their true origin. Several millennia have passed since they called Elysium home that they now consider it the place of their genesis. Neither a world on its own nor a simple conduit to other dimensions of the flesh, Elysium sits in the spaces between realities. Its streets, structures, and guiding lights visible only to the divine. Its architects still remain unknown. The celestial city followed the same design as any other city built by mortal men. The streets weaved in, out, above, and around the large, towering spires that reached out to the heavens. With neither doors nor windows, each structure simply moves like a set of living organs to accommodate its guests. In the center lay the heart of Elysium. Its beat could be heard as each echoed across time and space, where stars were made and destroyed upon its whim.

With the heart of Elysium now flooded with over a thousand Seraphim, Moloch stood his ground at the center of the great antechamber while Samael, Raphael, and Gabriel watched from a distance. Moloch watched as his brothers and sisters gathered around him from all directions. They flew about and took their place within the core. When all had settled, Moloch was able to speak. He looked around at his brothers and sisters and closed his eyes before parting his lips. "The bane of our father has been taken."

The crowd exploded in an uproar. Tendrils spread open like razor-lined wings and flesh burned to a boil as Moloch broke his silence. "The Abyss have stolen our lifeblood, they have ravaged our worlds and now they take from us the last remnant of our father."

Moloch knew that his words would cause such a heated commotion. "We have given our language, our design, our blood to mortal men. They have served us well. Now we must purge them and the Abyss alike. We must go to war!"

Samael stood near the entrance of the chamber and watched as the Seraphim cheered and screamed in bloody vengeance. His hands gripped the hilt of his scythe as he spread his wings and disappeared into the void of space. He set his sights on a world of blood, fire, and death that Azrael now called home.

* * *

Lights from the living forest could be seen penetrating from beyond the swirling walls of fog. Elizabeth, Charon, and Daemos drew closer to Baphomet's temple as they kicked their newfound slave along in front of them. Minos was barely able to move as he bled from the fresh hole carved into his face. Elizabeth pushed and shoved him along without a single care.

"I hope you are enjoying yourself, wench," Minos blurted out. "When my masters find me, you will all perish."

Elizabeth ignored his advances and continued to push him forward. Charon and Daemos stopped at the edge of the forest to listen to the newly formed rumble in the distance. Faint shapes could be seen twisting and winding back and forth. More clearly now were they able to see the glowing shroud of Seraphim tentacles as they changed shape into a darkened pair of tattered wings.

Minos called out to the Seraphim. "I am here, my lords. Your servant awaits."

Elizabeth planted her fist against Minos' face so hard that she felt bone snap. Daemos and Charon moved closer to Elizabeth as they knew the severity of the lingering threats waiting in the mist. "We must turn back and find refuge," Daemos told Elizabeth.

With those words, Daemos, Elizabeth, and Charon turned their heads toward the sound of the slaughter and saw a figure approach them from the thick of the fog. Samael revealed himself in all of his death-shrouded glory. His face was covered in the skull fragments of over a dozen different otherworldly creatures. His wings were not merely the same tendrils that the Seraphim sprouted, nor were they the oversized leathered claws of the Abyss. They were made of bone, feathers burnt to blackened coal, accompanied by mechanical gears and two-foot-long razor scythes jetting from the apex of their joints. They rose above his head like a crescent halo framing the face of death. His hands were wrapped in the dead skins of countless other foreign species, as was the robe he wore to cover his identity. His body armor was the living definition of pain and suffering. Human skulls lined his shoulders as living chains kept them in place. With each breath he took, the screams of a thousand dead souls could be heard trying to escape his mouth.

In all of her heroic bravado, Elizabeth turned her attention to the new threat at hand. "What is that?"

Daemos turned towards his brother and straightened his form. "Samael, the living death."

Minos crawled up to Samael and placed his hands before his master. "You have come. Kill these wretched souls. I will forever serve you."

Elizabeth readied her blade and stared into the lifeless void of the Seraphim god of death. Her grip tightened and her skin came to a freezing halt.

Daemos laid his hand out and lowered her blade with a solemn gesture. He walked up to Samael and looked into the dark red orbs that could loosely be described as eyes. "For as long as I have known, Samael has been one of us. He wears a keepsake. A shard of bone, a scrap of metal, a child's finger, on him, on his armor, as a map to the infinite deaths he has witnessed. Samael my brother, you have changed much over the years," Daemos proclaimed.

Samael kept his gaze upon Daemos as he shifted his eyes from Elizabeth to Charon and down to Minos. "And you travel in the company of traitors and vagabonds," Samael said in an echoed baritone voice.

"You know not of the events that have conspired here..." Daemos was cut off by Samael mid-sentence.

"Where is Azrael?" Samael asked.

A tinge of stress and doubt came upon Elizabeth, Charon, and Daemos as they weighed their options for telling the truth or resorting to further lies. Elizabeth stepped forward and kept her composure while she gave her answer. "Azrael left. He told us nothing more of any location, nor did he give meaning for his absence."

Samael looked at Daemos with an abhorrent expectation of some hidden truth.

Daemos looked at his companions and lowered his head. He took a breath that sounded all too human. For a moment, Samael almost doubted if Daemos would say anything. "She is telling the truth. We know not of where Azrael travels."

Minos took the pause in their gesture to try to gain the favor of his assumed rescuer. "He flew across the red sands to visit the witch Lilith," Minos said as he smiled and nodded at Samael, hoping to be saved and taken back to his sanctum.

Samael placed his hand on Minos' head and gestured for the failed judge to arise. Minos arose and stood before his master. Samael removed his hand and lowered it towards Minos' stomach. Within a split second, Minos felt his intestines leave his gut and fall to the ground. Samael reached inside Minos and set his organs ablaze. The judge screamed in pain as his blood came to a boil and his flesh cooked from the inside out. Samael gripped tighter until the last beat of a mortal heart gave way.

Charon clenched his teeth as he knew that he would not ferry Minos across the void to another life, for his soul had just been consumed. The natural order had further been disrupted.

Samael's eyes opened up like a pair of blistering suns. His wings spread wide as he gripped tight the scythe that he used to reap life. His calm composure had shifted to one of offense and urgency. Samael spread his mechanical wings and took to the skies, flying with great haste towards the east.

Elizabeth glared at Daemos and turned her back on Charon as well. "This changes nothing. Our path lies before us." She walked into the thick of fog and back towards the living forest which Baphomet calls home.

"We must make haste and warn Baphomet before either Azrael or Samael discover what lies beneath Lilith's domain," Charon yelled out.

Elizabeth turned back around and walked up to Charon. "What else does Lilith hide?"

Charon looked at Daemos and Elizabeth and explained the witch's true nature. "Lilith gives petty show with her harem. The mortal men and women are but pleasures of the flesh for her. She uses her harem as a distraction."

"Distraction from what?" Daemos asked.

"The old gods can never truly die, only lie dormant. They can be watched over or given different shape and form. Tiamat flooding the seas with her essence, Jehovah now trapped as living flame. The gods still walk amongst us," Charon said.

"What is your meaning? How did Minos know this? How do you know this?" Daemos demanded.

"Lilith is a watcher of the gods. She was given this task by Moloch long before you began using Azrael to hunt his own kind. Moloch appointed his own watcher, Minos. We all saw what Minos had wrought. With the horror that this world has seen, it will pale in comparison if Azrael is able to break Lilith. He will find more than a few rebellious souls in her prison," Charon answered.

Elizabeth changed her expression from that of a look of concern to a maniacal grin. She said nothing as she walked off and continued into the thickness of fog and dust. Charon and Daemos followed not too far behind.

* * *

Azrael's eyes burned with a torrent of hate and unrepentant violence. The flames from the blade of Jehovah grew wild as he held it high above his head. Mercy was a vacant notion as Lilith cried and pleaded for mercy.

"Your death will not be swift," Azrael said to Lilith as he brought the blade reeling down towards her tear-drenched face.

"Wait," Lilith screamed. Azrael stopped himself from murdering the witch to hear what she had to say. "There are secrets here, secrets even I keep myself from wanting to discover. The torments and horrors that lie beneath my temple are far too great for anyone to lay their eyes upon. Even for a world destroyer such as yourself," Lilith said.

Azrael satiated the flame of the living blade and stowed it away in a sash to his side. With his nerves calmed, he thought to himself with a more clear and rational mind. "I will be the judge of what horrors I wish to invoke," he said as he walked up to Lilith and picked her up to her feet. He could see genuine fear in her eyes that he had never witnessed before. For a moment, he wondered if the powers held beneath his very feet should stay sealed away.

"Please do not do this. Find another way," Lilith pleaded to Azrael, as he held her in the tight grip of his callous hands.

Azrael knew that there were other ways of going about defeating the Seraphim. He could wage war for over a thousand lifetimes and finally be rid of their tyranny. He knew that it would be possible to fight them for all eternity and never leave them with the risk of extinction. It was not an everlasting war that made Azrael make his decision. Flames had burnt his flesh long enough for him to be done with the meaningless act of war. He was now guided by the hope of their extermination. As he looked into her glassy eyes, he spoke. "No. Show me."

Lilith looked at the hilt of the living blade that sat at Azrael's thigh and knew that only a monster capable of merciless slaughter would be able to take the weapon away from a Seraphim. She no longer felt the need to plead for her life.

"If I do this, if I show you, there will be no going back to the old ways. You will have no choice but to finish what you start. This can only end with your death and the death of every living being in existence," Lilith said in a much calmed-down tone.

Azrael repeated once again, "show me."

Lilith closed her eyes and took in a deep breath. Her hands traveled over Azrael's chest and down to his thighs. She slid her fingers over the hilt of the divine blade and felt the power of creation burn hot within its grasp. Lilith unlatched the fastening to the weapon and held it in her palms so that she may take in its wonder more carefully. Slowly, she opened her crimson eyes and stared at the fragment of bone that acted as the core of such a glorious instrument of destruction.

"I hold in my grasp the key to damnation. I never thought it possible to wield such power," Lilith said as Azrael examined the awe and shock on her face. "It has been a thousand lifetimes since this key has seen the light of my domain. Never have I thought it to return," she continued.

Azrael looked at her, confused and curious. "This weapon has been here before? Moloch has been here before?"

"It was he that gave me eternal life. I drank from the nectar of shadow and live in darkness. In return, I provide him and his legion with living vessels to possess at will," Lilith answered.

The scent of death and fornication filled Azrael's senses as he looked around the harem while Lilith gave her lecture. While upon his entrance, he only noticed the rampant acts of sexual abundance. He now noticed another, more sacred act amongst the mindless mortals. Women gave birth during the orgy as children carried the newborn infants away to various chambers throughout the temple. The moans of pleasure from climax and release had earlier hidden the cries of the newborn. What he saw was an endless supply of flesh in production for the Seraphim to claim at will.

"I was deceived. I thought my pleasure to be a gift of the gods. The touch of darkness upon my lips that gave me eternity had stricken me barren. I only serve to entice these creatures into lust. My curse is one of the flesh. I can not consume as they do. I do not feed upon the merriments of wine and lamb. Their blood is my life. Every turn of the moon I must drink from them," Lilith said, as crimson tears began to pour from her eyes.

Azrael took the blade of Jehovah from Lilith's hands as she wept against his chest. There was something familiar about her blood as he caught its scent while it rolled in streams down her face. He did not catch it before, but was now able to make sense of things. Her mortality was taken from the Seraphim with the blood of the Abyss. She was fed their dark essence so that they may find her at any given moment in time. While she still had the shape of a mortal woman, her skin was pale, and her hair a deep dark red from the infected demonic blood. While she was not able to transform as a true creature of the Abyss would, she bit down with sharpened fangs and razor-tipped talons on her fingertips when she fed. She was a child of the night, a grotesque half-breed to the Abyss, and a thing of sanguine and dangerous beauty to mortal men and women. Lilith continued to sob in intermittent spurts as Azrael took pity on the cursed creatures he kept his company with. He let her finish and held her by the shoulders while she wiped the blood away.

"This sword belongs to my enemy. The same enemy you have a pact with. Open his prison doors for me. Allow me to let loose the fury that hides beneath this place. Let me end our suffering," Azrael said.

Lilith turned around to stare at her throne. A hundred fingers, tentacles, and phallic objects of desire pulsated as they awaited her return. She walked up to the smoldering chair and lowered herself upon it as she turned back around to face Azrael. He watched as the protruding objects twitched and penetrated her loins. She moaned and gasped while her gaze stayed fixed on his. She held her hand out and gestured for Azrael to come closer as a serpent attached to her throne slid in and out of her dripping sex. With a set of heavy moans, she spoke in broken phrases, "When I...reach my limit...plunge the blade...within me. Let me...spill myself. Your gate...will open."

Azrael held tight his grip on the blade of Jehovah. He watched her body writhe and tremble with each thrust from the living effigy. Her breaths began to shorten as she let herself go. Her hands began to follow her flesh as she dripped with a salty sweat he could smell from a mere few feet away. The dark red tint of her hair was a stark contrast to the pale smoothness of her undying skin. Lilith took in a deep breath and closed her eyes as her chest expanded and contracted at a more rapid pace, her breasts flush with ecstasy. He waited and kept his composure as she moved herself closer to climax. When Lilith opened her eyes, she flung her head back and dug her fingernails into her thighs while the wetness of her womb gushed out from inside her. At the exact moment that Lilith came, Azrael unleashed the living flame of the blade and plunged it deep into her womb. A scream of both pleasure and pain overtook the inner sanctum. The flames of creation met with the waters of life as Lilith's insides were caught ablaze. Blood and other bodily secretions made their way to the floor as droplets of living fire followed suit. A thundering roar could be felt coming from beneath Azrael's feet as he removed the blade from Lilith's body. The mixture of blood, fire, and sex coated the cracks in the floor as the tendrils, hands, and teeth that made up the bulk of the bodies of Lilith's throne began to tear into her flesh. Claws were dug deep into her loins as she was ripped open, womb first, then thighs, chest, and head. She exploded from the inside out as her flesh framed the edge of her throne, which now acted as an entrance to a gaping void of unknown terrors. Her body became a doorway of blood and torn organ. Azrael backed away and stared in anticipation as the gateway to the Seraphim prison had now been opened.

Screams could be heard from beyond the darkness as the figure of a woman, naked and bloody, approached. It was Lilith, made whole once more by powers unknown to either of them. She stepped forth and slid a finger across the remains of her former body, licking a droplet of blood from the frame that was made from her skin and bone. Lilith took in a few deep breaths as she gained her composure and let her body heal. The restructuring was made possible by unseen forces in the dark. "You...have done it," Lilith said.

Azrael walked up to the fatigued witch and placed his hand on her cheek and spoke, "Feed. When I return, we will cleanse this world." He gathered himself and set off to enter the large cavernous opening that had formed in the back of Lilith's temple. Azrael stared down into the darkness and wondered what savored delights might await him. The sting of hot winds come out from beneath the gateway. There was no majestic creature to greet him, no threats to keep him away, no force to otherwise invite him into this domain. There was only the endless void of darkness ahead of him. He had known this place and was prepared for whatever sights he may see on his way.

Lilith raised herself from her throne and walked over to stand by Azrael's side. She had not seen the entrance to the underworld in over a thousand years. She remembered when last she was witness to its opening, feeling the same pleasure and pain, as it was Moloch who had stuck her with the sword. In that time, the void of the underworld was barren. The prison was still vacant until the Seraphim took their old gods and placed them in the deepest pits of time and space. She felt regret to agree to become the lock and warden to their deeds. She watched now as Azrael took his first steps toward the place that no other being had seen outside of the Seraphim. "Wait," Lilith said as Azrael was now half cast in shadow.

Azrael stopped in his tracks for a moment to turn back and face Lilith. He said nothing as he let the look on his face convey what she already knew. He gave her one last chance to send him off with a warning or what other information she held.

She only had one last thing to say before Azrael took his descent into the darkness. Lilith turned her body away but kept her head facing Azrael as she told him, "Abandon all hope."

XVIII. God Of Emptiness

The slaughter had begun. The cracking of bone and slicing of flesh had become the tempo and melodies by which the living forest played its orchestra. Lives of both Seraphim and jackal were reduced to nothing as both clashed sword and spear against one another. Baphomet watched from beyond the shadows as the greedy, vengeful hands of the Seraphim lay her temple under siege. All was lost to the creatures of the living forest.

Like a roaring thunder, Elizabeth and her two companions ran through the thick of fog and twisted trees and into the heart of battle. She wasted no time finding a weapon as she vacated it from the dead hands of a jackal. She swung and cut through Seraphim armor with a fury unseen to mortal eyes. With each slash and cut of her newly acquired blade, she bathed herself in their divine blood. Breaths were slow and steady as anger pulsed through her veins, its bloodlust coming through the tip of her spear. Release came from the back of skulls, through the parting of ribs and the slicing of bellies. Of those she did not mortally wound, others retreated and took back to the skies. "Flee like the cowards you are," she yelled out at them.

"We must get to the temple before the Seraphim," Charon said with concern.

"Agreed. This madness is my brother's doing. The fool is waging a war he knows nothing of," Daemos added.

Elizabeth wiped her blade clean on the corpse of a dying Seraph. It held its hand out, its human form melting and peeling away, giving sight to the black-eyed, tentacled creature beneath. She stood over the dying creature before she looked it in its large, invasive eyes. "Consider this mercy," she said before sending the entirety of her blade through its still-beating heart.

"Elizabeth. The temple. We must go now," Daemos said.

Elizabeth picked up her composure and walked past Daemos and Charon, making her way to the base of Baphomet's temple. Charon stayed behind as Elizabeth and Daemos made their way up the corpse-riddled staircase. Daemos stopped in his tracks and turned around to take one final glance at Charon. Elizabeth stopped and followed suit.

"You can not follow, can you, ferryman?" Daemos asked.

Charon looked at the two of them and then turned his head towards the shores of lost souls where his ship stay docked. "No. My journey ends here." Charon turned his head back towards the two warriors. "There are plenty of lost souls that will be needing my guidance. Fix what your people have wrought."

Daemos nodded and continued his way back up the never-ending stairway. Elizabeth began to follow as well, but stopped for a moment to look back at Charon once more.

"You have a pure soul. Do not let what happens here change that," Charon said to Elizabeth. "He will need you to keep your strength. I fear this will not be our last meeting."

With those words, Charon turned towards his ship and disappeared into the fog. The light of his lantern faded from view and almost as soon as he appeared to them, he was gone.

"Come now," Daemos said to Elizabeth.

They arrived at the final footstep atop the spired temple and made their way through the now-demolished gateway. The bodies of both jackal and Seraphim soldiers littered the once-holy sanctum. Elizabeth stopped at the pool where Azrael had been blessed by Baphomet only days earlier. She thought of their time together and his hands upon her while they fueled each other's desires from spending centuries apart. Now the disemboweled corpse of a Seraphim lay in its waters, defiling this once-sacred place.

"Baphomet!" Elizabeth yelled out. "Azrael has gone to the east. He has seen Lilith." No response was given. "Your children will be free, but she hides secrets as well. What of these secrets shall we fear?" she asked herself, waiting for a handful of seconds that seemed to take an eternity. "Answer me," she demanded.

"Something is not right here," Daemos interjected.

"I come to give warning and she ignores me. I have guarded her lands for all my life and not once asked for an audience. Now that her lands are invaded, she hides," Elizabeth said to herself.

"No," Daemos said. "She is not hiding. She is held hostage."

Elizabeth and Daemos stepped closer toward the dark chasm that Baphomet used to slip in and out of meetings. They saw a slight glow emanate from beyond as Baphomet's cries could be heard getting louder. Slowly, the goddess appeared before them. Behind her, Moloch pushed forward while she still sat upon her throne. Elizabeth readied her weapon while Daemos quickly took a closer examination of his surroundings. The walls were fortified as the moon roof was occupied by Seraphim snipers that lined its opening. The collapsed entryway was now home to a legion of armed sentries only to follow Moloch's commands.

Moloch held in his grip a sword made of mortal hands. He trembled with rage at the mere touch of it, for he longed again to wield the power within the flame of the sword of Jehovah. He slid his primitive weapon down Baphomet's spine and teased her with the promise of pain. "Baphomet, the mother of the Abyss," he said as he drew in closer. "The mother of death," he said as he plunged the sword into Baphomet's back and out of her chest. The blade exited between her breasts as hot black blood spilled out and onto her multi-sexed organs below.

Elizabeth cried out and ran to the goddess. As Moloch pulled the blade out, Elizabeth held her hands over the wound to try to stop the bleeding. Baphomet took Elizabeth's hands with her own and looked her in the eyes.

Baphomet spoke, all pain now gone from her voice. "This life is but an instant. Our children will live through us. Be with Azrael," Baphomet said.

Moloch laughed and taunted those at his mercy. "How touching. Mortal words from an immortal soul. Or...what was once thought immortal," He said as he gawked.

Baphomet took one final breath and told Elizabeth, "And murder the Seraphim race."

Moloch let his rage take over as he swung his sword into Baphomet's throat, sending the goat-headed goddess to fall at Elizabeth's feet. He looked at Elizabeth and Daemos as he signaled his soldiers to surround them. "It seems a mortal prison can not hold you. I can not just simply kill you either, as you will find some way to come back. I do remember you now, girl," He said as he paced around Elizabeth. "You will pay for what you did back at the tower of that wretched judge. I was foolish to believe that you were somehow insignificant and to leave you with Minos, the failure. No, you mean something deeper to Azrael. And when he comes for you, he will bring my birthright with him." Moloch then walked over to Daemos. "I am so disappointed by you, dear brother. We were to build a kingdom in our father's image. Create mortal men in his image. We would be fed for eternity. You have instead chosen the path of exile."

Daemos spoke up for the first time against his brother. "What you are doing, Moloch, is condemning us all. Do you believe you will be free to feed as you please? You are a fool to think the Abyss are the only threat to our kind. You know nothing of what lives beyond the stars, beyond our small corner of creation."

"And you know, dear brother? You have seen these threats? That there are gods and men beyond us?" Moloch walked up to his brother and whispered into his ear, "Then show them to me."

Daemos looked down at Elizabeth, who had ceased to resist or say a single word. She held herself in a state of concentration while the Seraphim bound her. Moloch made his way over to her as ethereal bonds were placed on her wrists and over her mouth. He looked Elizabeth in the eyes and spoke, "Do you remember the words you spoke to me in your last prison cell? Where are your jackals now? Where are your thorns to break my stronghold?"

"You fear this girl? This simple creature that you must bind her?" Daemos asked Moloch.

"I will show fear when there is something to fear. Take them away. Our kingdom awaits its newest guests," Moloch said, as he and his brothers took their prisoners away and into the heavens above.

* * *

Silence. The acrid stench of nothingness filled the spaces between flesh and eternity. All around was a constant force of motion that neither came nor went. Hope and fear had left this place long before its creation. It was a prison without walls. A fortress built on empty ground. Each footstep was greeted with a solid form of earth beneath but, upon further inspection, there was no ground below. Only the eternal panoramic of darkness swirled about.

Azrael crept along his path as if he had a set goal to reach. The reality was that he was lost more so than ever. Had he turned around at some point? Was he climbing or falling? In this place, the dimension of nothingness, he had only his imagination to guide him. His heightened senses, his power of flight and speed, meant nothing in this darkened shrine. He spread his wings and arms out, hoping to feel some sort of barrier. A trace or clue to his surroundings. All he could find was the pulsing of his veins and sullen gasps of his breath. Time left its meaning behind as well. It could have been days, weeks, even years that he would spend in this place. Perhaps the secrets held beneath Lilith's temple were a prison meant for him. There were no guards, no cells, and no way of escape.

He let his mind race at the thought that maybe this was his trap. That the Seraphim had finally captured their prey. He turned from thoughts of survival to despair. Despair became anger and anger turned to relentless pursuit. For the first time in a long time, Azrael understood what it meant to feel mortal. When his heart began to crack and his arms grew limp and fatigued, he finally heard something. Or so he thought. It could very well be his mind tricking his senses. It was a faint, scratchy sound. Like nails dragging across wet stone. Soon it was followed by a hiss of wind and the beating of life. There was something watching him.

Almost immediately, Azrael realized his mistake. The creature did not appear by surprise. It had been there from the very moment he set foot inside the darkness when he stepped through Lilith's eviscerated body-made portal. He quit trying to find his bearings and simply froze himself in place and allowed the darkness to envelop him. His wandering and searching had proven to be the cause of his absence.

Heat filled the stillness of the newly formed air. Azrael turned to see a pillar of living flame grow from the void of nothingness. From behind the flame peered the head of a lion. Its teeth dripped with fervent salivation. Its mane spread about as a radiant sun tipped with razor quills. Limbs resembling that of a mortal man stretched out from the slithering body of a serpent. The beast was always there. It watched, growling and hissing, as it slid its way toward Azrael. It grew in size, three times that of a mortal man. The lion-headed beast opened its mouth and spoke in a thousand tongues, unknown to most. Azrael kept his composure as the creature circled him, speaking in unison its amalgamated language.

The fires from its eyes died down as its body began to contort and change shape. The lion's head cracked and reformed into several creatures before taking the guise of a simple mortal. Its serpentine body did the same. Its form was near flawless. All parts of its new human anatomy were sculpted to functional perfection. Absent from this form was any and all hair, as well as any distinct features. Skin white as the brightest star covered the creature's sculpted physique. Missing was any color from the eyes, instead adorned with milky white orbs that seemed to focus on everything at once. Not quite a female nor a male, it moved with a strength only seen in the strongest of warriors. For all intents and purposes, this sexless creature could pass for a mortal given the proper attire.

As the naked, sexless thing walked up to Azrael, bits of cloth and other material seemed to latch onto its flesh from the beyond. It was now covered in a strange set of adorned attire resembling something of what Azrael knew to be royalty. The thing then walked over to a newly formed pillar of flame. This fire was set upon a pile of scorched earth. Around the flames there formed an enclosure to satiate and control the inferno. Beneath their feet, a spread of red cloth had materialized. Azrael looked as walls came into existence with candles springing up from countertops and shelves formed beneath. Books lined a massive wall behind them and soon, a strange melody could be heard coming from beyond the now-completed room.

"It's music," the being said as it walked over to a table and poured its nectar into an ornate glass. Its voice was calm and gentle, yet precise and stern.

Azrael took a few seconds to comprehend his new reality. He walked around the room and felt the stained wood surfaces to be sure his mind was able to perceive what he was seeing.

"Everything here is real. Go ahead and see for yourself," the being said as it sipped its drink. "I quite like this surrounding. It's very much...relaxing, I believe, is the right word. Oh yes, you do understand me, I hope. Unless, of course, you wish me to choose a different form of communication."

Azrael stopped his investigation and answered the being.

"No, I understand you. What I do not understand..." Azrael was cut off before he could finish.

"Is everything else? What you do not understand is everything else you were going to ask, correct?" The thing sipped its drink and continued, "Well, yes, I'm sure you have plenty of questions. And answers will come...in time. Please, sit." The strange being walked over to the table and poured Azrael a drink as well.

"I have no time for this," Azrael said.

"Oh...you have no time? Well, that is quite convenient. As I understand, you have enough time for feasting, fighting, and fucking. All I have is time. Now sit."

Golden embroidery adorned a large red chair built by the hands of a master craftsman. Azrael moved slowly into the chair, always keeping his eyes on his new companion. He still had difficulty believing what he was seeing. "Where am I?"

"Ah yes. The first relevant question. You are wherever I wish to be. And that is no riddle. This place does not exist in your reality," said the being as it sipped its wine.

"Who are you? Why do you speak so...strangely?" Azrael asked.

"You're very good at this. I can see why you were chosen to kill, defend, and do unspeakable things to billions of living creatures. To answer your question, I am...me."

"I have no time for riddles."

"It's no riddle. I am the motherless and the fatherless. I was born with a birthmark of cinders. No being has come before me. I choose to create what I will at my own whim. I want to know love, hate, life, and death, to wade in shit and fuck as I please. If something does not exist, it's because I simply haven't experienced it yet."

Azrael looked at the being as it drank from its glass. There was nothing about it that was outright threatening nor comforting. Everything about the creature seemed to defy logic. "Then you are the creator of all?" Azrael asked.

"Oh, by no means would I claim that. I am simply the creator of what I create."

"You are not of the Abyss, nor are you Seraphim. Tell me then...does this hold meaning to you?" Azrael pulled the hilt out from under his sash and stood up as he lit the sword of Jehovah. Its flame illuminated the room as the being walked over and stared into its divine light.

"Now that certainly is something...special," it said.

"Then you know what this is and what it is capable of?" asked Azrael.

"Of course I do. I helped create it," the being answered.

The revelation sent Azrael into a state of disbelief. If this creature was in fact telling the truth, he could end the peril of all living creatures once and for all. The coming of a great war and the bloodshed that would follow could be averted. Hope, it seemed, could be a reality that he never thought possible. All of his years of torment and rigorous pursuit had come to a halt. "This weapon is the cause of more pain and death than any force I have seen. Take it. Destroy it and end this madness," he said.

Examination came with a price as the being took the fiery blade from Azrael's grip. "Creation is the breath of free will. Memories hold the threads that tie us to one another. What I create, I cannot destroy," the thing said as its hollow eyes stared into the world-destroying weapon.

"Then undo your words of creation. Reverse the natural order and send us back into oblivion." Azrael grew louder and more fervent with each passing word. "Your power means nothing if you allow these atrocities to go beyond your will. I have killed against my will and I shall no longer be held in thrall to yet another false god."

Wings spread from Azrael's back, followed by the revealing of his serrated whip tail, black-tipped claws, and layered horns. He reared himself in preparation to undo the life of this creature while taking his prize back with him.

Before Azrael could make a single movement, the being stuck the tip of the fiery blade into the ground, sending a shock wave of pain and relentless motion throughout the room. Walls shattered and crumbled. Tables, books, chairs, and other ornate items burst apart in a series of explosive bursts. Beneath their feet, the ground became a boiling cesspool of blood and oil.

The thing began to pulsate as its form cracked and gave way to misshapen oddities. "My children grow upon the pillars of creation. Their flesh is my flesh. My mind is their will. Defiance bred from both the Seraphim and the Abyss are the musings of lesser children. And my children are fucking with the natural order."

As the self-proclaimed god transformed its shape, its words echoed hundreds of voices throughout the darkness. Beyond the empty reaches of this new reality, creatures older than recorded time came into sight. Slithering tendrils farther than the length of an entire army were attached to a thousand layers of pain as eyes the size of planets looked on from above. The serpent coiled around its form as it fed upon its own tail and spat out the blood of mortal men. Another towering beast made its appearance as tusks rose from beyond the nothingness and led to a mouth that chewed upon the remains of the damned. Wings spread and covered all, as dead eyes were ripped and peeled from a hundred faces of enduring hatred.

Azrael stared in horror as, for the first time, he witnessed the true revelation of the gods. Around him were the reanimated, world-devouring carcasses of Tiamat, Abzu, Marutuk, and Kingu. Their corpses were the plaything of their warden, held in this empty prison of darkness for purposes beyond his understanding.

"These children are now your legacy. Abzu, my beloved prince, was slain by the jealous hand of his son Marutuk, the watcher of time. The first act of free will. Tiamat begat Kingu to avenge her brother Abzu. Marutuk slain Kingu as well. From the blood of Kingu, mortal men were created to serve the will of Marutuk." The being continued to change form into a mass of undefined flesh and unnatural composition. "Tiamat chose self-sacrifice to ensure survival. Two souls emerged, Jehovah of the Seraphim and Leviathan of the Abyss. Jehovah begat Moloch and Leviathan begat Baphomet. You are a bastard child of Baphomet. You are her legacy. I will not undo my legacy." The thing, now a fully formed creature of dissidence and chaos, took the sword of Jehovah and devoured it. As it swallowed the flaming blade, the air around grew cold and stale. The history lesson and revelations of Azrael's bloodline were further expanded by the growls and hissing laughter of yet more creatures beyond his vision.

In front of Azrael, he watched as the sword of Jehovah gave newfound life to the creature that once took the shape of a nude pearlesque creature made of exposed white muscle before him. His body was now a slave to the dark, shattered into a thousand pieces of flesh and cinder. Behind him came a familiar song of pain and anxious hunger.

"Your destination is set, young death dealer," a different but familiar voice said from beyond the expanse of darkness. Echoes of eternity traveled upon the fury left behind by the old gods. "The child has returned the key. Balance will be the forefront by which we will call our campaign. Destiny has grasped your will and driven you into our embrace once more. Will you join us for our feast?"

Revelations made their appearance as Azrael witnessed a thousand wet teeth accompanied by hurried claws and frenzied tails. The Abyss began to surround him and pull at his flesh. He fought them off one at a time, trying to escape their hungered state. With the corpses of the old gods fallen back into nothingness, a more familiar form took their place. Leviathan made his presence known for this grand reunion.

"You seek refuge from yourself. The beast and the jackal are here with us. Your journey has proven its merits through your determined pursuit. I ask once more. Will you join us for our feast?" Leviathan asked Azrael.

Azrael took a moment to calm his nerves and sedate his muscles. The Abyss continued to tug and pull at his flesh, but he now realized it was never out of fear, hunger, or threat. They were pleading with him. Their sharpened claws tugged at his skin for attention. It was guidance that the creatures were seeking. The towering god was released by his masters to restore the very balance that the Seraphim had corrupted. With the sword of Jehovah now consumed, the Seraphim had no means to claim an unfair advantage. The scale of justice was now placed on even footing for both Azrael and his enemies. Azrael spoke, "Your prison was never meant to hold you. It was built to house my arrival, to protect you from a weapon made by a jealous race that murdered their own father. I see now what I am. And I hunger for Seraphim blood."

Thousands upon thousands of creatures of the Abyss flew upwards, past Azrael and out of the darkened chasm. A continuous roar of thunder and crashing rock belted up from the brittle earth as legions of rabid Abyss took to the lands and skies. Wings, tails, and talons spread their nightmare visage as wave after wave of beasts clawed their way out from the mutilated tombs below. Azrael followed suit as Leviathan rose up and into the gray void above, his towering mass still embedded into the ground. A mass storm of fire and electric symphonies engulfed the apex of the towering god. The heavens were now covered in a thick layer of black ash and poisonous fog. Almost all light extinguished from the sky as the Abyss made their presence known to the inhabitants of the dead world. A world revealed to be the birthplace of all races. A world the gods called Tartarus.

XIX. Reign In Blood

The shrieking screams of winged beasts carried their tune as a thousand claws ripped their way up from the dirt below. Legions of Abyss crawled and climbed over one another to get a long-awaited glimpse of the surface of a world once called home. They scratched and tore away at rock and stone to make their way to the surface. Amongst them, the amalgamated form of Leviathan broke through several crevices, sending over a dozen towering forms of his flesh to the skies above. With every breath Leviathan took, each of his massive towers bellowed out red flame and black smoke, creating a new atmosphere. The Abyss continued to pour out from the fiery depths and into the lands as the now dominant force of nature.

Azrael made his way out amongst his brothers and sisters and spread his wings to join them in their pursuit for blood. In the distance, he saw a slaughter in waiting.

Thousands of Seraphim soldiers came down from the skies as they prepared to face a glorious onslaught. The winged serpents of the Abyss had long waited for this moment. And with the blowing of trumpets and the growling of ancient tongues, the two races finally met.

Ethereal steel cut its way into the ash-gray flesh of the Abyss. The Seraphim used their weapons as an advantage to rip through the first wave of the Abyss. They plucked the Seraphim warriors from the sky and brought crashing down to the ground below. The hulking brutes of the Abyss whipped their tails up and snatched their foes mid-air. Claws the size of a man's arm tore into Seraphim flesh while massive jaws chewed through their armor. The living tanks of the Abyss fed upon the fallen Seraphim. Each Seraph that fell tried its hardest to leave its mortal shell behind. Once exposed in their true form, the winged serpents in the sky grabbed them as well and tore open their enemies' chests, exposing and clenching their teeth into a black Seraphim heart.

The Seraphim began to change their tactics. They split their approach between both an aerial and ground assault. Those still in the sky flew above the Abyss and came down with the intent of an ambush. As they came down, their vision was blinded by the toxic cloud of death exhaled by one of the many towers of Leviathan's form. Dozens of Seraphim sky soldiers were caught in the fiery black clouds. When they finally emerged, they fell to the earth not as threatening instruments of destruction but as engulfed carcasses set ablaze. The Abyss roared and cheered as they watched their enemies fall to a fiery grave. Ten thousand millennia of dormant vengeance fueled their rage. Unable to take flight above to the heavens, the Seraphim glided their form closer to the ground war below. They came down and tore heads and limbs off of their Abyss attackers. For every one they killed, half a dozen more ripped their way out from beneath the earth.

The fighting had escalated from hundreds of one-on-one confrontations to a multitude of uncoordinated battles. The fields of slaughter were now no different from any other world Azrael had waged war upon. These ancient creatures of time had now begun to fight like mortal men. Weapons of steel and bone were no longer part of the conflict. Hands made into weapons beat in skulls and gouged out eyes in a myriad of exquisite slaughter.

A group of five Abyss set their forces to tear a Seraph apart one limb from precious limb at a time. Two other Seraphim warriors held down their enemy while pulling its head off with their hands and tentacles. No matter what direction Azrael looked, there were unspeakable acts of death and murder. The violent path of mortal men did not come close to the hatred each of these species subjected towards one another.

More scouts sent by the Seraphim ran into the mountainous region now covered in both the black and red blood of these ancient foes. Lightning shattered the sky as acid rain began to fall from the poisonous clouds set forth by Leviathan. Upon the horizon, the orange stain of the fiery depths rose against this murderous backdrop. Still, the Abyss fought off their Seraphim attackers. They would fight and die if needed to keep their enemies from making further advancements.

After what seemed an eternity fighting an unthinking, animalistic foe, the Seraphim began to realize their mistake. The Abyss were not fighting on pure instinct alone. They were carefully coordinated, and each push to attack, as well as sacrifice, was made with careful consideration. The Seraphim had gravely underestimated their foe.

Azrael came down from his furious charge in the skies and landed upon a protruding cliff overlooking the battle just a few hundred feet below him. To his left and his right, a horde of Abyss came up behind and stood watch by his side. He looked up at the black clouds above as the pouring rain began to fall harder. His eyes wandered back down at the fighting below. "They are blocked from passing into the heavens. They have no choice but to push through us." Azrael turned around and saw his brethren listen with keen ears. Their natural form was almost identical to his winged bestial state. Their eyes, black as midnight, with claws to match, and skin gray as a morning fog. He gestured to those on his right, "Take flight and round the Seraphim to the path up the cliff." He looked at the bigger, taller creatures of the group. "You will stay here and clench the Seraphim when they arrive. They will try to retreat. When they do, I will be there to meet them." And with his command, the Abyss followed. Azrael took flight and ripped his claws into a few Seraphim he met on his way around to flank his targets. He watched his orders take shape. His allies had drawn the remaining Seraphim on the ground over to the passage which he kept his legion waiting.

The Seraphim fought and murdered their way around the edge of the blood-soaked cliff. Once they reached the top, they were met with over two dozen hulking beasts of the Abyss. They began to retreat down the cliff, as Azrael had predicted. Once at the cliff's edge, the Seraphim spread their tentacles and made a desperate attempt at flight. Azrael came down and sliced clean the tentacles of one of his enemies. The Seraph screamed in agony as another creature of the Abyss ripped its throat from its neck. The Abyss cheered as they killed the Seraphim one at a time. Azrael aided further in the fight as he sparred and dodged attacks with ease. Eventually, he pummeled his opponents into oblivion.

Finally, only one Seraph was left. He crouched, wounded and beaten, as he spat up blood and pieces of his host's flesh until it fell off. Parts of his Seraphim form could be seen coming through from underneath his host. "We...only...wanted...order," the Seraph said as it spat up more blood.

Azrael walked up to the wounded warrior and crouched to meet him at his level. Before he spoke, another creature of the Abyss walked forward and grabbed the Seraph by his throat. "We never wanted your order," the Abyss creature relented. He held the wounded Seraph up and cracked his neck with a single, crushing grip of his massive, stone-like hand.

The battle had been won. Not a single Seraph that had engaged the Abyss was left alive. The landscape was littered with the slain bodies of the Abyss as well as both the host and native bodies of the Seraphim. As the Abyss cheered on their victory, the rain had begun to cease. Soon, the clouds would part ways just enough to see the red-orange glow above.

In the distance, Azrael heard a hundred screaming echoes. He turned around and looked up at the sky, past the clouds.

Samael came down like a comet hurling through the atmosphere. Behind him followed more Seraphim warriors. His wings spread open like a raging beast ready to devour the air. His scythe stayed gripped in his claws as he reared it up and took his aim at Azrael. With only mere seconds to react, Azrael dug his heels into the rock and took his full Abyssal form. Samael crashed into Azrael as the two of them were flung several hundred paces across the ragged, rocky terrain. While the two of them went tumbling through the landscape, Azrael's Abyss allies engaged the new Seraphim threat. The ones that followed behind Samael were better equipped to handle their rivals. Still, they were outnumbered by the sheer force of the Abyss. This battle reigned in further blood and shedding of skin.

* * *

Disorientation had begun to pass as Elizabeth gathered her surroundings. She knew little of the destination and even less of how she had arrived. Three guards of the highest Seraphim order detached ornate clamps from her hands, feet, and waist as they picked her up and laid her upon a clear crystalline table. She looked over to where she was released from and saw a clear object in the shape of an egg. The thing pulsated with a luminous shell and engines of living flame. It was how they brought her here, across the stars and through the cosmos. They strapped her to the table and raised its base so that they may be able to further bring her to the inner workings of their lair. The Seraphim guards raised their hands, and the table raised with it. Her vision, still blurred by the strain of interstellar travel, was seared by the blinding white light of her captors. Their large black eyes peered out from beyond their domed heads. They had shed their mortal shells to work in their true Seraphim form. Their long fingers and warm touch made her skin tense up in fear and anticipation. They examined her face, neck, and torso in morbid curiosity. Before they could go any further, she heard voices and footsteps enter the large cavernous room. It was a rough mumbling at first but, after a few moments, their sound became recognizable.

"It is not too late to end this madness," Daemos said to Moloch as they entered the room.

"Our brother Samael has the situation under his control. Soon he will arrive to greet us and he will bring my sword back with him," Moloch said in an assured tone.

The two men circled their way around the room, passing through thickets of green mist that came from several organic vents near the floor, as they took turns greeting their Seraphim brethren. As Daemos passed Elizabeth, he saw her, still gagged, looking back at him in disgust and confusion. He gave her a slight nod, as if to silently say that he had a plan underway, yet unknown to her. She wondered why they had decided to keep their mortal shells while the others shed their fleshly skin. While in her train of thought, Moloch walked up to her, the stink of his host's decaying body filling her senses.

"You need not worry," Moloch said to Elizabeth as he placed his hand on her cheek. "If I wished you dead, you would not be here. My...hubris blinded me before. You were with Azrael on every world I brought to ruin. For so long, I thought he searched for Baphomet. It was you. I was a fool to think he would stay alone in his thoughts for so long. No, of course, he would find...companionship, no matter how futile. With you, of all creatures. Though I still do not know why. And that, my dear, is what I intend to find out."

Moloch signaled his brothers to bring Elizabeth with them and follow him and Daemos down the halls of Elysium's secret chambers. Her living coffin floated and moved as if it were submerged in liquid. She saw the carvings of countless alien worlds in the stone that held this fortress together. To mortal eyes, it was a thing of beauty and intimidation. The hall she traveled down was lined with large black arches made of some material she had never seen before. Based on her surroundings, she could have been inside the carcass of some planet-sized beast by the look of its organic structure. It seemed as if everything in this place was crafted from the stars themselves. Even the slightest of objects seemed to have some sort of life to them. Everything from the floor to the ceiling seemed to pulsate and move. There were no calculated angles or straight lines, as with things crafted by the hands of men, yet there was a touch of perfection to how all the pieces fit together. What may have been an even and flat walkway to her was a winding and climbing corridor to the Seraphim. The most haunting of thoughts to her was that any idea of escape now seemed impossible. All she could do was take in any and all information she could. So she closed her thoughts and opened her mind to listen to her captors.

Daemos stayed close to Moloch as he kept his gaze on Elizabeth. "A war wages below and we are yet back in our home. Even if Samael does prevail, what then will you do?"

Moloch entered a large room, enough to hold a thousand men, with an ornate altar in the center. Daemos and Elizabeth, accompanied by her three guards, followed. On the altar lay a large bowl thrice the size of a man's torso. Inside boiled the blood of mortal men. Moloch stared at the crimson soup and gathered his thoughts.

"The Abyss have been released. This I know. I can feel it. Even you, dear brother, had to know that Lilith would not be able to contain them forever. This day was destined to come. And you speak to me of war," Moloch said with a grimacing tone. He walked around the altar and swirled his finger in the bubbling nectar. With a single taste of mortal blood, he closed his eyes and felt a shiver run up his spine. He looked at Elizabeth and spoke with his vision set on her. "Blood. Life. Essence. Nectar. Whatever name you wish to call it. It is the source of everything. Even the gods must adhere to its call as it pumps through their veins. You may call forth a beast, you can change shape and even bring forth that which was once dead. Do you know why that is?" he asked Elizabeth as he walked up to her, a slight drop of blood seeping from his lips. "Because blood does not lie. You may change your flesh, you may pretend to be that which you are not, but the blood, it will never lie," Moloch said to Elizabeth as he peered up at Daemos.

Daemos walked around the room and examined the altar as well. He looked at his brother and knew that Moloch was hiding something. Whatever his intention was, Daemos would soon find out. "You do know that this is the very thing our father warned against. It is not enough that you wish to destroy them, but you are sacrificing our brothers as well," Daemos said to Moloch.

"So now you grow concern for your kind dear brother? Was it not you that took that damned child and raised it as your own? I often wondered how he was able to search out and be sent to all of these worlds you believed to be inhabited by the Abyss. As it turned out, there was never any such creature on any world you sent him to plunder. Instead, all he found was her, always...her," Moloch said as he paused and looked back over at Elizabeth.

"What is your point, brother? I did what needed to be done. I found Azrael as a crying babe and nurtured his lust for the hunt. Is it not what we wanted? To be sure of our safety in all of creation? I used the blood rituals our father taught us. He was always under my control," Daemos said.

Moloch walked over to Elizabeth and stared into her eyes. He signaled the three guards to leave the room as he grabbed a blade hanging on a nearby wall. He made a slight incision on Elizabeth's arm and tasted her blood. His mouth burned as he spat the blood back out and onto the floor.

"No Daemos, you did not fail after all. He did find the Abyss," Moloch said as he stared back at Elizabeth. "Where did you say you found Azrael again?"

Daemos looked at his feet and thought of the dirt and muck he stepped in when he was first given the child. Azrael, along with his siblings, had already been given names. Daemos took the boy and was later accompanied by the boy's brother and sister.

"He was abandoned while I still had rule over Abaddon. He was left bloody and silent. He had the mark of our father upon his flesh. I had assumed that one of our brothers had delivered him to me as a sacrifice. The child's blood was different. I knew he could be trained as a weapon," Daemos said, as he carefully crafted his lie.

"Of all the foolishness you have accused me of committing, this by far surpasses that. Never once did you think it to be false settlement? He was left for you to find on purpose." Moloch closed his eyes as he let his thoughts gather and all became clear. "It was Baphomet. She sent him to you. How blind we have been."

"No, I gave Azrael the blood of the Abyss so that he may gather their scent and hunt them," Daemos shouted out.

"All this time, brother, you have been raising the son of our enemy. And you let him find the one other mortal infected by the disease of the Abyss," Moloch said as he glared at Elizabeth. "But do not worry, even with newfound revelation, Azrael will still come and I will be here to greet his demise."

Tremors began to overtake the room as Moloch placed both hands over the blood altar. A thousand screams of pain and echoing madness came up from the ground below. Where the altar once stood was now a vortex of dark energy and torrential mist. From beneath the shrouded fog, bodies began to twist their way upward toward the sky. Their form was contorted, yet rigid. As the mist began to settle, it was clear that the bodies that made up the living cage were of Seraphim origin. Hundreds of them had taken to a stone-like form to create a cell that no living creature could hope to escape from.

"This is my final sacrifice of my brothers. When Azrael does arrive, he will have no choice but to call this place home," Moloch said as he adorned the towering cell made of flesh and tendril.

* * *

Dust and fog were split apart by the shimmering steel of a crescent blade attached to a staff made from the mechanized intricacy of bone and gears. Armored hands with sharpened claws gripped the weapon as it slashed through the air, each time missing its target. Red eyes peered out from behind a mask made of the bone fragments of a dozen creatures from other worlds. Wings spread against a muck-covered cloak that hid much, but not all, of Samael's steel and bone patchwork armor.

Azrael dodged each of Samael's attacks with fluid movement. He countered with claw swipes and tail whips of his own. Each opponent managed to inflict only mere scratches upon the other. Their combat was more of a choreographed exposition of skill than a cold-blooded fight to the death.

Against the backdrop of Seraphim on Abyss slaughter, they waged their dance macabre. When one would attempt to take to the skies, the other would bring him down. Samael pounced above Azrael to gain a greater advantage from above, but was grounded by a tail that wrapped around his booted foot. In return, Samael brought Azrael down with the blade of his scythe as he attempted to take flight. They tugged and tore at each other while the hissing cries of war bellowed all around. Hundreds fell to either blade or claw while they still slashed and thrust their hate at one another.

Bodies fell like rain against a fiery sky. White-hot lightning cracked the air and charged its electric pulse beneath ash black clouds. The winds of battle were infected with the taste and scent of death. As the bodies piled up, so too did the ensuing storm.

Closer to the throes of agony were Azrael and Samael as they continued their assault on each other. They began to sacrifice technique and safe footing for an opportunity to inflict damage. Azrael had struck first. While the bladed end of Samael's scythe had missed the apex of Azrael's horns, claws were sent shredding across bone-laced armor. Samael lunged back as his ribs were torn apart. Once again, Azrael lunged forward, only to be met with the stinging pain of sliced flesh. The edged sickle had penetrated deep into Azrael's chest as it slid across bone, thus spilling precious blood across Samael's hidden face.

"The living flame. Where is it?" Samael demanded as Azrael shuttered back. Holding his wound, Azrael's flesh began to entangle upon itself as his body healed. Samael once more readied his scythe and flung the excess blood from his blade to the ridged rocks below.

Azrael began to laugh as his foe came forward once more. "I have discarded that accursed weapon. The old gods keep hold of it as we speak. You are too late," Azrael said with a heavy, breath-laden laugh.

Enraged, Samael charged at Azrael with pure rage. Azrael reared back and spun his body around to Samael's side. He kept his wings open to disorient his foe and keep the scythe guessing. Samael swung like a rabid beast with no purpose and let his guard down. A leathery tail caught Samael's foot and tripped him over his own skull. As he came crashing down, he sent the end of his weapon into the rocks below and found his footing once more. As Azrael came to attack again, he was met with a second slash, this time to his back. With wings spread, Azrael turned to face Samael and cut open a piece of his shoulder armor, a pauldron made of a skull foreign to these lands but grafted with Seraphim steel. He cut deep with the bone edge of his wings into Samael's flesh. Blow after blow, Azrael did this. Still, Samael found the strength to rise up and counter his attacker. It was not long after his armor had been weakened that Samael had begun to spill his own blood. No longer was he able to contain his composure and rely on his mortal host body to keep him propelled for battle. With a final thrust of his scythe, Samael lunged toward Azrael with great purpose. Azrael allowed the edge of the blade to skewer him through the outside of his thigh. In doing this, he was able to reach in close enough to grab Samael's weapon and release it from his body. He pulled the scythe from his flesh and threw it deep into the ensuing inferno. The storm had claimed Samael's only weapon. Not one to give in to defeat, Samael relied now on his gauntlets to beat his war cries into Azrael's flesh. They did nothing to slow him down. Azrael was able to overtake Samael with ease while his wounds once more began to close themselves. In desperation, Samael hurled his body at Azrael, hoping somehow to render him null, so that he may have a fleeting moment to recover his scythe. As they tumbled over the edge of the cliff, their tirade ceased.

Samael awoke to the pulse of thunder and defeat, something that he seldom felt. Time was lost amongst the swelling and blackness of pain. His spine had been cracked with monstrous force, yet he was still able to crawl. Behind him, Azrael followed at a steady pace. He watched the Seraphim reaper of death crawl away and towards the direction of his precious scythe. With long, slow steps, Azrael kept pace. He allowed Samael to crawl like the vermin he saw inhabit the dirt. Blood came pouring out from Samael's mouth as he hurried away, pulling his body forward one arm at a time.

Finally, it was in sight. The scythe had been lodged between two rocks. Next to it lay the body of a dozen Seraphim and a handful of Abyss feeding upon their prey. They had not taken notice of Samael. Once they had seen Azrael follow the crawling Seraph from behind, they flew away and allowed their master to continue his pursuit.

The weapon was now within grasp. Samael reached out his hand and touched the bony exterior of his scythe. Before he could fully grasp it, Azrael placed his foot upon Samael's hand. Bone cracked under the pressure of Azrael's clawed foot as Samael growled in fury. He knelt down next to his foe and turned his body over. Samael shrieked in pain as he was placed on his back. Azrael stepped on Samael's chest and reached his clawed hand toward his face. He ripped away the bone-made mask and threw it aside. Before he had a chance to see into the eyes of his prey, Azrael picked the scythe out of the rocky crevice and claimed it as his own. He turned to face Samael and raised the weapon above his head as he readied it to come down onto Samael's skull. When he set his eyes upon Samael's face, he dropped the scythe and stood still, as if frozen in time. He had half expected to see the corpse of some unwilling mortal taken as a host by a Seraphim assassin. To see gray skin lined with dead veins and eyes black as a starless night. It was not to be. What he saw was something less of a threat and more familiar than he had expected.

XX. Reunion

A torrent of memories began to flood in as Azrael looked into Samael's eyes. They were not the blood-red orbs he had expected to see. With the mask of death now stripped from his flesh, Samael's true face had been exposed. There were no signs of Seraphim infection or possession as his skin was not gray nor tainted. What Azrael saw was the face of a man, mortal and weathered as his own. There was no mistaking the resemblance. Though lacking the black mane of hair that he wiped from his brow, Azrael saw his reflection, cracked and torn, staring back at him. There was not a single strand of hair on Samael's head, nor a sign that there might have once been life within his body. He was the living death.

Samael coughed up strands of congealed blood as he crawled his way up and onto his feet. He let his hands follow the coarse rocks toward his fallen weapon. With a firm grip, he used his scythe to lift himself and face Azrael. The two creatures examined each other and followed the lines of their faces in morbid curiosity. Before either could utter a single word, the ground below began to quake and rumble with the force of a thousand drums.

The earth split beneath their feet and eruptions of rock and fire were thrown toward the sky. A wall of flesh-made darkness crashed up through the crater and touched the grayed-out heavens above. Leviathan had sent one of his many pillars of living agony up from the depths. The towering wall of glistening black flesh slithered and swayed while fire and smoke danced at its base.

Azrael had assumed that the ancient god sent forth his appendage to reclaim him as his own, or perhaps smite Samael now that he had been beaten to a weakened state. Instead, a sliver of molten blood began to tear away at the base of the flesh tower. It opened as a wound, but of its own accord, as if to expel some foreign body. The gash widened as a torrent of boiling blood rushed out and spread throughout the ground, covering the immediate landscape. Azrael and Samael found themselves standing in a now rancid lake of hot crimson expulsion.

The threat of further violence was sated by the lack of pursuit by the escaped Abyss. Samael saw not a single creature yet could feel their black eyes upon him, watching, waiting. Ahead of them, they saw the gash in Leviathan's flesh pulsate further. From behind the wound was a hint of movement. Not from Leviathan, but something lying in wait.

Fingers, long and white, pushed through the gash. Blood fell on milk-white flesh, rendering it a deep red as each limb broke through. The wound in Leviathan's flesh revealed itself to be a doorway. The form that emerged was female and human in nature. She stepped lightly out from the towering god's innards and placed her delicate feet on the blood-engulfed ground. She was completely nude except for the red expulsion that dripped from her skin. Her hair was a series of long black threads covered in the same blood as her host. She opened her eyes and approached both Azrael and Samael. Once the blood had cleared and her face became recognizable, Azrael stared in shock at the woman before him.

"Sophia," Azrael said.

Sophia walked up to Azrael and smiled as she placed her hand on his cheek. She continued her way to Samael and gave the same gesture in kind. "My brothers. Azrael. Samael," she said while adoring both during this long-awaited reunion. "We are made whole once again."

Azrael gazed up and looked around the landscape he had helped to create as well as destroy. The world he had arrived on was not the same world he now set eyes upon. It was then he realized that he was standing in the birthplace of his gods.

Sophia, blood still wet and hot on her lips, spoke, "You have done well, my brothers. For so long, have I looked after you. For so long, have you suffered at the hands of our enemies." Sophia leaned into Azrael and closed her eyes as she took in his scent. "You have found your birthright. Tis a joyous reclamation."

Azrael stood in confusion, not knowing whether this was another trick by a vengeful god or if, in fact, this was his sister and if she spoke the truth. Azrael stepped forward and further examined the tear in Leviathan's flesh. Before he could ask his question, Samael had done it for them both.

"What are we?" Samael asked.

Sophia began to make her way back to Leviathan's towering doorway, but stopped at its base and turned to face her brothers. "We are the living blood oath between the gods of flesh and fire." Sophia looked up towards the sky and let her memories flood in as the time for revelation was due. "To know what we are, we must know why we exist," she said.

Azrael and Samael looked at each other, then back toward their sister. They knew they never belonged with the kind by which they were raised and, recently discovered, held hostage.

"Baphomet. She created us. But why did I never know of Samael? Why not reveal that to me? Why the need for secrecy?" Azrael asked Sophia.

"Because of Moloch," Sophia answered with a fervent groan.

Samael looked at his armored hands and felt his bones crack and tense beneath his gauntlets. He had always known he was not natural born to the Seraphim yet carried out their duties without question. Once his lust for death surpassed even those of his adopted Seraphim family, he was raised to the mantle of death itself.

"Moloch," Samael said to himself with his fist clenched and his jaw tight.

"We are all family, my brothers. And as a family, we must protect each other, even from those we share blood with," Sophia continued.

With those words, Azrael made his final grave revelation known. He deduced the line of succession from his time on this world. The statues of the elder gods from the ruined cities, the murals, and the bloodletting and conjuring of ancient creatures gave him his answer. And with it came the truth.

"You know, do you not, brother?" Sophia asked Azrael.

Azrael looked to Samael and then to Sophia. "Moloch is a distant cousin to Baphomet. How have I not seen this?" Azrael asked himself.

"That, my brother, is our connection. Tiamat, the very serpent that gave life to this world, begat Leviathan and Jehovah. In turn, Baphomet was born of Leviathan and Moloch from Jehovah," Sophia confirmed to her brothers. "Had Moloch not slain his father, Baphomet would not have created us."

Samael broke his silence once again. "We were born out of fear."

"Yes, brother. Moloch had created a weapon of pure annihilation. Every creature on every corner of creation feared for their existence. We then were born of Baphomet," Sophia exclaimed.

Azrael stared at Sophia with a puzzled look on his face. "I hold the soul of the Abyss, you hold the soul of mortal life, and Samael the soul of a Seraphim."

"That is so my brother," Sophia answered.

"How did Baphomet create us? The Abyss do not have the power of possession. They have not the means to steal the essence of the Seraphim to infuse it into a newborn mortal," Azrael demanded.

"You already know the answer," Sophia said.

Azrael and Samael watched as Sophia made her way back through the gash leading back inside Leviathan. Sophia turned to see her brothers one last time and smiled as she made her way through the crimson doorway and back into the innards of her god.

Samael looked at Azrael as their alliance was now sealed with blood and bond. "Baphomet did not act alone in our creation. She was aided by one of the Seraphim," Samael said to his brother.

Azrael looked off into the distance and past the horizon towards the direction of the Temple of Baphomet. He looked back at Samael and said a single name, "Daemos."

Before any further plan could be hatched, they heard the sound of hissing growls and demonic laughter. The Abyss had come out of hiding and began to surround them. By the thousands, they swarmed like a flock of mad locusts and blacked out the sky. While some stayed circled above, others landed next to and surrounded Azrael and Samael. One came forward and spoke.

"You conspire with our enemy?" the creature asked in a cracked and low groaning voice.

"No," Azrael answered. "I conspire with my brother," he said as he spread his wings and changed to his Abyssal form.

"Heresy," the creature yelled out as it lunged at Azrael.

Before Azrael could counter, Samael sent his scythe thrusting through the air, impaling his brother's attacker.

Samael walked over to the creature and dug his claws into its skull, tearing flesh and bone away from muscle as it screamed in agony. He placed the fragments of its skull upon his face and let his Seraphim blood shape his new mask. The rest of the Abyss kept themselves at bay and simply watched from afar. "I was not born of the Seraphim. I am not a son of the Abyss. I feed upon mortal life. I am the face of death. I am Samael," he yelled out with a newfound strength.

Azrael stood next to his brother and spoke, "Join us or perish."

Legions of winged Abyss made their way down and landed at Samael and Azrael's feet. A single creature stepped forward and uttered the word "follow." It spread its wings once more and took to the sky. Azrael took flight as well, and Samael, with wings spread, followed suit. Before long, they, with an army of Abyss, made their way across the battle-worn landscape and back toward the Temple of Baphomet.

* * *

Echoed screams carried their songs through the blighted dungeons of Elysium as living mist danced around the fervent tortures that bellowed and hissed their tunes. The distinction between artificial and organic material had begun to fade into obscurity. Glistening walls pulsed with fragments of bone and stitched wire that seemingly had no end in sight. The resemblance of digestive innards crept their way around the arch of the ceiling and followed their way down the stretch of hallways that split apart like capillaries from veins and those from ebony arteries.

Elizabeth imagined herself to be no more than a single droplet of blood being pushed along in this living nightmare. She breathed in the fervent, toxic fog, still held in thrall by her captors to the tomb she lay upon. Gagged and silent, all she could do was watch as she was guided by an unseen force that kept her afloat, accompanied by her Seraphim guards. She imagined that this place was secret to even the highest of the Seraphim order. These were not the grand exquisite chambers of Elysium. Absent were the golden spires, lakes of raw starlight, and windows to the never-ending cosmos. She found herself in a darkened cocoon made to house the vessels of the flesh.

By the hundreds, she could see translucent coffins held in place by intestine-like tubes that coiled around the base of each captive shell. Inside were the preserved remains of mortal men. Their bodies were kept fresh, virulent, and intact for further use. Each pod moved and swayed over one another in an assembly line of flesh and programmed machination. As she was eventually brought to the center chamber, she too was propped between two other coffins holding the bodies of the newly damned. Her eyes wandered around the grandiose dome-shaped room. She noticed that she was the only female present and that her coffin was different from the others. Her fate was not to be shared with the men she kept company with. She wondered where, if any, of the females had been taken. The thought that she was misplaced had crossed her mind, but it soon left when she realized that her captors had placed her where she was to bear witness to their unending glory.

Still held in thrall, all Elizabeth could do was watch. Above her, a single Seraph came floating down, like a feather, weightless and delicate. Its tendrils spread open and its black, soulless eyes eventually met with hers. After staring at her for a moment, it glided to a coffin across the chamber. The shell opened, exposing the dead flesh of a man inside to the vacuum of this place. It placed its hands on the dead man's chest and proceeded to push itself inside the corpse. The thing struggled and twitched, convulsing heavily with each push. Soon only the creature's tendrils were seen, all six, protruding from the dead man's backside. Elizabeth had witnessed the act of Seraphim possession. The now living corpse walked out from its holding cell and examined its new body. His fingers cracked and heavy breaths were drawn like bellows of smoke being released from a freshly kindled fire. The dead man floated, as a Seraphim possessing one would, over to a pulsating panel on the wall above the row of coffins, and reached inside. He pulled out a set of armored boots and a second set of external bones to cover his flesh. She watched as the Seraph armed itself to match those of its brothers. Often she would wonder how the Seraphim were able to replenish their numbers and find new hosts at such a rapid pace.

Upon further investigation, she looked above and below her cell. She saw not only the bodies of mortal men but hundreds upon thousands of cocoons, all holding the carcasses of creatures she had never seen before. Her mind led her to question how many other countless worlds these creatures have plundered and harvested for their supply of hosts. With her thoughts now in full control of her body, she fell into slumber and awaited whatever fate the gods had so seen fit to bestow upon her.

* * *

The midnight air cracked with shrieks of cold lightning and tumultuous thunder. An orange glow pierced through from behind gray storm clouds as the devil in flesh, and death incarnate, shared the skies side by side. Behind them followed a horde of rabid and bloodthirsty creatures of shadow bent on vengeance. Their wings moved like giant fins of the great beasts of the sea, creating gusts of wind that hissed and pushed at the land below. Trees swayed while rock and stone weathered beneath their strength. Like a swarm of locusts, they engulfed the landscape in their majestic fury.

Not far now was the once-hallowed temple of Baphomet. Mother to these beasts, though none have seen her in the flesh or given ample opportunity to praise her glory. She was but a myth in the tongue of the Abyss. A nocturnal goddess spoken of only in shadow.

From the distance, Azrael, Samael, and their army of Abyss could see now see the temple. Its roof was a gaping hole while fires whipped their frenzy toward the skies. Bodies of both Seraphim and Baphomet's jackal children littered the temple and surrounding structures. The scent of death still lingered in the air, as it was all too apparent that there were no survivors. Azrael and Samael headed directly for the once majestic domed roof of Baphomet's temple, now caved in and open to the starlit night sky. They, along with a handful of Abyss, landed inside the temple while further scores of Abyss circled the skies above. Others made their way to the grounds around the temple to keep watch. Azrael and Samael took a moment to mourn for the fallen and look for any signs of life. Azrael walked over to the pool he and Elizabeth had shared their pairing not but a few days prior. Once a crystalline body of pure life-giving liquid, it was now a grave to Baphomet, the blood from her corpse swirling in the waters she now lay in.

Azrael knelt by Baphomet's corpse and placed his hand on her head. Knowing he was somehow responsible, he closed his eyes and felt regret for the first time in ages. "I will fix this. You will not be forgotten," Azrael said, while he stood up and turned back around to face Samael.

"All were slaughtered. None spared. This was Moloch's doing," Samael said through his mask as he followed the spatters and trails of blood up and around the walls.

Azrael looked amongst the corpses for Elizabeth and Daemos as he wondered if they had shared the same fate as the others. Samael caught a glimpse of what his brother was investigating and gave his answer before Azrael was able to ask.

"Moloch took them. Your female and my...brother Daemos are at Elysium," Samael said.

"I know," Azrael said as he stared up through the torn-open roof and at the sky above.

"There is nothing left here for us. We must take the fight to them," Samael exclaimed.

The two warriors walked out from this place of suffering and made their way down the steps of Baphomet's final resting place. They joined the rest of their brothers amidst the carnage and felt the breeze of the surrounding woods push against their flesh.

"Bury the dead. Baphomet and her children deserve to return to the dirt from whence they came. Do not let them rot above the soil," Azrael told the crowd.

A single Abyss spoke out, "And what of the Seraphim?"

Samael turned his head and looked at the corpse of a Seraph soldier, its body ripped apart and contorted. "Burn them," he said.

As Azrael and Samael began to conjure a plan to enter Elysium, a familiar hiss and clattering of hooves approached. Azrael turned his head and looked past the thick of trees and shadows of the living forest. He saw a creature approach with the body of a man and the head of a jackal. Beside the creature was a hound. Three heads sat upon a hulking form while growls and snarls let loose a breath laced with the acrid stench of blood and acid. Before long, Azrael saw clearly that the figures that approached were Belial and Cerberus. They came forth, Seraphim blood still dripping from their teeth and claws.

Belial walked up to Azrael and threw a broken weapon, that of a Seraphim war scythe, to the ground. He looked at Azrael and spoke, "I never doubted you."

Azrael could not help but release a small smirk as he was reassured by his actions at the sight of his brother-in-arms. "I hoped you to be among those I set loose. I am grateful to have been right."

Cerberus took his place by the corpse of a jackal as he gave aid to other Abyss currently digging graves for their cousin race.

Belial walked over to Samael and examined his face while taking in the scent of both Seraphim and Abyss blood coming from his flesh. "Sophia was right all along. The brother thought to be lost, hidden amongst the Seraphim. I thank you, the mantle of death. I believed us to be trapped with the old ones, in that darkened shrine beneath Lilith's temple."

"Why wait so long for escape? Leviathan has guided me from the shadow since I arrived on this world. What whispers have you heard while held captive?" Azrael asked Belial.

"Whispers of divine retribution. Yet you entered the domain of the slain ones and brought a weapon feared by all. With Moloch's blade in the depths of the lost void, Leviathan now no longer fears the Seraphim. When the ground cracked above and the scent of fire and flesh filled me, I knew you had returned and that we would reclaim the surface once again," Belial exclaimed with excitement.

"All is not finished. Daemos helped in your escape. It seems he, as well as other brothers of the Seraphim, fear Moloch has lost his way as well. He has taken Elizabeth and I fear he will discover Daemos' betrayal. I must find my way to Elysium," Azrael explained.

Samael stepped forward and slammed his scythe into the ground and stared at Belial and then Azrael. "We will leave this place under your command. This world is in need of salvation. Rebuild the once great cities. Remove the memories of Minos, the false judge, and free Lilith from her torment. I leave you in charge of this task," Samael said to Belial.

Belial nodded his head and looked back at Cerberus. "Cerberus will once again guard the doors to the great city of Dis. I alone can not rebuild," the beast said.

Azrael walked over to the steps that led up to Baphomet's temple and stared at the already decaying ruins before his very eyes. The Abyss stopped their grave digging and spoke amongst themselves. Whispers were carried throughout the horde as a handful of Abyss departed from the group and headed toward Azrael, Samael, and Belial. One creature, a hulking form of leathered bone and insect-like appendages, came forth. Upon its shoulders sat a single head with a face in the center and two more, one on each side. The center face resembled that of a man, while the one on the right side was that of a decayed rabid jaguar. The one on the left had the scaled visage of a reptile.

"I am Baal," the creature spoke in a very well and articulate voice in contrast to his monstrous appearance. "Allow me to be your lord of whispers. I have spent countless millennia with my brothers and our father in that tomb to the east. I remember the days before the last days when the Seraphim wiped clean our kind from this world."

Another creature came forth and soon another until there were five more alongside Baal and Belial. The creatures stood beside one another, and one at a time, presented themselves.

The first was a towering muscular form of a man, skin gray and cracked with black veins and fiery eyes. He resembled the demonic form Azrael took when he changed his shape, with protruding horns and a tail though, absent wings. Claws sat upon oversized paws while his hooves dug into the dirt. "I am Asmodeus. I have served Lilith. Allow me to drive forth our enemies by temptation and vengeance."

The second creature stepped forward. At first, its shadow cast the shape of a mortal woman, but further reveal showed it to be a creature of lies. Its figure had the breasts, hips, and limbs of a human female however, its face was that of a serpent. Sharpened black eyes pierced from behind tightened skin and small slits where a nose would otherwise sit. Upon its head were thin strands of coarse tendril that reassembled something akin to hair. "I am Pythia, Mistress of prophecy. I foretold your coming to our brothers. May I tell of your retribution to our children as well?"

Azrael nodded as the third creature stepped forth. He walked up to Azrael with a nobility rarely seen amongst the Abyss. He was not in nude flesh as his brothers were, but wore the scavenged armor of those he slain. His form was almost completely that of a mortal man. His limbs were slightly elongated and his mouth, like that of dried fruit. He licked a small amount of blood from his fingertips as he looked up at Azrael and cracked his bony fingers and joints. "I am Mammon. That which I see is that which I take. That which others see and do not take, I coerce to take. Allow me to build your armies, on this world and the next."

Next to Mammon was a creature with eight wings and the head of a jackal similar to Belial and Baphomet. Only upon his brow was a row of horns that grew in size the farther they sat towards the back of its skull. The size of his arms and their muscles dwarfed all others in comparison. Three tails splintered off from his spine as he stomped and slithered toward Azrael. His voice was thunder incarnate as he spoke. "Astaroth. Son of the Abyss. Born of the lords of Tartarus, the first world before all worlds. I will feed on Seraphim flesh."

The last creature to approach was that of another female. Unlike the other, she had the form of a human woman. Her skin, like all Abyss, was gray and tempered hot. Her veins were cracked beneath her skin. On her shoulders, thighs and head were elongated scales that looked much like the black feathers of a bird attuned to the night. She had a set of wings covered as well in the same long, black scales. Her tongue was a long black tendril that slithered and hissed its way past her lips and down between her breasts. She perched upon a mantle next to Azrael as she spoke, "I am Camio. My voice can soothe and persuade any to my bidding." She stepped from the perch and changed her form to resemble that more closely of a man, still with the same attributes. "Or perhaps I shall speak in a firmer tone and command my will," Camio said while standing with her male form in full effect. With her words set upon Azrael and the others, she reverted back to that of a female.

Azrael looked at his new generals, the new dukes of his now-forming empire. Belial, Baal, Asmodeus, Pythia, Mammon, Astaroth and Camio. They stood before Azrael and pledged their allegiance, and that of all Abyss, to his side. Samael released his scythe from the ground and walked over to Azrael and took in the sight of his new circle of seven.

"Gather yourselves your dukes and generals, and grow your legions as well. The Seraphim are many, and the Abyss are but few in number. In time, we will erase their stain from creation," Azrael told his generals.

Samael looked at his brother and watched as Azrael's generals disappeared into the night. With their future now secured by the seven generals that have appointed themselves the watchers in shadow, Azrael and Samael were now ready to leave for Elysium. Taking one last glimpse at the world around them, they spread their wings and took to the skies. They flew past the surface and into the dark cold of space. Once beyond the shadow of the world below, Azrael turned to see the red and orange planet he left behind. Never had he seen their world from beyond, amongst the stars. He wondered if the Seraphim felt the same wonder and excitement when they traveled between worlds. With nothing but the vast seeming emptiness of space ahead of them, Samael guided Azrael to one of three stars that gave off its crimson luminescence to the surrounding worlds. Samael became that of a comet, flying towards the sun at a speed far beyond anything most living creatures could ever fathom. Before the flames of the star could engulf him, he tore his way through time and space. He disappeared moments before touching the infernal surface of the red sun. Azrael followed close behind his brother. The shock wave created by Samael tore his flesh and ripped his body to pieces. He was pulled apart one atom at a time, feeling only the sting of creation course through his veins. And before he could compose himself, Azrael had disappeared with his brother into the dimensions between dimensions. The skies above Tartarus were empty and silent once again.

XXI. Into Elysium

Echoes stirred and traveled, whispering their secrets throughout the hidden chambers of Elysium. The world fortress housed the remaining bulk of Seraphim sentries that had returned from spreading their divine retribution and ordained academics throughout their finite section of creation. Made up of over twelve dimensions and guarded by twelve gates, it lay hidden within the ethereal dust of the cosmos, all linked by a single core. None that wandered beyond the gates have seen the core, as its contents were beyond the comprehension of even the most divine of beings. At constant the kingdom expanded each passing cycle, adding to the strength of the Seraphim and their conquest. Devoid of name, each pillar of Elysium acted to serve a specific purpose. There did lay one, in secret, far away from the inner web of Elysium. The thirteenth pillar, a tomb made of flesh and suffering, held for the world slayer Moloch and his closest generals, to house his secrets and conjure up plans of absolution that once acted as the origin for his patricide.

Moloch sat cross-legged with his hands upon his knees and fixated on the tower of writhing flesh in front of him. Chains, twine, and serpentine coils held over a hundred bodies in place as they moaned and cried for release. Rivers of blood and other fluid ran down the flesh tower and into the bottomless chasm below. He kept his mind clear while he stayed focused, sitting on a pillar in the center of a bottomless chamber. Surrounded by darkness, the only light that shone through came from a small fixture hundreds of feet above him and illuminated his position. There were no doors, nor any entrance or exit to his chamber. Only the pillar he sat upon and the void of space below. As a being of light, he engulfed himself in darkness, becoming ever-corrupted by the nature of his enemies.

Soon, the darkness gave way to the winding sound of arrival. He recognized the clattering of armor and spreading of angelic tendril. Gabriel had disturbed his silence. With tendrils spread and armor cracked, he held his own weapon of shadow. Gabriel floated down and stood next to his brother.

With his eyes still closed, Moloch spoke to Gabriel, "Tell me they have been driven back into shadow. If even for a passing moment, lie and tell me they have been driven back into the depths whence they belong."

Gabriel looked down at his brother, his host's skin cracked and bleeding streams of rotten black blood. He saw the deepening rage hidden behind his brother's meditation and peered at the tower of bound flesh that wailed and echoed in their presence. "No. We have been overrun. For what numbers we had, they had thrice what I could command."

Moloch clenched his fists and tightened his jaw, focusing on the pain of his human host body. "The soul of our father. The key to salvation. My instrument of divine retribution has been found?" he asked Gabriel.

"No. There was no sign the great bringer of order was upon the fallen. Or the living," Gabriel answered.

Moloch opened his eyes and stood up. With each movement, his host body cracked and bent in a manner unnatural to the living. He took in the surrounding darkness and looked down at his hands, beaten and bloody, with scars still present from his last encounter with the Abyss. "Then Azrael has left my birth rite within the darkened chasm. It is either the worst mistake he has made, or the wisest," he said, still looking at his ravaged palms. Moloch looked back up at Gabriel and knew that time would soon come to confront their enemy. "I have held onto this form for long enough, dear brother. I shall find a new skin and mold it to my appearance. There are whispers and traitors amongst us. We must be ever vigilant if we are to reclaim what is rightfully ours and continue to bring order to the very core of existence. I await the return of brother Samael, as he will surely have disposed of Azrael. If not, Azrael will surely find a way here. I will not make the mistake of undermining his resolve a second time. We have something he wants. Go now, blow your trumpets, Gabriel. Prepare our brothers."

With those words, Gabriel took flight and gave his leave through the celestial opening above. Droplets of Seraphim blood fell from Gabriel's wounds as he made his way above Moloch before disappearing into the cosmic void of space. Moloch took a moment to stare at the pillar of flesh once more before shedding his mortal shell. He followed Gabriel and left his meditative chamber, the echoes of the dying still ringing like a funeral bell.

* * *

The silence faded as pieces of reality and lost memories began to make their way back into Azrael's mind. He was stuck between the places of life, death, and the weaving of dreams. His mind moved with the punishing resistance of his flesh. Infernal heat and the freezing sting of death pulled at his insides while a deafening silence polluted his ears. For a moment, he had forgotten that he was without sight. Where his eyes once were now sat empty orbs that pierced with the pounding of a thousand nails being hammered into his skull. He gripped his head and screamed out in pain, yet no sound left his mouth as his body curled up in a mass of exposed muscle, vein, and bone. Still, his flesh was ripped away and reformed at constant. He defied those that came before him, alone and ill-equipped, to travel within the gateways among the stars. He convulsed and spat up innards that reformed anew. And again he spat up his innards, only to be reformed inside his fleshly shell. He did this, at constant, for what seemed a hundred lifetimes. Memories were further torn and re-introduced.

He found himself back within the confessed limits of reality. Mud and dirt gave way beneath his feet while rain and thunder clamored their songs above. Men shouted and yelled while the crunching of bone and slicing of flesh overtook the ensuing storm. Azrael followed the all too familiar sound of battle and headed up a hill and over to the edge of a rocky cliff. The falling waters washed away the rain from his feet as he took in the stale air and peaked over the cliff side. There were thousands of men, some dressed in steel cages and others in the bones of their enemies. He watched as they penetrated each other's soft bellies with weapons of sharpened edge. The rain was not enough to quell the bloodletting as rivers of crimson rose beneath their feet. He had seen this particular battle before. In the center of the chaos, he saw one man, a warrior dressed only in a pair of greaves covering his legs and feet, and a burnt sash around his waist. The warrior had plunged the end of his weapon into the chest of another man, staring into his dead, sullen eyes. He then pulled the weapon out as he twisted and turned, murdering all those around him. This warrior had not chosen a side to fight for. He simply killed with efficiency and complete resolution. Those that crossed his path were neither given the chance to escape nor surrender. Azrael felt his gut churn as the sky turned a darkening red and the rain soon turned to a downpour of torrential plasma. Soon, all was covered in the blood of the gods. On the distant horizon, he saw the shadowed forms of the old ones rise above and into the setting sun. He returned his gaze to the battlefield and saw that the bodies of over a thousand men had vanished from sight. Left standing now was only the single warrior. Azrael looked at the warrior and saw into his own mind. Even while administering the touch of a butcher, he was always truly alone. No longer did Azrael find himself standing on the edge of the cliff, looking down. He stared at the sea of blood beneath his feet and at the towering gods in the distance. At any moment, he believed he would be conjured back to Daemos. He would rip his way through another girl set aside for sacrifice and made to feel comfort by his sister, Sophia. Time and reality had ceased to exist where he now stood. As he focused on the setting sun, it began to blur. It streaked and raced across his vision like a spinning wheel with himself caught in the center looking out. Once more he looked at his hands and saw skin tear away. Soon after, muscle was torn in snapped strands and veins unwound from their housing. Bone shattered and turned to dust and his mind was once more cast into darkness. And in an instant, he saw light.

Over a billion stars invaded Azrael's vision as he spread his wings and reared his claws. From out of oblivion, his body reconstructed its physical form. Behind him, the heat from a dying star dissipated and left its mark. He caught himself, for the first time, floating with a direction in the cosmos. All around him were clouds of green, red, purple, and blue gas. His tail swerved and slithered as he swam through the celestial springs. With his memories now coming back, he turned to his side to see Samael racing beside him. His brother looked over and gave a slight nod to reassure their journey through the inner dimensions of creation had been successful. Azrael's last coherent memory was that of following Samael through the ever-burning core of a crimson star. It was the stars themselves, he realized, that were the gateways for the Seraphim. If they could harness the power of the heavens, then so too could the Abyss.

They flew, with wings spread and blood as their destination, through a giant nebula and past the darkened pulse of a nearby cluster of shattered stone. All around them, with countless lifetimes of travel, were far-off worlds. Some barren and others still teaming with both new and old life. Unknown to the creatures of these uncharted worlds, were the gods of a new age as they approached their destiny.

Further into the cosmic storm, they flew. Streaks of concentrated gas whipped about while towers of crackling electric current materialized amongst the ethereal fog. Azrael followed his brother as they drew closer to the lower gates of Elysium. It was nothing that could be seen physically but felt as one approached. Soon they left behind the ensuing storm and entered through what seemed to be an atmosphere surrounding the planet-sized city. Azrael took in the sight of this magnificent structure. He saw twelve layers of carefully crafted architecture weaving around each other. None of it seemed to connect, yet each section fit above, beside, and below the next. To an outsider, it had the appearance of an abandoned planet left halfway through its creation.

Towers of bone and gathered stone shot out in every conceivable direction. Beyond the natural exterior, he could see signs of advanced technologies that he had never witnessed. Through the gaps in rock and stone, he saw great pillars and structures made of artificial materials. Steel pillars and electric pulses swam throughout the inner workings of this world. There was a serene order to the chaotic design. Upon closer approach, he could hear the rumbling of living engines as the fortress moved and swayed. It breathed while its innards expanded and contracted like that of a living organism. And as such, he would soon pass through the outer atmosphere. It was as an electric barrier that acted as a membrane to protect this grand design from the elements of cosmic storms.

Samael led his brother to a collection of pillars that covered the southern hemisphere. They landed on what was a solid surface made of a reflective material that mirrored the stars above. Azrael looked down at his feet and saw that he was standing on the heavens themselves. Without a definite surface, the pillars stayed afloat, kept in a state of suspended animation. While jagged and rough, the floating pillars were each unique in size and shape. Some were no bigger than that of a small child, while others towered above and grew to the size of a castle tower. Yet each one, over a thousand in all, had its own shape. The material from which they were made was unknown. Even their architects remained a mystery. They simply acted as a buffer for the upper atmosphere before reaching further into the inner workings of Elysium.

"Beneath the reflecting shimmer of these pillars, on this, the twelfth circle of Elysium lay eleven, each tethered by the great unity. Each passing gate shall give way to their chambers. Beware, though, for the eyes of your enemy will be watching," Samael said as he closed his wings and took in a shallow breath of celestial air.

"And at what pillar would Moloch hold his captives?" Azrael asked.

"Creatures of flesh are held within every facet of Elysium. Each great pillar is home to countless tombs that house the shells we use as mortal flesh. Moloch keeps himself, and those within his command, within a storm born of lost souls, held behind a thirteenth gate," Samael answered.

Azrael looked around at his surroundings, the mirrored rocks passing by his vision, set against a starry galactic backdrop. "Which of your surrogate family would know how to find him?" Azrael asked.

"Moloch keeps his secrets close. More so than any of the Seraphim. His trust has waned over the passing years. He keeps with him Gabriel and Raphael by his side. They answer only to him and perform their duties without question," Samael said beneath his death mask.

"And where would I find them?" Azrael asked Samael.

Samael kept silent and turned his head toward the distance of the surface of Elysium. From there, he could hear the echoing bellows of a war horn. It rang out from beyond the core and carried its tune through the cosmic winds. "Listen," Samael said.

Azrael tilted his head and pointed his ear in the same direction that Samael kept his concentration on. He heard the same ringing melody.

"Gabriel has blown his trumpet. The tides of war beckon our calling. All Seraphim will gather at the core to re-solidify their place in this sacred space. You must call the attention of a beast within these walls and draw the Seraphim out before you can reach Gabriel. I shall attend to Raphael," Samael said.

"And when I find Elizabeth, if we are able to escape this place with our lives, what of your brother's pursuit?" Azrael asked Samael as he stared off into the cosmos.

Samael walked up to his brother and looked him directly into his eyes. "Leave this place, Azrael. Take her. Find yourself a world far away from these petty warring factions. We have all suffered enough at the hands of our enemies." With those words, Samael slammed the blunt end of his scythe against the surface on which they stood. It quaked and sent tremors through the many caverns of the pillar they stood upon. Beneath them, they could hear the thundering growls of an ancient beast. "The guardian of the great throne. Once a great weapon of Jehovah, now reduced to nothing more than a rabid monster living within our shadows."

Azrael turned around to see a dozen massive tentacles rise from behind the floating surface he was standing on. Four pairs of elongated human arms rose up with the tentacles and grabbed him as well. The creature wrapped its tendrils around Azrael's legs and drug him toward the darkness. He was swept up and pulled down into the darkened caverns that were hidden inside Elysium.

Samael took a few lasting moments to watch his brother get swept away by the beast before once more spreading his wings and taking to the skies. He flew off towards the core to meet with his brothers at the beckoning of Gabriel's horn.

* * *

The beast pulled and prodded at Azrael's flesh as it took him deep into the bowels of Elysium. All around them, rock was blistered and broken as it hurled itself through the caverns. Azrael fought off the tentacles and ripped away at the corrosive hands holding onto his flesh. He freed his upper body and beat his fists into the creature's writhing sides. With every hit, the beast swayed and crashed into the walls of this ever-tightening tunnel while also gaining momentum. As the two of them raced through the inner workings of Elysium, Azrael was able to catch brief glimpses of the rest of this artificial world through cracks in the walls to the right of him. He saw quick flashes of light accompanied by ornate and exquisite machinery. Bringing his attention back to the beast, he did what he could to keep from transforming his body into its Abyssal form. The tunnels had grown too tight, and they moved at too fast a pace for him to take on a more monstrous physique. He continued to rip and tear at the beast's tentacles until his whole body was freed. While the beast roared and screamed through the caverns, Azrael climbed his way up its back before realizing its torso was but three all intertwined into one. He dug his fingers into its spinal cord while continuing to make his way up toward the massive creature's head. With no choice left, Azrael contorted his flesh and shifted his muscle and bone to take his demonic form. He kept his wings tight to his back and sent his tail skewering into one of the beast's torsos. He tore his claws into the beast's flesh and pulled up as if guiding an animal to obey a command. The beast screamed out and crashed through a wall ahead of them. Rock and debris flew out as the two of them fell into a large chamber. Beneath them, a pool of shallow liquid awaited their eventual landing.

In a thunderous quake, they fell into the illuminated liquid. Waves were sent up and crashed against the inner walls of the chamber. Before a single droplet of water could fall back to its origin, Azrael had lunged head first towards the beast. Like a strike of lightning, he was shot back against the opposite wall. The beast raised one of its many heads and hissed at Azrael. It untangled its monstrous form and spread its body open to show a sign of dominance and intimidation. The base of its body, a series of more than a dozen giant tentacles, stay submerged in the pool while its upper body, three humanoid torsos with two arms and a head each, swerved and weaved amongst the still-falling rock. Azrael reared himself and prepared for attack. The beast charged at him, a creature nearly eight times the size of a mortal man, and tore away at solid stone as if it were rotten meat. Azrael spread his wings and dodged each attack. The beast raged and swung its arms, tendrils, and sharpened fangs. They played their dance macabre, while the cavern still fell apart all around them. Azrael picked his moments carefully and chose with precise timing when to strike. For every dozen attacks he dodged, Azrael tore his claws into the beast's flesh for a single strike. He used the beast's unguided rage to his advantage. He allowed the beast to expose itself and its weaknesses. There would be no final killing blow but instead a slow and steady bloodletting. Eventually, the beast was no longer able to support its own weight as it collapsed and fell face-first into the now blood-stained pool of crimson expulsion. Finally, there was silence. The last stone had fallen from the opening above and the beast made not a sound but for the movement of short breaths. Azrael flew to the opening above and looked down at the defeated creature one last time before following the tunnel out and into the great expanse of Elysium's inner chambers.

* * *

The meeting within the great hall was short-lived by the thundering echoes of battle. The Seraphim knew that their enemy had arrived. Samael approached his brothers as they discussed their plans for swift retribution. Raphael kept the meeting organized as he stood guard by the entrance of the great hall. Words of vengeance and plans for war made up the bulk of the conversations at hand. Amongst them, Daemos gave his conjecture as well.

"Samael. Judging by your stride and the sound of conflict, I am to believe you have brought our enemy here?" Raphael asked as his brothers awaited an answer.

Samael looked around the room, his brothers perched against the protruding fixtures that stemmed out from the walls. "He has come. The guardian of the throne has relinquished our enemy," Samael answered.

Before Raphael could give his thoughts to Samael's answer, Daemos spoke in his place. "Then it is settled. Therion has defeated the last of our enemies." With those words, Daemos raised his hand and gestured a sign of victory to his brothers. The Seraphim in the great hall cheered and rallied their war cries. Whilst the cheers went on, Samael looked back at Daemos and kept with him a silent oath. They knew it would be no more than a matter of time before their claim to victory would be short-lived. Raphael kept his gaze upon Samael and Daemos as he suspected their reveling to be in haste.

"I will attend to brother Gabriel and cease the calling of the horn. Moloch will expect the seizure of a corpse as well," Raphael said to Samael and Daemos as he gathered himself and took off through the open domed roof above.

Samael knew that the charade would come to an end soon and that he would have to face the Seraphim with his true brother by his side. He looked at Daemos and wondered if he, too, would be able to fulfill his end of their treachery.

"Come, let us find Azrael's corpse and bring revelation in person," Daemos said, as he walked past Samael.

* * *

With nothing more than instinct and the unrelenting will within, Azrael made his way through the inner workings of Elysium's vast network of hidden tunnels. Each led to a different chamber of horrors. He saw Seraphim experiments on mortal hosts, some living, others no more than an eviscerated corpse. Curiosity got the best of him as he continued through the innards of his enemy's home. Each tunnel he traversed gave way to an opening above a room, which allowed him to view these experiments from a safe distance and in secret. He now knew why the Seraphim favored mortal hosts.

There was a serene sense of unity in how the Seraphim worked. They would lay their captive prey upon a table held afloat by some unseen force. Men, women, and children were spared no special treatment. No visible bonds or restraints were used as these unfortunate souls seemed to lie on their backs upon these floating coffins willingly. The Seraphim would work and examine their prey in their true form. Perhaps it was their enlarged hollow eyes that held these mortals in thrall. Always, they would succumb to their gaze. The Seraphim would work, always in groups of three, on their victims. Those that survived were taken away for further experimentation. Of those that did not survive, they were removed by guards wearing a suit of mortal flesh. Every fiber of Azrael's being told him to follow the trail of those still breathing from their torture. He knew, though, that he, as always, would find the answer he sought by following the trail of the dead.

Azrael waited for his moment. On his own, he could find his way out of these caverns in no more than a few waking hours. He had precious little time to spare, however. Below him, the screams of a wailing child began to whimper and were eventually silenced by the cold, gray hands of a Seraph that removed a long sharp object from the child's neck. They took the corpse away and into the further recesses of their citadel. Azrael followed above in the winding tunnels. As he traversed deeper into the pits, he could feel the air getting thicker as the sound of industry began to grow louder and more thunderous. Before long, he lost sight of those he was following and instead found himself on the edge of a larger inner sanctum. He could hear the rumblings of an entire world on the other side of the wall that he had now been blocked from passing. With his claws reared, he scratched and tore away the surface to break

through a new opening made of his own hands. With each puncture,

sharp light pierced through the damaged stone wall. Eventually, he

broke through and the wall ahead of him came crashing down. He

put his hands up to protect his eyes from the white-hot fiery light

that hit him like a thousand suns. Once the blinding light had finally

settled, and he was able to focus his vision once more, he was able to

take in his surroundings. He saw that the tunnels he traversed were

the innards of part of a larger outer structure that acted as a barrier to

the true world of Elysium. And thus he gazed upon its glory for the

first time. What he saw shocked, horrified, and astounded him.

Elysium was more than just a mere set of gargantuan pillars housed

inside a world-sized shell. Though on a limited frame of time, Azrael

could not help but take a few moments to realize the horrific secret

as he took in the view of his enemy's home world that had just been

uncovered.

XXII. Hall Of The Great Horn

Where there had once been the drumming of war-beaten hearts now lay only the cold stillness of death. All life had faded from existence and darkness fell upon the face of the deep. No living creature had yet been privy to lay claim to any world known nor yet witnessed by mortal eyes. Only the rustling of shallow tides and crashing waves gave their voice to the stars. An endless ocean of red-hot blood covered the landscape as a new consciousness sprung to life below.

In a shallow gasp for breath, a new form had broken above the surface. Air had been taken into newly formed lungs while black clouds parted their ways to open up to a crimson sky. The creature became self-aware of its existence. Cold hands wandered over naked flesh as blood was wiped away to reveal a soft pearly shell. Not knowing what it was, or why it had emerged, it had only the view of others like it rising from the depths to compare itself. It saw hundreds of other beings like it rise from an ocean, the same color as the red sky above. They were each in different sizes and shapes, some with round soft bodies that held a delicate form and others with hardened bodies that stood taller than the others. This creature had seen its resemblance in those with softer, rounded shapes. While still grasping for meaning in this storm of blood, and the flesh it held, with it came trace memories and knowledge of the world around.

It knew it was female. She looked around and saw the others become aware of their existence as well. Each of them noticed the others while fixated on the towering structures of bone that protruded high above the ocean's surface and towards the sky. As the mass of people looked up, they soon felt the waves ripple and tremble. With the rumbling of a thousand quakes, a massive tower of charred flesh and bone rose high above the surface of the sea. It stood the height of more than a hundred men with over a dozen appendages slowly wading in the wind as it looked to struggle while keeping its balance. She was witness to the first coming of Leviathan. With its rising, all of the men and women that had surfaced with her were pulled down into the depths below by the thousand-eyed monster of the deep. Behind her, she could hear the wailing of a far-off voice. Faint at first, but louder it grew with each passing second. From above the clouds, she saw a great fire approach. It grew beyond the size of the sun and soon entered the fabric of this world. Though she saw only flame, inside the towering inferno was the shadow of another creature similar in shape to the current god towering above. It was the father of the Seraphim,

Jehovah. They stood above her, looking down at the mortal creature.

As quickly as the two gods appeared, they too took their leave.

Leviathan to the sea and Jehovah to the skies. Only she was left to

witness the birth of a new world, as life fed upon life.

Though simply lost in her thoughts, Elizabeth knew the dream she had was all too much a reality. Her time held captive by the Seraphim allowed her mind to further dig into her ancestral blood memories. She remembered witnessing the first pilgrimage of the Seraphim into the cosmos. The Abyss had stayed behind to claim the world, flooded by the blood of Kingu, that gave mortal life as their own. She remembered the bones lining the surface of the ocean to be that of the former god. Its blood spilled over the entire surface of the planet, thus giving life to the first race of mortal men. Beyond the coming of Jehovah, father to the Seraphim, and Leviathan, lord of the Abyss, she too knew of their connection. That the two races were not mortal enemies locked in an eternal struggle, but lost cousins that had forgotten their true origins. Origins that if traced farther back would show mortal men to predate the birth of both the Seraphim as well as the Abyss. She knew that somewhere Azrael was apt to find her, and they would reignite the proper course of nature.

* * *

It was a magnificent sight to behold, the structural makeup of Elysium. Though the current home of his enemy, Azrael could not help but feel a tinge of awe as he gazed upon the true face of their cosmic fortress. He saw each pillar as it stayed afloat, held in place by a series of tunnels attached to another corresponding pillar. Each pillar was about the size of a large city built by men, able to house more than a few hundred thousand per structure. At first, the placement of each pillar inside the hollow planet seemed to be set at random points. After careful examination, he saw that Elysium's design was not random nor made by chance. The fiery tunnels that connected each pillar acted as a series of neurons made to relay information between each one. He could no longer deny to himself that what he saw was the remnants of their dead god. They had built their entire society deep in the reaches of space within the very core of what was left of their creator's physical mind. The levels of the pillars started from the outside in. He had been escorted by Samael to what they believe to be the twelfth pillar. Azrael stood silent as he listened to the bellowing of the great horn. It echoed like a hammer felling a thousand strikes of thunder throughout this world. Without further hesitation, he spread his wings and made his way to the next, the eleventh pillar.

Azrael flew slow and steady between the mass of wiry tunnels and corridors that connected each grand city. Many of the Seraphim traveled inside the ventricular tunnels instead of the vacuum outside. Only once in a great while did he have to hide against a pulsing conduit or protruding structure made of bone to avoid being seen by a patrolling guard. The eyes of the Seraphim seldom peeked outside the pillars and their tunnels as their hubris did not allow them to think an intruder could come into their home and, at the very least, break past the reflecting shell of Elysium's exterior. Though he had no walls to block his path, the openness of the space outside the pillars was a maze of its own. He had only the rumbling sound of Gabriel's horn to guide him.

Before too long, he saw a mass of Seraphim traversing away from what looked like a large core that held a great chamber. It appeared to be a sort of meeting area. He watched as hundreds of Seraphim left this chamber and headed back to the surrounding pillars. Whatever distraction Samael had provided had come to an end. Azrael would have to make haste and follow the bellowing trumpet before Gabriel met with his brothers. As the trumpets began to fade, he could feel the tension of fear rise in the air. Though his and Samael's plan had seemingly worked, there was still the wonder of doubt that he would invade this place unnoticed. And with that, the horn ceased to blow. Not a sound except for the hum of the stars could be heard within the negative space of Elysium. Azrael took a few moments to examine his surroundings. It was unsettling how similar the scale of his enemy's home resembled that of the void. There was no definite point of reference to determine any sense of direction. His guidance relied on feel and instinct rather than what was relative to what lay above or below. Azrael closed his eyes and let his senses take him to follow the vibrations from the echoes of Gabriel's horn. Fear and uncertainty were replaced by the old will to kill as he felt himself come closer to the echoing pillar. Azrael

opened his eyes as he broke through the thick membrane that

covered this, the seventh pillar of Elysium.

The former symptoms of vertigo that had overtaken Azrael's

mind while outside in the vast negative space between the pillars

were now gone as he entered this place. Beneath him, he could see a

grand structure set atop a vast network of pipes and hollowed bone.

Farther towards the horizon of this isolated world within a world, he

could see the steel and former flesh dig deep beneath dirt and rock.

It was as the surface of any other planet. He kept his wings spread as

he flew below toward the top of a grand spire. On top, he saw the

source of the Seraph's calling. The grand horn was made of a series

of hundreds of large pipes, made from the same bone and steel that

dug into the landscape, pointing towards the heavens. It stood atop a

central spire the size of a grand castle that was surrounded by five

other smaller spires, each with a barrier that acted as a connecting

hallway back to the center chamber.

Azrael made his way through an opening in the roof and into the bellowing chamber, where Gabriel had called forth the Seraphim with his horn. After what seemed an eternity, he shifted his body, with bones and flesh cracking back into place, to his mortal human form. No longer hiding the element of surprise, Azrael heard only the clashing sound of his boots against the stone floor, while his drape fluttered and swept about as he walked up to the port of the horn. Behind the piston chamber, he saw Gabriel. He was wearing the skin of a mortal man, as most Seraphim had now become so accustomed. Though fixated on his work, Gabriel was still unaware of Azrael's presence. Azrael used this to his advantage to sneak up on the unsuspecting Seraph. He softened his footsteps while Gabriel shut down the great horn. The creaking of steel and bone hid Azrael's approach.

With the turn of a knob, Gabriel felt a hand grip tight around his throat. Azrael turned Gabriel to face him, and the two locked their gaze upon each other. Gabriel saw the rage and fury within Azrael's eyes, but knew that death was not his first choice. Azrael held Gabriel high above himself and squeezed tight around the throat of his prey, letting only enough release for him to speak in short spurts. "I will ask you this but once. Moloch took with him a mortal woman. Where?" Azrael demanded.

Gabriel began to form a series of grunts that Azrael expected to further form a series of words. He loosed his grip on Gabriel's throat and allowed him to speak.

"Raphael," Gabriel answered.

"Where is Raphael?" Azrael responded, now more agitated by a further setback.

As Gabriel struggled, Azrael awaited a second answer. Azrael's patience waned as his temper began to overtake his senses. He had come this far, only to be led astray yet again. "Where is Raphael? Answer me," Azrael demanded further.

With a tightened grip on Gabriel's throat, there was no use in Azrael's mind to let his enemy continue breathing. He clasped his hand as Gabriel tore and fought at Azrael's arm. During his plea for escape, Azrael saw his prey's eyes widen. He had less than a split second before he felt the crushing blow of a Seraphim war ax tear into his backside. Azrael flew across the room as Gabriel was inadvertently released. Holding onto the fresh wound, Azrael got up and turned to see his attacker.

"You wish an audience with me?" Raphael asked as he picked his weapon back up and slung it over his shoulder. Gabriel pulled a sword from beneath his sheath and joined his brother by his side. Both Raphael and Gabriel walked around Azrael with their weapons drawn and spread their distance to surround him. Azrael got back up and brushed off his wound as it slowly began to heal and close back up. He tried changing his form, but the blow from the ax had damaged his body more than he thought. Only small adjustments were made to his bones as he pushed hard to release his tail and horns. He was too weak to bring forth his wings or harden his exterior.

"Perhaps you should have tightened your grip," Gabriel said to Azrael.

Raphael kept a steady pace as he circled his prey. His eyes fixated on the half-transformed man-creature of the Abyss. "I claimed your head as a trophy once before. I will do it again."

Azrael pulled himself completely to his feet and gained his composure. He gripped tight his fists, cracking knuckles and shifting bone while turning his focus back and forth between Raphael and Gabriel. With a final gesture, Azrael felt the muscle and bone in his neck crack as he tensed his shoulders and readied himself for battle.

* * *

Neither trust nor loyalty was questioned as Samael and Daemos walked down the pulsating chambers of the tenth pillar. They made their way towards the hollowed caverns of the surface that sheltered all of Elysium. There, they would expect to find the remnants of Azrael's intrusion.

Silence held the air captive while they traversed deeper into the caverns of Elysium's guarding shell. Each knew that their allegiance to the Seraphim was now in question. The details of their betrayal were suspect, though. Motive could mean the difference between eternal imprisonment or unending damnation. As they came closer to the underbelly of the surface, they could see the remaining damage in the surrounding walls done by Azrael's confrontation with the throne guardian, Therion. Pieces of rock, bone, and rubble still fell from the covering dome. A faint light from distant stars could be seen shimmering through holes made by their fight. The two of them followed the path of destruction to the grand cavern, where the apex of their battle came to an end. Samael and Daemos saw Therion lying in a pool of its own blood mixed with the waters of Elysium. Behind Therion stood Moloch, stoic and shrouded with complacency.

"The beast still breathes life," Moloch said as Samael and Daemos entered the cavern. Moloch slowly made his way around Therion while keeping a hand on the beast's flesh. "He was but one of many. While our father still reigned, he, along with the other great Seraphim beasts, stood proudly by his throne. Our father's rule was grand and just," Moloch said while still keeping his hand upon the shallow breaths of the beast. "I do not regret what I have done. If not for my sacrifice, the Abyss would have overrun us. We would be no more than a feast for their rampant appetites. I kept this one, Therion, to keep guard still. Though the throne is no more than a symbol now, this beast still guards it with its life," Moloch continued.

Daemos stepped forward and looked around at the damage caused by Azrael's battle with Therion. "No one is questioning your resolve, brother," Daemos said.

Moloch closed his eyes and took a deep breath in his mortal body while focusing on his still-beating Seraphim heart. "You have grown too fond of your pet, dear brother. Though I gave us the strength to cleanse the worlds we visit, it was you that our brothers placed faith in. Faith to harvest each world where mortals dwell. To purify those that we found infected with the Abyss. Yet, no worlds were ever found to be harvesting those dark creatures. Only mortal men and women. Always, only mortal men and women. Why, brother?"

Daemos felt his mortal heartbeat at twice the pace of his true Seraphim heart. He looked over at Samael, who stood like a statue, saying not a single word. "There was never any way to be sure. When I found Azrael..." Daemos was cut off by Moloch mid-sentence.

"I know you did not find him. He was given to you," Moloch interjected. "How could you do such a thing? Barter with our enemy? What is your blatant excuse? Use one of their own to hunt their own?"

With truth and lies now out in open air, Daemos felt no need to continue his facade. "I was not chosen by faith alone, brother. Was it not you that came to us with the promise of eternal salvation after you slain our father? Was it not you that saw all others aside from the Seraphim to be a threat? It was on your testimony that we harvest and possess mortal vessels so that we may preserve our own bodies. You had us take on mortal names and speak their mortal tongue. You have forgotten what it is to be a creature of time and space. Both mortal and Abyss had no means of acting as a threat to us, yet you saw them as one yourself. I never ordered you to cleanse those worlds in the purifying flames of our father. You did that of your own accord."

Moloch stepped forward and up to his brother. He placed his hand on Daemos' shoulder and took in a deep breath before he spoke. "That I did, dear brother. However, it was not I that conspired with our enemy."

Before Daemos could interject and give his reasoning, he felt the sharp sting of pain course through his body and release from his chest. He looked down and saw that Moloch had sent a blade through his heart. Daemos looked at his brother in dismay and slowly began to try to tear his Seraphim body away from his mortal shell. Moloch held Daemos close and did not let him leave his host's body. Moloch clenched his teeth as he twisted the blade further. Still, Daemos struggled, knowing that before long his true Seraphim heart would die after the mortal heart he possessed gave out. As he stayed held in bondage and dying, he looked over at Samael, who looked back with the same stare Azrael once gave him. Somehow, within his mind, Daemos knew that Azrael was Samael's true brother. With his dying breath, Daemos leaned in towards Moloch and whispered into his ear, "You keep your enemies close, brother."

With the final beat of his angelic heart, Daemos was released and dropped to the waters at his feet. Moloch let him fall beside Therion as he removed the blade from his brother's corpse. He walked up to Samael, who stood cold and still. "Samael dear brother, we must be careful whom we place our trust in. It was brother Daemos who had conspired with our enemy. I know it was you that led Azrael here, but it was Daemos that conspired to let him pass into our home. I do not blame you, for I am sure you were unaware of our brother's treachery."

Samael kept his composure as he answered. "Daemos knew nothing of the true threat he created. His ignorance was his downfall. Azrael will not get far," Samael said.

"You are right, brother. Azrael will be met with swift retribution," Moloch stated.

"Therion?" Samael asked.

"Let the beast feed upon the corpse at its feet. In time, it will heal, and our guard will prosper once more. For now, I must confide in you. Azrael is loose amongst our people. I will underestimate him no longer. Go now beneath our great house and bring his woman to the doorstep of oblivion. Wait for me there," Moloch told Samael.

Samael took his leave and wandered out into the darkness of Elysium's hidden chambers. As Samael lost himself to the darkness, Moloch spread his tentacles and made his way to meet with Gabriel.

* * *

The first swing of Raphael's ax had near missed Azrael's throat. Behind them, Gabriel drew his blade. It shone with a brilliant shimmer as its golden glare reflected the light of the sky above. The blade swung in almost perfect harmony with the pendulum swing of the ax. Azrael dipped and weaved his body as he dodged each strike. Both Raphael and Gabriel had charged their onslaught with an almost choreographed perfection of unified combat. When one would finish with a thrusting strike, the other would be midway through with the next incoming threat. Their speed and precision were unmatched. As long as Azrael could, he held off their advances. Not until after more than a hundred failed attempts had Raphael finally gotten a cut, although shallow, into Azrael's forearm.

Raphael lifted his intricately designed crescent-shaped ax to his head to taste the blood that dripped from its edge. "This is the nectar of the Abyss? How sweet your end will taste," Raphael said as he licked the blood while it fell to the cold gray floor at his feet. Its sting burned at his tongue, sending trails of smoke to rise from his mouth.

Gabriel circled around behind Raphael, and past the pipes that made up his calling horn to the Seraphim. It took him twenty paces to walk completely past the piston chamber of the organ before he was opposite Raphael while Azrael stood, still bleeding, in the center of the lavish pipe room. Gabriel kept his sword close to his side as he took no chance to allow Azrael to launch a counterstrike. "Your wounds are open for us to see and we see that you are neither man nor beast. You sit between the edge of mortal and Abyss. You are an abomination," Gabriel taunted.

Azrael felt his heart beat faster with each step his foes took around him. Though he tried, he was too fatigued to fully change. Still armed with nothing more than his horns and tail, he shifted his feet and moved the sash around his waist aside. The blood from his arm fell onto his tattered clothes and mixed with the red from the cloth around his waist. He had relied too often on being able to change his form since his rebirth in the city of Dis, at the center of Acheron, by the cleansing fires. His blood had always shared that of the Abyss, yet he fought for several millennia as a mortal man. Countless armies had fallen to his feet and been laid bare for the gods to see before he had any ability to become a creature of darkness. Azrael closed his fists and lifted his head as the bleeding began to slow down. He looked at Raphael, still gloating, then at Gabriel. They were monsters, Seraphim possessing mortal bodies. He would fight them as a mortal, he decided. Azrael tensed his muscles and retracted his claws and horns. His tail whipped forth and pulled itself back into his spine, leaving only a tear in the cloth by his back. Both Raphael and Gabriel looked at him with curious eyes, not knowing what his intentions were. Perhaps he was tricking them? He had done so in the past by allowing Raphael to remove his head, feigning ignorance of his ability to resurrect on his own. Once fully reconstructed as a mortal man, Azrael took his stance and did something had never done in battle to an opponent. He smiled.

Like the silent whispers of gushing wind between leaves, Azrael jumped forth and propelled himself towards Raphael. He knocked the Seraphim down and pulled the ax from his hands. Behind him, Gabriel rushed to his brother's side and dropped his blade down toward Azrael. With Raphael's ax in hand, Azrael lifted and blocked Gabriel's strike. Locked in their stance, Azrael twisted the handle of the ax and flung Gabriel's sword across the chamber and over the edge to the mass of rock and bone that held the structure in place. He then turned his attention back to Raphael and cracked his jaw with the ball and mortar end of his own ax. Gabriel picked himself up and kicked Azrael, digging his armored boot into Azrael's back. With the ax still in hand, Azrael ran at Gabriel and knocked him to the ground, breaking the ax into multiple pieces.

All men were now on equal footing as their divine weapons had been dismounted and rendered obsolete. Raphael and Gabriel picked themselves up while Azrael stayed by the base of the grand horn. He kept his focus on them, never letting either one have the opportunity to take his flank. Like rabid animals, they hissed and snapped their jaws at each other. No longer was this fight going to be clean and by the standards set by the high class of Seraphim order. Raphael led the charge while Gabriel followed behind. He sent a kick toward Azrael's face that was blocked, knocking him to the floor. Gabriel came through less than a moment later with a flurry of fists aimed at Azrael's brow. Every other hit made contact at the cost of Gabriel's mortal ribs, feeling the hard crunch of bone snapping by Azrael's hammer-like blows. Azrael grabbed Gabriel's wrists and sent the top of his skull to meet his opponents. Gabriel fell to the ground, blood pouring from between his eyes. Raphael lifted himself into the air and circled Azrael with his tendrils spread. Hard as he tried, Raphael missed every swipe he charged. Azrael jumped to meet Raphael mid-air and pulled him down, smashing his face against the base of the horn. It echoed out and rang like the calling of victory.

Azrael lifted Raphael's head to his own and dug a rigid clawed thumb into his enemy's left eye socket. The Seraphim warrior screamed as his eye was pushed in and eventually torn and popped. Layers of ocular liquid and dark red mortal blood ran down his face as Azrael yelled, "Where is she?"

"Take the other, it is only a mortal eye and I will take another body to claim as my own," Raphael said as he spoke with both laughter and pain.

Blood poured between cold fingers, and Raphael was let go. Azrael set his sights upon Gabriel, who was crawling ever so slowly toward the edge of his chamber. He felt the sting of pain once more as Azrael dug his foot into his back. Azrael knelt and turned Gabriel over to face him. The bone that held Gabriel's jaw in place was shattered in more than a dozen areas. Azrael knew that he would not reveal the information he needed either. He opened Gabriel's mouth and grabbed his tongue. Azrael shifted the tips of his fingers into that of the black claws of his Abyss form and tore Gabriel's tongue from his mouth. Rivers of blood came pouring through as the Seraph screamed.

"I know you will find yet another host to claim as your own. For now, feel some mortal pain," Azrael said, before he dropped Gabriel's tongue to the ground. Behind him, he heard a new set of footsteps. These were the steps of someone who was confident and knew the price of defeat. Azrael turned around and saw Moloch approach from down one of the five halls connecting to the structure. At any opportunity, Moloch could have dropped from the skies above or intervened. He, however, chose to approach Azrael as his equal. Moloch entered the chamber and faced Azrael. The two readied their stance as the inevitability of battle loomed in the air. Death had finally come to claim its stake.

XXIII. Fall From Grace

Hidden within a sea of stars sat a world unlike any other. Once the body of a living god, it had been stripped and laid barren, only to be colonized and reignited by its own offspring. Molded and reformed to take the shape of the worlds which these creatures visit and steal life, it has become home to them. The outer shell, once the epidermis of an ancient deity, had become the first of twelve pillars that made up the living world of Elysium. Beyond its gates sat eleven other pillars, all connected by the reconstituted neural strands of their god. Further in, to the deepest reaches of the core, lay a great storm, the very epicenter of what was once the life force of this being. In this maelstrom of living energy and trapped souls sat a great structure built by the Seraphim of the highest order. Its form mimicked that of the greatest cathedrals and castles built by man. Inside, it held the dark recesses of their race and the space necessary to conduct their experiments on mortal flesh. It allowed for retreat, deliberation, and meditation. It was their thirteenth pillar.

Through feigning ignorance, Samael was able to keep

Moloch's trust. He traveled to the structure he had helped create at

the very heart of Elysium. Beneath the onyx gates, and grand halls of

the divine palace, lay the catacombs of the damned. Mortal hosts

were taken from various worlds and held as possessions to be used

for experimentation and study. It was here that Moloch conducted his

research into the limits of mortal flesh. Unlike other Seraphim, he

and his generals were able to mold and manipulate the flesh of their

hosts to suit their bidding. Samael was one of the first to be fitted

with a mortal host body. Though able to survive in the deep vacuum

of space, it was discovered that the Seraphim frame had a weakness

to the harsher environments of the physical world. Born as majestic

creatures of light to live amongst the stars, they were once nameless,

able to weave their path between all dimensions. Like all species,

though, they had a natural predator in that of the Abyss. Though their

enemy was not able to traverse the stars, they did keep their

blessings to the dimensions hidden within the darkness. It was not

until one of the Seraphim sacrificed their own father and built a city

from his bones that they began to learn the art of physical

possession. And with the taking of mortal bodies, they too took their mortal names and language. It was over the course of a thousand lifetimes that they learned mortal secrets and played mortal games. They took on once-mortal names such as Gabriel, Raphael, Moloch, and Samael. Others simply stayed the Seraphim course and lived within their new home in their native form. Those that wished were conscripted by the one called Moloch, into the Seraphim army, to spread out and hunt the Abyss. It was their oldest, Daemos, that had devised a plan to use a child of the Abyss against their own kind. Instead of a single child, Daemos was presented with three. The nature of this deal was hidden from all, and a web of lies was formed to protect the identity of the children. And though he never found what he was tasked to discover, Azrael did find the very thing he was looking for. A woman he had met on a distant world, in a distant lifetime that was somehow tied to him by blood and memory. And now, beneath the catacombs of the thirteenth pillar, she had been brought as a captive for the Seraphim to bring their enemy out of hiding.

Samael arrived at the entrance to the dungeons. To the mortal eye, it looked as if it were a forest, with every tree covered with over a dozen coffins starting from the base and moving like a spiral staircase toward the ceiling. The ground was thick with a hazy fog that acted as an atmosphere for those still living in their tombs amongst the damned. Their cries and moans could be heard like whispers beneath the electric hum of Seraphim technology. Insect-like arms made of steel and bone picked and pulled at both the living and the dead while they lay in their tombs. The dead were stripped of their clothing and flesh while the living were tested to the limits of pain. The Seraphim used whatever they could scavenge from their prey to reconstitute and make as their armor. Samael felt the eyes of his surrogate brother's stare as he walked by. Some simply hovered over their victims, their large black eyes staring back at those screaming in agony, while others simply fondled the bodies of the deceased. He knew this place was a chamber of torture that not even he intended to become. He continued forward, headed to a chamber saved specifically for the most dangerous prey, the Abyss. Though they had never captured a creature of the Abyss, they had still prepared a cell for if they ever did. In this same room, they kept their next best hostage, the woman whom Azrael had set himself upon to find.

Amid a dark and foggy haze of green and blue light given off by the electric pulse of starlight and luminescence of trapped souls, she lay before him three stories high in a special tomb of her own. Elizabeth was still unconscious from the twisted poison fog of this place. With the Seraphim still watching and prodding, Samael made a careful gesture to spread his wings and fly ever so softly up to Elizabeth's coffin. Some took notice while others did not. Those that did saw nothing out of place as Samael had come here on many a past occasion to retrieve a body for either Moloch or Daemos.

From high above, he released the translucent hatch that held Elizabeth in place. Streams of cold mist and amniotic fluid poured out from her tiny cell. He carried her out, her fragile body covered in nothing more than the tattered rags of her stolen armor now torn to shreds. With her unconscious body in his grasp, he lowered her to ground level and past the prying eyes of his adopted siblings. He traveled back the way he came, through the intestine-like catacombs and past the lacquered ribbed walls of the cathedral's underbelly. Ahead, he could see a pulsating light marking the exit of this stench-ridden jail. He would make his way out and up the steps to a grand terrace at the center of this fortress. There he would place Elizabeth's body overlooking the panorama of the ensuing storm that hid the thirteenth pillar from those unsuspecting.

With his task complete, it was only a matter of time before he knew that Azrael would arrive, either alone from gathering the information he needed, or as a prisoner of Moloch. No matter the outcome, Samael knew what it was he must do. Elizabeth would be used as bait to lure his enemy in and together, he and his true brother, Azrael, would kill Moloch and end the real threat to existence. Samael stood by Elizabeth's side with scythe in hand, prepared for the battle to come.

* * *

Eyes stayed locked as the inevitability of confrontation came drawing closer. Moloch kept his composure strong and hardened while Raphael and Gabriel picked themselves up and limped to his side. The two of them cracked their host's knuckles and reared their teeth as they prepared to join their brother in glorious combat. Azrael took note of his surroundings and kept the base of the horn to his back to not allow himself to be surrounded and overtaken by his three foes. He backed away, not in a sign of weakness or retreat, but to give himself an open advantage. Knowing that the strength of Seraphim combat was in quick hit-and-run strikes, he led them to believe that he was misjudging their tactics. Azrael had guessed right. Raphael and Gabriel licked their wounds and separated away from Moloch. Before they could deliver a single blow, Moloch made a sweeping gesture with his hand and nodded his head to Raphael, then over to Gabriel. The two wounded Seraphim looked at their brother in confusion. Moloch turned around and faced his back to Azrael. This was not to be the fight Azrael or his enemies had expected. Moloch spread his tendrils and, with back still turned, nodded his head and took to the skies.

Begrudgingly, Raphael and Gabriel followed their brother high into the clouds and past the atmosphere of the seventh pillar. Azrael knew that this gesture was meant for him to follow. He gathered enough strength to change his full form at will and become the beast within. With wings spread, he too took to the skies and left the seventh pillar behind as nothing more than a bloody memory. Once more, Azrael found himself in the space between the pillars of Elysium. Each world-sized pillar seemed so much bigger than he had originally thought. Perhaps it was his haste in following Gabriel's horn, but he was now able to take in and fully appreciate the sheer scope of the believed Seraphim home world. He stayed close while Moloch traveled, accompanied by his wounded brothers. They would occasionally look back at Azrael and scour at his very presence.

Deeper into the core of Elysium, the four of them flew. What was once darkness lit up by thousands of neuron-made tunnels soon began to drift into fog. Azrael felt his chest grow heavy and, after what was left of the purity of the vacuum of space, had become a dense and shrouded cloud. He could see flashes of green and bright blue light in the murky fog ahead of him. Soon bolts of electricity dashed by without warning. All around, he heard echoes, voices guided by misery and confusion. They sang the same tunes as those collected by Charon. Only these voices were lost. Further, into the blackened clouds, he flew, still following Moloch. At times, he knew not if he was being led into a trap or if Moloch had finally given up trying to best him. Lost in thought, he flew through a patch of green light. Not knowing what it was at first, he shrugged off the encounter as any other insignificant event. When his vision cleared, he saw the structure that Moloch had been leading Azrael towards. It was a massive multiple-layered city all on its own. It sat flat, like a disc being held up by tight strings. From the center out were grand towers piercing the heavens. Beneath the city was a network of caves and tunnels. He saw that from these tunnels flowed the same green mist.

Only it was not a simple conjuring of illuminated fog. In the mist, he saw faces and shapes. It was the by-product of mortal suffering and concentrated energy. He had arrived at the thirteenth pillar. A place constructed and fueled by mortal souls.

The souls of the damned swam and prodded at Azrael as he neared the entrance to a cavern at the underbelly of this haunted place. Moloch and his brothers had landed at the broken floating steps that led into the bowels of these caverns. They waited for Azrael, who was caught fending off hundreds of confused souls pleading for help, to arrive. He pushed his way through and landed next to Raphael, who was still holding the gaping wound on his face left by their previous encounter. Once by his enemy's side, Azrael changed back into his mortal form and followed them into the dark caverns.

All four men kept silent as they passed through the stagnant tunnels beneath the thirteenth pillar. It was a place that smelt of death and decay. Echoes coming from the screams of mortal souls filled the air of this oversized tomb. What had been a series of narrow and windy corridors soon opened up to a vast array of massive chambers lined with the bodies of mortal men and women. Azrael looked at this collection of life in shock and awe. He now saw where the Seraphim had kept their supply of mortal hosts. Though able to possess on will, this place housed bodies that were tempered and made to be worn for an extended period. Azrael knew he would not be so lucky to find Elizabeth with ease in this necrotic maze, thus he kept a sharp eye as he searched the surrounding walls.

Moloch, leading the pack up front, knew that Azrael must be scanning the scenery around him for his woman. "She is not here," Moloch said, with his back to Azrael. Raphael and Gabriel made a slight nod to each other when Moloch spoke.

Azrael kept silent for a few moments before finally breaking the air around him with his voice. "This is your purpose?" Azrael asked.

Moloch nodded his head and smiled to himself as he realized Azrael's naivety. He spoke to Azrael as an adult would to a child. "You know not the sheer number of worlds that are home to these mortal men and women." Moloch took his time to stop and examine a body latched by hook, chain, and mechanical claw on a wall next to him. It was that of a boy nearing adulthood. The boy was alive, but only by the artificial tubes that had been shoved down his throat and into his lungs to keep his blood pumping. "Without the aid of these contraptions, it would be no more than a corpse. On each world we find them. The young, the old. The wealthy and the desperate. Their lives are so fleeting and fragile. Creatures made with delicate precision. Unlike you or I, they have no allegiance to anyone but their kind. I envy them in a way, their design, their bonds of duty never set by their creator."

Azrael looked at the boy as well and saw fear and pain in his eyes. The boy gripped his hands tight, yet was unable to move his body to break himself free. Azrael kept silent as he continued to listen to Moloch speak.

"I remember this one in particular. Yes, I remember you, boy. When we took him, he had forced himself upon a female, a few years younger than him. She had sent her prayers to us, and like the saviors we are to these unfortunate beings, we took him. We took her as well," Moloch said as he turned and continued walking down the path.

"Why?" Azrael asked.

"Tell me, Azrael, why are we here?" Moloch countered with his own question.

"Is this some sort of trick?"

"No, no trick."

For a few moments, Azrael pondered Moloch's question. He wondered if he had meant it as a rhetorical response or a defined query of their current situation. "Because we are meant to be," Azrael answered.

"Because we are meant to be," Moloch repeated in a dampened tone. "What is it do you think these creatures are meant to be? They were never meant to be. You and I know this better than any of our brothers or sisters. We have both seen what these mortals do to their own worlds. No matter their advancement, whether they live by flame and stone or sit upon machines and in cities of electric pulse, they each share one goal. In the thousands of worlds you and I have both cleansed, it was by their hands that they brought destruction upon themselves. For a time, I truly believed them to be a greater threat than the Abyss. Oh yes, the Abyss may live in the shadows beyond creation, but I can attest that even my sworn enemy has never turned on their own flesh."

Azrael looked at Moloch and at the bodies held, forced upon hooks, in this Seraphim prison. "You reveal nothing I have not already witnessed. We both have spilled the blood of many a mortal man and woman. They are a weak and broken species. I assume you have a point?" Azrael asked, as he set his eyes in a deepened frown upon Moloch.

Moloch walked past his brothers and over to Azrael. "Why a mortal woman? You returned to Baphomet. Is it not in your blood to propagate your species? I know you are no mortal man. I know you are a creature of the Abyss. How my brother concealed, and hid you away, in the flesh of a mortal for so long eluded me for a time. So why then do you sacrifice yourself for a mortal woman? I know she has struck a deal with Charon. It is the only way that one with a mortal soul can resurrect on another world. So answer me Azrael, why her?"

"Keep collecting mortals from each corner of creation and you might eventually find your answer," Azrael said, as he shoved Moloch aside and took the lead.

* * *

The clamoring of footsteps grew louder while Samael waited on the enclosed terrace overlooking the swirling storm of souls. Next to him on the reflective black marble floor, Elizabeth lay, still unconscious and lost to a world of nightmares. With little choice but to be a silent observer, he awaited the arrival of his brother, along with the clamoring of Seraphim taunts not too far behind. His expectation was broken once Moloch entered from beyond the large black doors that guarded this palace of death. Behind Moloch, Raphael and Gabriel followed with Azrael, not too far behind.

A final creak came from the closing palace doors. The onyx skulls that made up the mass of their structure fell to shadow as the shimmering light from the electric storm was sealed. With a loud clash, the doors were now shut. Azrael looked behind him, his view piercing the distance of a thousand feet back to the entrance he was led through. He turned once more to follow his foe into the bone-made palace, taking in the radiance of each and every curve of its architecture. Their footsteps echoed loud and taunt. Further, as they traveled, so too did the size of each room. From narrow halls to open meeting rooms and eventually their journey's end, the great expanse.

Ahead of them stood Samael, set against a backdrop of a massive balcony that oversaw the very storm of souls that acted as a veil to hide this terrifying place. By Samael's feet, Azrael saw Elizabeth, still and lifeless, yet taking in small bouts of air into her lungs.

"I know she shares your blood," Moloch said to Azrael, as he looked at Elizabeth's fragile body as well. "Mortal life cannot call upon the shadow. Yet she has. In the tower once held by Minos, she sacrificed a human child and used her blood, her tainted blood caused by your fornication, to summon forth a serpent of the Abyss. You and this female have been a thorn that I have been unable to pluck. Now here you stand, and here she lay," Moloch finished.

"We are not the creatures you think us to be," Azrael quickly interjected.

Moloch turned to Azrael and looked his enemy directly in his eyes. "You have taken something from me. I was arrogant to think I could ward you off and keep her in bondage. I will offer you a solution. Guide me to my birthright and place in my hands the tool of my destiny. Do this and I will leave you and this...woman, to flee to whichever world you find, far away from the world of shadow."

Azrael kept his stare into Moloch's cold, black eyes and shifted his vision over to Samael and then to Elizabeth. Samael gave a slight nod toward Azrael, as if to signal that he would strike if given notice. Azrael made a slight gesture with his hand, out of Moloch's vision, for Samael to keep his charade, no matter the outcome. Samael knew that his brother's answer had already been set. Azrael knew as well that Moloch was keen on what his response would be. "Your birthright. The weapon you created from the tattered bones of the father you murdered," Azrael said, as he took in a deep breath. He continued, "I remember everything, Moloch. I remember cleansing every world that I was sent by Daemos' bidding. I remember seeing her for the first time, wondering how such a frail creature could harm me, that which could not be harmed. I remember spending an entire lifetime on those worlds, only to hold her as she burned along with everything else in my sight. I was blind to why each world ended in flame. You have tried and succeeded at murdering me and entire civilizations a thousand times over. Entire species worshiped you and your kind as their gods, while they feared me as their devil. And for what purpose? To cleanse your small corner of creation of a threat that was imprisoned more than a million lifetimes ago? How quaint the thought must be that you are forced to rule now, with even footing."

Blood came to a boil as Moloch's knuckles turned white from the tension in his bones. Azrael's words stung like the piercing end of a tempered blade. He knew that Azrael would never reveal the whereabouts of the blade of Jehovah, yet he could not simply toss the beast and the female to the winds of fate. Slowly the heat from his Seraphim form began to eat away at the pale-skinned mortal shell he wore. Slight tears were made on his skin as his wavy blonde hair began to fall out in small patches. Azrael saw this and knew he dug deep and cast Moloch into a place he could not simply bargain his way out from.

Moloch gave a final plea for Azrael to side with Seraphim reasoning. "Then join us. You are not like those other beasts on the world below. It is simply your blood that is tainted. You have seen the terror that they will spread. Join us and I will ensure that neither you nor that woman will be host to terrors. We can cleanse your blood as well as hers. We can end your torment, Azrael. Those creatures that you have bled with. Have they not shown you only pain and suffering? We do not wage war against them for petty disputes such as territory or dominance. They cannot be allowed to spread. The Abyss will devour all within their path."

Azrael looked down at his hands and gave careful consideration to Moloch's offer. Though he had been put through more misery by this creature, there was a solemn truth to his words. Azrael looked once more at Samael and Elizabeth. In a strange twist of fate, the Seraphim reaper of souls and a woman born over a thousand lifetimes had become his blood. Azrael thought of his sister, Sophia, as well. The thought of her being nurtured by Leviathan, the magistrate god of the Abyss. For the first time in his life, Azrael knew that he had those he could call upon to share his bond. "As I see it, Moloch, this crusade has been led by you and by your hand alone. Your...pets...would be lost without your constant willingness to sacrifice them for your own need. I think I will take Elizabeth and leave. Perhaps when I am feeling more generous, I will come to our calling and reveal to you where your precious weapon lay," Azrael spoke with newfound confidence smirked across his face. Raphael and Gabriel kept their composure as they watched their brother let anger and fear overtake his body. Moloch did all he could to keep himself from snapping out of control, but it was of little use.

As Azrael turned his back to Moloch, he saw Samael continue to stand guard next to Elizabeth. An unexpected jolt of pain ran up Azrael's spine as he felt bone and sinew snap from the thunderous crash of Moloch's fire-tempered boot. Azrael fell to the ground and held his back with a grimace of pain. Moloch leaned in and prepared to strike. Once close enough, he saw that Azrael had feigned his injury. Within an instant, Azrael sent the sharp edge of his wings shooting out from his back, slicing through the flesh of Moloch's host body. A streak of crimson nectar flew out from Moloch's chest and across the room. Moloch backed away and signaled to Raphael and Gabriel.

"Go beneath, bring all those below as so above," Moloch shouted with his still-breathing host body.

Gabriel left the way they came and Raphael followed.

Moloch picked himself up and looked over at a wall on the far side

of the room. He contemplated making a run for a sword that hung

like a trophy in the center of the ascending staircase behind Azrael.

While fixated on the potential weapon, Azrael came hurling at full

speed, knocking Moloch into a stone pillar behind him. Debris flew

across the chamber as the two of them fell back into the hallway

behind the terrace chamber.

With barely any mortal flesh left on his body, Moloch used what energy he had to keep himself whole, to not expose his Seraphim form. Azrael was relentless with his attacks. He sent his claws into Moloch's face and tore chunks away from his brow and cheeks. Moloch did what he could to fend off Azrael's attacks, but he came forth as a devil possessed. Muscle was broken and shredded from Moloch's forearm as he held it in place to protect his head. While concentrating on Azrael's flurry of clawed attacks, he failed to notice the tail that swiped him off the ground. Azrael lifted Moloch into the air and held him close as he ran him through more columns in the observation hall. The roof and foundation began to crumble all around, while Moloch's body was tattered with each crashing blow. He was thrown around like a sack of flesh against the walls and pillars of this grand cathedral. In an act of instinct, Moloch began to crawl out of his host's body. He exposed his Seraphim arm and two of his tendrils. Azrael sent his demonic foot, covered still by his stolen armor, into Moloch's back. With claws extended, Azrael dug into Moloch's native Seraphim flesh and held him up to face him eye-to-eye. Symmetry had been torn as Moloch's left eye was still an intact green and white mortal orb, whereas his right eye was black and pointed like a teardrop at the ends. Hot breath left Azrael's hissing mouth as he growled his rage while still holding Moloch up to his extended height.

Beaten and broken, Moloch was thrown back into the terrace room where Samael still stood watch over Elizabeth. Moloch shook and shivered as he slowly crawled away from his pursuing enemy. Azrael had finished toying with his prey as he headed for the defeated Seraphim. He could hear Moloch's black heartbeat beneath the dying rhythm of his host's mortal heart. Moloch used what little strength he had to raise his bloody and mutilated hand up to Samael. Perhaps it was the finality of the situation or the thundering pulse of battle that had sent a shiver of life through Elizabeth's veins as she slowly began to hear the sounds of shadow and light waging their war ahead of her. She knew not if she was still locked in a dream or if she was somehow finally freed of her bonds. A single twitch of her waking eye gave her a defined answer.

Azrael approached with a single goal in mind as he neared

Moloch. With nothing more than pure hate fueling his desire, he

knelt down at the Seraph and pushed his claws slowly into an open

wound. Moloch screeched in pain while Samael moved slowly

toward them. Samael looked at Moloch, then at Azrael, and raised

his scythe high above his head. Moloch had believed that Samael

intended to bring his weapon down upon Azrael, but the reaper had

other intentions. The moment before Samael was about to lower his

crescent blade into Moloch's heart, he heard a sigh and an intake of

air behind him. Samael turned around while Azrael raised himself

up. Elizabeth had awoken and was now surrounded by the Seraphim

guards that Raphael and Gabriel had been commanded to bring to

Moloch's aid. Soon more than a hundred fully armored Seraphim

warriors had flooded the terrace with both Raphael and Gabriel, now

in new host bodies. Elizabeth looked around her and saw that they

had brought weapons she had never seen before. One carried a

mechanical tool that moved like a set of jagged teeth upon a chain,

another carried with him a set of pipes that spat flame far beyond the

eye could see. With each second that passed, more flooded in. She knew that there was little choice but to have Azrael give chase.

Azrael lifted himself from Moloch's body while Samael lowered his scythe. Still, in his Abyss form, Azrael saw Elizabeth standing at the edge of the terrace looking out upon the storm that surrounded the entirety of the thirteenth pillar. With little to no hope left for escape, Elizabeth knew that her only option would be further imprisonment. That Azrael would once again be forced to do the bidding of the Seraphim, only under a different master. She turned to look at Azrael, who was now surrounded by over a hundred Seraphim soldiers. While she had no doubt that he could best them in combat, she had little hope that their numbers would fall so fast being in their native world. She looked into the storm and then back at Azrael one final time.

She waited for her eyes to look into Azrael's and at that moment, she said, "Find me."

Once her words passed from her lips, she threw herself into the storm. Azrael screamed as he pushed his way past the army of Seraphim that surrounded him. He dove over the balcony and into the raging cyclone of lightning and souls. Ahead of him, he saw Elizabeth fall deep into the blackened clouds as her skin was lit up by the blue and green flashes of electric pulse and lost souls. They both fell, not knowing the direction they were headed, only that the palace of death was now a distant memory behind. Elizabeth reached her hand out to Azrael as she fell further away. Azrael returned the gesture and reached out as well. As they pummeled through the storm, Azrael saw Elizabeth spend her last few breaths, unable to take the harshness of the celestial environment. Both extreme heat and cold winds whipped at Elizabeth's body as her clothes, and eventually, flesh, were torn away. Azrael kept his focus on her face, in her eyes, as she grimaced in pain. With a final push, his outreached finger touched hers. It lasted no more than a second before the storm tore her body to shreds as Azrael flew through the ashes of her corpse. When the last piece of her flesh raced past his own, he saw, but for an instant, the small burnt heart of his unborn child. He screamed out in a rage that all of Elysium could hear.

Behind him, the bodies of a thousand Seraphim gave chase in a

vortex that swirled like the closing of a dead star. No matter the

direction Azrael continued to fall, he was surrounded by over a

dozen of these torrents made from Seraphim flesh. He was soon

engulfed and trapped in a prison of bodies. Their skin hardened and

came to a freezing halt. Azrael was able to rip and tear his way past

many, but their numbers did not seem to come to an end. They grew

colder and froze like the deepest lakes of Tartarus. Eventually, his

body, still trapped in its Abyssal form, was frozen in place within the

nexus of Seraphim flesh turned to crystal and ice. The quiet stillness

of the storm had returned as Moloch's prison that held his enemy had

now sat under the thirteenth pillar.

* * *

Though victorious, the Seraphim did not celebrate. Samael knelt beside Moloch and picked him up to his shoulders. Moloch limped, holding his mortal innards while keeping the strength of his Seraphim form. His soldiers gathered around as they watched their beaten brother walk up the stairs overlooking the terrace and into the storm. Moloch looked over the edge and saw, deep within the tempest, that his living prison had successfully ensnared Azrael.

"Your plan worked, brother," Samael said as he joined Moloch by his side.

"My plan. Yes," Moloch said while he coughed up both Seraphim and mortal blood.

"The woman has been vanquished and your enemy is lifeless and within your watchful grasp," Samael continued.

Moloch, barely able to still stand from his wounds, looked at Samael with a discerning eye and wondered whether it was truly Azrael that he intended to drop his scythe down upon. "Yes. It seems our enemy is a threat no more," Moloch said. He turned around and looked at the legion that came to his aid. In the crumbling chamber, he saw hundreds of warriors, armed with weapons made to inflict pain and worship. They looked back at him as he barely held onto his flesh and gave allegiance to both him and Samael. Raphael and Gabriel stood amongst the crowd as Moloch held his head high and ripped himself from his mortal flesh. He spread his tendrils and took off into the deep, dark recesses of space in search of the answers he so desperately needed.

* * *

Beyond the dark reaches of space, the ferryman guided his vessel. It mattered not if moments had passed or an entire lifetime, new souls were brought to their destinations. Charon watched as a thousand more boarded his ship. He saw one in particular that took his attention. He looked at her and nodded a slight smile before heading to the helm and guiding his ship across the stars.

Out there, beyond the reach of celestial tyranny, breathed a world infected with mortal life. A small blue orb that gave off its light to those that would seek it. Untouched and unclaimed until its people would be ripe for the taking. To be shaped and molded by the hands of those that wished it so. It is on this world that gods both old and new would find a place to wage their bargains. On the first days of this world, darkness would fall upon the face of the deep and it, too, would hide amongst the shadows of the abyss.

Made in the USA
Columbia, SC
15 November 2024

829cfafc-f3a7-4206-9063-cc54dda18a0fR01